A DEATH OF COLD

A DEATH OF COLD

JIM SELLERS

GREENBOLD

Published by Jim Sellers
info@jimsellerswriter.com
www.jimsellerswriter.com

ISBN 978-0-9948414-3-8 (pbk.)
ISBN 978-0-9948414-5-2 (mobi)
ISBN 978-0-9948414-4-5 (epub)

Published in Canada

Cover art, design, typesetting: Magdalene Carson / New Leaf Publication Design

To Zoë, Christine and Stephen

Now is no time to think of what you do not have.
Think of what you can do with what there is.

— Ernest Hemingway, *The Old Man and the Sea*

Awake to the Nightmare

BANG, SCRAPE.

A sharp noise woke Jacky out of his troubled sleep. The sound was distant but clear enough to rouse him from his dream. His consciousness was slow to gel, still lost in the confusion of his chaotic nightmare. He dreamt he was imprisoned in a vortex, falling and spinning, unable to control his movements while the world exploded around him. He heard the banging in his sleep, but it ceased when he woke. He assumed it was part of the dream.

Waking didn't clear his confusion. Everything was dark; he didn't know where he was or what had happened. Every part of his body was cold and numb. He was lying uncomfortably on a cramped bed of some kind, his legs curled up with his head pushing against a hard, cold wall. He blinked to clear his vision, but his eyes were crusted over. He tried to rub his eyes to clear them, but his fingers were so frigid it felt like someone else's cold hand was touching his face. His legs ached and he tried to move them to get more comfortable. They were bound up in something; he was unable to move his lower body except for his toes. He tried sitting up but he was being weighed down. He tried to force himself free of his binds, but the exertion made his head hurt.

Suddenly, the noise returned. It was loud and very close, starting somewhere over his head and continuing downward toward him. His heart raced. What was happening? Where was he? He lay frozen in fear and unable to free himself from the tight space he was squeezed into. He was focusing on the noise as it came closer. It dragged, like claws on metal, descending closer to his head. He pulled at his bindings, trying to move away, but the wraps around his legs held. The sound came even with his ears, then it stopped. He held his breath, bending his neck to see what it was. The sound was replaced by a loud hammering; something was trying to break through the barrier between it and Jacky. As he stared, a bright light pierced the darkness, burning through his retinas faster than he could close his eyes. The pain was severe but it pushed the clouds from his mind and he remembered fully where he was, and what was happening before he blacked out.

His fear of the unknown was quickly replaced with terror at the reality that was flooding into his conscious mind. In a panic, he kicked off the blankets that had twisted around his legs in the night. It wasn't a dream; it did happen. He no longer felt cold, or pain, or confusion. He was driven by a desperate need to escape, to get out of there and run. Pulling free of the last of his constraints, he stood up but immediately collapsed as his legs folded uselessly beneath him. They had no circulation and the muscles ached for blood as he struggled back up to his feet. A flood of pins and needles poured down his legs as the circulation gradually returned to his veins. He was still wearing his boots, which added dead weight to his already weakened legs. He saw no one else in the darkness as he pulled himself forward, using on the tops of the seats for support. Where had they gone, were they all dead? His brain was still clouded, this time with a searing headache as he dragged himself toward the exit ahead of him, his eyes stinging from the bright light shining in and his slow legs protesting every step. Breathing fast, his blood awash in adrenalin, he forced himself toward the light and out the doorway.

The outside world exploded around him in a blaze of sunlight, glaring white snow as he bolted through the doorway and past others standing outside, their voices melding together in an audible blur as he ran. He didn't stop to find out what was going on; he didn't want to know. There was a single thought running through his mind and pushing him on as he ran to get out, to get away from danger. He didn't know where he was going; he didn't know where he was. He heard voices behind him, someone yelling. He pushed madly ahead through knee-deep snow toward the clear, open field directly in front of him. One second later he was face down in the snow. It took a moment to realize he had been tackled and his attacker was on top of him, weighing him down. Jacky struggled and kicked to escape. Several other voices were calling excitedly behind him and a familiar voice was yelling in his ear.

"Stop, dude, calm down. You want to kill yourself?"

The voice and the thick, muscled arms belonged to Rick McCribbon, the biggest guy in the group. He was holding Jacky down in the snow so hard so that any movement on Jacky's part caused a wave of pain up his back to his shoulders. Rick was taller and more intimidating than other guys his age. He was only sixteen, the same age as Jacky, but people often assumed he was much older, including a few bartenders if you believed Rick. Being held helpless was embarrassing enough, but Jacky was forced to look ahead at where he was running and saw that, in another few steps, he would have been running on air as he fell off the edge of the mountain to his death far below. The reality of it, along with the realization that Rick had just saved his life, made Jacky feel sick. He pushed hard to get out of Rick's grip.

"Get off." Jacky struggled to no avail. He heard others catching up to them.

"Let him go, Rick," Jacky heard a girl's voice yelling.

"Ouch, hey," Rick's grip loosened as he reacted to someone pulling him off.

Jacky sat up quickly, gasping for air. He saw Rick being forced up by Nadine, one of the girls in the group. She was holding his arm painfully behind his back as the others crowded around them, staring in fear or disbelief. Rick twisted to get away from Nadine's vice-like grip and howling in pain as she held on to his arm. The confusion and dizziness caught up to Jacky as he bent over and threw up, spitting out acid. He was burning inside, both from the running and his embarrassment. He could hear more people coming up behind them and yelling. Mr. Stewart, the band's manager, was leading the charge.

"Okay Nadine, you can let him go," he called. She did but kept her eyes on Rick. Mr. Stewart crouched to check on Jacky who was still bent down on all fours.

"You didn't have to be so rough, you jerk," Jacky said, looking up at Rick.

"He was running to the edge; I had to tackle him," Rick whined to Mr. Stewart as he rubbed his sore arm. His voice was raised as if he was worried. Jacky didn't believe him. He knew Rick was loving the attention, being the hero. He also wondered just how strong Nadine had to be to be able to pull Rick off like that.

Mr. Stewart exhaled loudly, "Yes, yes, I saw. Thank you for stopping him, Rick." Mr. Stewart had been the band's manager for years. Jacky had no idea how old he actually was, but, in the bright sunlight, his manager looked older than ever. His eyes were red rimmed, and the bags under his eyes were puffy. His face was drawn and lined; he clearly had very little sleep.

"What's going on, here?" asked another man, his voice deeper and more commanding. Jacky looked up and saw the co-pilot standing next to Rick and staring accusingly at Jacky. The other man was taller and had silver flecks in his coarse, dark hair and his thick moustache. His stiff, lock-jawed expression gave him an air of intimidation, of command.

"Everything's fine, Mr. Connelly. Jacky just woke up confused." Mr. Stewart said, examining Jacky's head.

"He overslept," said Connelly. "He should have been up earlier with the others clearing the site."

Mr. Stewart was still checking Jacky's head and looking in his eyes. "Jacky had to stay up a lot later than the others last night." He was staring into Jacky's eyes and talking to him. "You took a nasty crack to the head and we had to keep you up to make sure you didn't have a concussion. How's your head this morning?"

"Hurts," Jacky mumbled, turning away.

Mr. Stewart called out to the others, "Go back to the plane now everyone; please keep working." Then, helping Jacky up, he said, "You scared the hell out of us. Where were you running to?"

Jacky looked down, brushing the snow from his clothes and hiding his embarrassment. "I woke up confused—and scared. I thought we were—I thought it was still happening," he kicked the snow away from his boots and looked at Mr. Stewart for his reaction. The manager put his arm around Jacky's shoulders, leading him back to the site.

"No Jacky, fortunately that's over with at least. We're all safe, mostly. We have a few injuries, lots of cuts and bruises, a few noses that may be broken. Unfortunately, our flight attendant fractured her arm and the pilot took a bad hit to the head; he's still unconscious. They're the most serious of the injuries. Mrs. Walford and some of the band members are looking after everyone who was hurt. Everyone else is clearing the site and sweeping the snow off the plane so we can be spotted more easily from the sky."

Jacky looked up to see what was going on. The airplane they had boarded the day before for what was to be a two-hour flight crash-landed on this mountain and now it lay flat in the snow like a dead whale. The members of the band, twenty-four kids around his age, along with a few adults, were busy clearing snow from the outside of the plane and the area beside it. Looking at the plane brought memories of the night before rushing back to Jacky's mind, and he was gripped by violent shivers. They were falling, out of control; people were screaming. Jacky was hanging on to the seat but he lost his grip and fell when the plane dipped sharply to one side and hit his head. He felt dizzy and his head started hurting again. He stopped and bent over, waiting to vomit again, but it didn't come.

Mr. Stewart steadied him by the shoulders. "You okay? Why don't you go lie down for a few minutes, maybe change your wet clothes? Then you need to come out here and start moving around, help the rest of the group clean up. Don't worry, Jacky; this is temporary. They're coming to get us."

Best of Plans

The band was supposed to spend one night at the island, play the concert and fly back the next day. But somewhere over the mountains between Vancouver and the place they were headed, their short trip turned into a long night of terror as weather and mechanical problems sent them flopping around inside the plane as it careened into the mountains and crash-landed on a ridge, in the middle of nowhere. The plane lay useless in the snow, one of its wings and the tail section untouched, while the other was crumpled and the front section flattened against the rocks. The inert propellers, which had stopped spinning long before the plane landed, towered over them like statues; impressive looking but useless.

From his vantage point, facing the landing site, Jacky could trace the sequence of the landing. They manoeuvred through the mountains, coming down between two peaks and just missing the solid rock face of the one they were on, into the trees that were bent and broken as the plane ripped through, then a straight furrow in the snow carved by the belly of the plane as it tobogganed down the slope, still moving fast enough that it could have tumbled down the other side of the mountain. A stand of trees had caught in the propeller and pulled the plane off its fatal course and drove it, nose first, into the rock face. All the evidence of the crash was scattered everywhere, surrounding the carcass of the plane, which lay on its belly like a beached whale. It was glowing in the bright sunlight as people clambered like scavengers over its body, cleaning off the snow and shovelling it away from the site with crude tools they had made from tree branches and whatever they could find on the plane.

He watched the faces of the band members as they busied themselves at their work. He saw the worried looks when they ran to see him; he thought they were worried about him, but they still had those same looks of fear as they pushed at the snow. Many of them glanced upwards to the sky repeatedly, hoping for a sign of rescue. They were afraid; it hadn't occurred to Jacky that they should worry about being rescued. There had to be locators on the plane; surely the rescuers were coming. He looked up at the sky himself, hoping to see something, but there was nothing up there.

His legs were aching with the cold, calling him back down to reality. He was standing in knee-deep snow, getting wet and doing nothing while everyone else was busy working. He retraced his steps back to the plane, still brushing snow from his clothes. The warmth he had felt after his excited run evaporated and he was shivering. He needed to get busy so he could warm up, but first he needed dry socks.

Back at his seat, inside the plane, Jacky allowed himself some time to rest. His legs were still cold, and his mood hadn't improved after being publicly humiliated in the snow. He sat in the nest that was his seat, surrounded by his coat, sweaters and airplane blankets that were wrapped around him. The newly cleared window meant he could read, except the only things he'd brought that weren't electronic, and dead, were a few comic books. He read through those in a few minutes, but it didn't relax him or help get his mind off his brush with death. That would have been a stupid way to die, survive a plane crash only to run off the edge of a cliff. Being stuck there with no means of escape was just as bad. The best they could do for activities was to sweep off the plane and wait around for someone to come and get them. That was pathetic. He pushed away the blankets and put on his coat and boots. He had to move, to do something to get away from his thoughts. His frustration with the situation only got worse the more it bounced around in his head.

He wasn't just angry at himself for running around like an idiot, or having to be saved by Rick McCribbon of all people, or being laughed at by the rest of them. It was the impossible situation he was stuck in that was burning him up. He had one goal that weekend, one thing he absolutely, positively had to get done, and he couldn't do it. After all of his planning and preparations, all he had to do was go online to submit his application and his problems would be over.

He spent hours before they left, preparing everything so he could just sign in, fill out the form, and upload the file of documents he packaged and had waiting on his Dropbox account. He knew the hotel would probably have wifi, or he could have used his phone if that didn't work. He thought he covered all the bases and had it all figured out. He never imagined that he might be in an airplane crash and never make it to the island. That one he missed.

There were maybe a hundred different things he could have planned to do if only he had thought, what if I can't go online this weekend and get it done? That possibility never occurred to him. The whole world was against him, apparently, and it seemed to be prepared to go to any extreme to stop him from accomplishing the only thing he wanted to do. The one simple thing that would change his life and take him away from there.

He stepped outside the plane, looked at the group sweeping snow and asked if anyone wanted to take a break. One of the girls handed him her pine bow and thanked him as she walked inside. Jacky took a swipe at the snow and it rolled down the side of the plane, into his sleeve, on his head and down his neck. He swore as the melting snow ran down his spine and soaked his arm. There was a lot of needles and junk in the snow and much of it ended up in his eyes. He tossed the branch down and scooped the dirt from his eyes. The others around him were laughing as they worked.

"I hate this place," Jacky grumbled as he picked up the makeshift brush.

Old Issues

Bagpipes; his life was being ruled by bagpipes. He had no social life because all of his free time was spent practising at home, or going to weekly band meetings, or playing concerts and fundraising for their travelling. The band travelled all the time; they were always going to competitions and Highland games and being invited to special events. They were victims of their own success; they were just too good at what they did.

Jacky learned how to play the bagpipes at thirteen. It started as an idea for him, something he could do for his father, who also played the pipes when he was Jacky's age. Jacky was fortunate in finding a generous and patient teacher, but Sergeant MacGregor, the director of the Police Pipe Band, didn't take excuses and demanded dedication. Once he started, Jacky kept working until he played his first solo performance at the opening of the National Police Games Competitions in a massive hockey arena with five thousand people—and his father—watching. As a result, Jacky was invited to join the New Caledonians, one of the best youth pipe bands in the country. It was a big deal to be accepted into the band. Finally, Jacky could say he was good at something and he loved doing it.

Three years later, Jacky was still at it. Playing the bagpipes had its advantages; it made him different from other guys in high school. Jacky liked showing off, playing them any chance he could, like games and special events. He learned the guitar and played in a rock band with some other guys in school, but he brought out the pipes and played the solos with them instead of the guitar, which was also cool. The first time he saw anyone doing that was the comedian Johnny "Bagpipes" Johnson, who played an Eddie Van Halen guitar solo perfectly. It was so wild; Jacky had to learn to do it. He got pretty good, copying some of the other great guitarists like Slash, Brian May from Queen and Angus Young from AC/DC. He was also started listening to "bagrock" bands like the Red Hot Chilli Pipers and the Dropkick Murphys, playing along with them note for note. It was fun, but that was the point. He was not having fun anymore.

Jacky had other things to do, like science, computer programming, and endless new video games he wanted to work on. It was impossible to have time for a school project when he was spending all his after school hours practising and performing on the bagpipes. He had enough. He tried quitting, but his dad said no.

And now they were stuck on a mountain.

Schemes

After a few hours, with its open door and cleared windows, the plane looked almost normal, except that it was lying in the snow. The wheels were still tucked underneath the wings. The other side, where the plane hit the wall of rock, was too badly damaged. No one cleared that side; there was no point. It faced the trees and the wall of rock, but you could also see the crumpled front cabin from the windows. They decided to leave them covered.

As time passed and the sun steadily climbed over the trees, centring itself in the sky, Jacky gradually acclimatized himself to his new surroundings. After his panic attack, and being crushed in the snow by McCribbon, Jacky worked a shift on the plane cleaning detail, sweeping snow off the rear section behind the wings. As he worked, his body temperature alternated from cold and frozen to hot and sweating. For a while, as he dug through the snow by the back of the plane, he opened his coat because he was sweating on top while his feet were numb from the cold. He climbed to the top of the plane and started clearing up there. The metal roof reflected the sun and warmed him to a uniform average.

Mr. Stewart was right about one thing, working did help take their minds off being afraid. When Jacky ran outside the plane that morning, he saw fear on the faces of the band members as they stared at him. Now, they looked tired or bored, talking about mundane things like relationships and TV shows. From his perch, he could see the group's collective efforts were starting to show on the ground. They cleared off most of the plane and the area to the side of it, right out to the edge. Someone had even put stakes in the snow at the edge and strung yellow tape around to warn them. *Not much chance of that plastic ribbon stopping anyone from going over,* Jacky thought. It was still a good idea.

Most of his work was done on the roof and he was enjoying the warmth, especially on his feet. He assumed it was around noon as the sun was directly overhead in the nearly cloudless sky. He refused to turn on his phone, hoping to hang on to any charge he could in case he could get a signal. It was hopeless to try and get a signal up there; they were too high for the towers to reach. He heard that clouds and weather inversions can amplify and redirect a cell signal. He was actually hoping for weather to come in, but, wouldn't you know it, it was clear and sunny.

They would probably be handing out lunch soon, but he preferred staying up on his warm spot to climbing back down into the snow. He stood facing the sun and let it shine on him. He could do nothing to change the situation now; it would be too late to do anything even if they flew in now and plucked them off the ridge. His hopes and plans were dead, so he might as well accept it. There was a line in the song "Me and Bobbie McGee," "Freedom's just another word for nothing left to lose." Once you've lost the fight, you're free. Might as well relax. He looked out at the place they had landed. Out behind them he could see the damage to the trees the plane had caused when it crashed through them. He could see the two trails that led back to the latrines they had dug. They didn't allow use of the plane's toilet to ration the water. From the front of the plane, he saw the steep drop they would have gone over if the trees hadn't stopped them. Over the edge, from his perch on top of the plane, he could look down and see the next set of mountains, probably miles away and at least a mile down. They were sitting on a ridge just below the tree line and Jacky could see trees covering the mountains right down to the valley. Down where the cell towers are. Maybe even people and telephones. And they had no way of knowing a planeload of people were sitting up above their heads.

Looking to the other side of the plane, all he could see was the side of the mountain, solid rock and lots, and lots of trees. He looked down into the forested area but he couldn't lean too far off the roof of the plane. He almost lost his balance and kneeled down to steady himself.

"What're you doing up there?" a voice called. Jacky looked and saw the co-pilot staring up at him with his usual scowl.

"I was clearing the snow off the roof and wings but I finished. Now I'm just looking around, and staying warm," Jacky answered.

"Well, you can come down now. We're serving lunch."

"I'll be right there," Jacky said. He pulled his phone out of his inside pocket and turned it on, "I want a couple of pictures first."

The co-pilot snorted and walked away. Jacky unlocked the phone, checked the battery (25 per cent) and made it look like he was taking pictures. He spun around to the other side of the plane, looked down, and zoomed in on the trees. He clicked off the phone and smiled as he walked to the wing and slid down off the plane to get his lunch.

All hope wasn't lost after all.

The trees that covered that side of the mountain were mostly pines of different sizes that grew close together, forming thick stands. From his lookout, he could see that the trees curved down around the rocky slope behind them. He saw that the forest grew all the way down the other mountains; there was no reason to think it didn't on this mountain as well. He saw that the clumps of trees grew out to the other edge of the hill and down the side. He saw the tops of trees growing farther down. If that was the case, all he had to do was hike down the trees to the bottom. The mountain couldn't be more than a mile or two down; he could walk that far easily. Besides, he didn't need to get all the way down. He only had to get far enough for a cell signal. There had to be cell towers down there; this wasn't Mars.

When he got down, everyone was eating. Lunch was cold half-sandwiches and fruit yogurt as they couldn't cook anything and the co-pilot wouldn't let them use the microwave on the plane as it would drain the batteries. It looked like they were planning for a long stay, judging from the small amount they were giving out. Mr. Stewart made it clear they needed to ration all the food and water for everyone, and had even taken their personal food and snacks for their collection. Jacky ate quickly and returned to his seat in the plane to prepare for his hike. Checking to make sure no one was watching, he emptied his backpack but kept some extra socks and gloves, just in case. He snuck a bottle of water out of the cupboard in the plane. He knew he would get in trouble if he was caught, but he was well past worrying about that. He had also secreted a few of his energy bars under his seat. He fished them out and put them in the bag. He didn't need anything beyond that and his phone. He squeezed the backpack as flat as he could and tucked it in front, under his coat, and walked outside, away from the others who were still eating lunch or standing around by the door. He picked up a pine branch and started brushing snow from the ground around the plane. He worked gradually around the back to the other side, continuing to brush the plane as he went and watching the others. Once he was out of sight, he dropped the branch, pulled out the backpack and slung it over his shoulders. He clambered slowly and carefully over the low branches and snow to avoid making any noise as he slipped into the trees toward the other side of the mountain.

And freedom.

5

Mother

For most of his life, Jacky's relationship with his father was at a distance. He understood that his dad's work required that he be away a lot—most days, into the night sometimes, and away some weekends. It was understood in his family—which was Jacky; his father, Murray; and his mother, Katherine or Kathy—that work was most important and it overrode everything, including games, special nights, and birthdays. Jacky accepted that and assumed most families were the same until he was old enough to understand that they were different.

Going to friends' houses and seeing how they lived made Jacky realize how much he differed from most of them. He had no brothers or sisters, no relatives that he knew of except for one aunt whom he rarely saw. He didn't know any of his grandparents—they had all died when he was young—and he had no cousins he could talk to or visit. His knowledge of his own family wasn't any more complete. He only knew what his mother had told him.

"My family came from Ireland originally," she said while he scribbled in his notebook to keep up with her. "They helped build most of the major infrastructure in the country, the railroad, the Welland Canal, the Trans-Canada highway. You name it, but they worked for almost nothing and no one gave them any recognition for their work. They were just cheap labour for the rich people to use so they could make more money." Her Irish temper would rise when she talked like that, and her face, normally pale white against her bright red hair and green eyes, would start to turn pink.

"What about Dad's ancestors?" He changed the topic. "Were they Irish, too?"

That calmed her, and she went back to making dinner. "No, his people were Scottish. They settled in Nova Scotia. His is an entirely different story. You'll have to ask him about it."

He decided he wasn't going to ask his dad if there was any chance he would get as angry talking about it as his mom.

"What about his parents?" Jacky asked. She had told Jacky earlier about her father being in the army and raising his three daughters by himself after her mother passed away when she was very young. He was sure she wasn't going to give him any more information than that. His mother spoke in non-specific generalities like "quite young" and "some illness" when she wanted to avoid discussing anything.

"Your grandparents lived in Nova Scotia, but I never met them. Your grandfather worked for the railroad and was away from home most of the time. There was a car accident; I don't know anything about it, but your grandmother was killed and your father ended up going to a boarding school until he finished and went to university. That's where I met him. He never saw his own father again."

Jacky stopped writing and stared at the word on the page. "Never?"

"No, your father never saw him alive again. They weren't close, apparently. Sad, isn't it?" she said, looking at Jacky. "Maybe you might want to ask him about it sometime, in the future."

He never did ask.

Jacky liked the way things were with his family. During the times when they were all together, they travelled, they would go camping, they went to movies and out for dinner in restaurants. Everything was planned and organized by his mother. She insisted they spend as much time together as a family as possible. She was the one constant in his life. She was just there when he came home from school, when his dad was out of town, when he was at home sick, or when he had problems with his school work.

Kathy Fraser was a writer. She worked at home doing freelance jobs for people, for magazines and websites. Jacky looked more like his mom than his dad. She was the same height as her son and had the same curly hair, although hers was more red while Jacky's was a dirty, straw-coloured blonde. She was so organized and so calm about things; Jacky rarely ever saw her get upset at anything or lose her temper. She could usually find a way around a problem, which was something that Jacky would need help with.

Jacky's life changed for the worse when he started going to middle school. It was strange, unfamiliar territory for him. After six years of going to the same school with mostly the same friends, Jacky was suddenly one of the youngest ones there. There were new kids at school, and the friends he had for years started moving away or finding new friends. He had to run to get to the different classes that were scattered around the big, two-storey building. His courses were harder and his marks started going down. He wasn't popular anymore and he lost all his confidence. His only support, his only real place of refuge was at home, with his mother.

Then he lost her.

As a kid, going to the same school for years, hanging out with the same friends and never having to face any real challenges other than a basketball game, life was great. Jacky didn't understand how anyone had problems with school, or life for that matter. As long as nothing changed, his life was perfect, or so it seemed looking back. By the time Jacky hit his twelfth birthday, he had life figured out. He would grow up and be a basketball player, maybe go into acting, because that was what athletes did, and then retire early and live off his success. It wasn't even work; it was fate.

His faith in fate and himself crumbled like a dust castle when he graduated from elementary to middle school. The classes were different, and the monstrous school was two storeys of three wings that spanned in different directions requiring the students to sprint between classes to avoid detention for being late. The courses were spread out over two days, each subject a hundred times more complex than the math, science, and history he learned in grade six. Instead of feeling he was growing, progressing in the subjects he learned, it felt more like he knew nothing and was starting from scratch. He was also forced to take subjects he didn't want to, like music and industrial arts—shop class. Instead of going home after work and relaxing in front of a video game, he hauled his books home every day with work to do.

He hoped his friends felt the same, looking for some kind of kinship, a group to offer each other support and remember the old days at school. Instead his friends were changing, moving away to different schools, or finding new friends. His best friend, Lenny, the guy he'd known most of his life, moved away with his mother when his parents got divorced. Despite his promise to do so, he never called, never messaged. He vanished along with every one of Jacky's happiness. The only constant that remained through all of those life-altering changes was his home and his family. His mother was always there when he walked in the door. His world remained a safe refuge at its core. Until she got sick.

Everyone got sick; it happened all the time. People get sick and they get better. Jacky's mother was a pillar of strength; she never needed help or asked for it. It never occurred to him that anything more than that could happen, not to his mother. First it was a cold, then the flu. She was in bed sleeping most days so Jacky and his dad looked after the cooking and shopping and the cleaning. It was comedic at first, like a Buster Keaton movie. Look at the goofy guys trying to do the work of supermom and suffering near miss disasters. Jacky waited, impatiently, for it to be over.

After a few days, she seemed to feel better. She was up and moving around a little more at a time. But the illness never went away completely, and she was never herself. Still, it wasn't until they saw a doctor and ran tests that the true reality of her situation became clear. She was admitted into hospital for surgery, and Jacky was suddenly alone with his father in their grim new world. Waiting and hoping, Jacky didn't know what to do next. Other than get up every day and do whatever he had to do. Life didn't care that his world was dark and hurting. The homework piled up. His dad still had his job, and Jacky floated in a lie, that she would be better, and somehow all of this would end and they could go back to life the way it was.

She had surgery; they removed a huge tumour from her brain and she was recovering. It was going well. She had radiation treatments; Jacky went with her to watch, and they gave her chemotherapy that made her sick. She was thin, her beautiful face shrunken to a skin-covered skull and her arms like sticks with fingers. Her voice was breath and a distant whisper of memory of how she used to sound. She had to be getting better; there was no reason to be living like that if there wasn't a purpose at the end of it. Jacky clung to this belief like a tether. It gave him a reason to face the next day.

"Jacky, get up, quick," his father roused him from his sleep. It was late, or early, and he was deep into sleep. He climbed out of bed and dressed, not fully awake and not knowing what was happening. The look on his father's face said what he didn't want to ask. He got to the door and saw the ambulance in the driveway, red lights flashing and rotating past the houses on the street and the faces of the people watching them in their coats and pyjamas. Some of the neighbours came over and talked to his dad with long, solemn faces, but no one spoke to him. No one told him what was going on, but he knew, or at least he thought he did. This was another setback for his mother. She needed more time to recover.

They got in the car and drove, not speaking as they followed the ambulance in the distance. When they parked and entered the emergency room, all was chaos. Noise and people talking, a TV blared in the corner and the PA system droned the names of doctors and medical teams over top of the noise. The lights were too bright, and the plastic chairs too cold and hard to get comfortable. His dad told him to wait there, but for how long? Jacky wanted to be with his mom, not stuck out there sitting next to an old guy hacking his lungs out.

His mother never treated Jacky like a child. She talked plainly to him and if there was something he didn't understand, she would explain or tell him to find out. Their relationship was one of honesty and frankness. She worried less about hurting Jacky's feelings than letting him think he was a child. That was why Jacky trusted her, implicitly. He didn't have that relationship with his father. Jacky's dad treated him like a child, holding back information, using euphemisms for words Jacky knew and understood. During his mother's illness, Jacky's dad repeated told him not to worry; she was going to be fine. He would also prevent Jacky from talking to her, saying she was tired and not to cause her any worry. Sitting in the waiting area at the hospital, his doubts about his dad were playing in his mind. If something were to happen to his mom, would he come and tell Jacky? Why did he leave

Jacky out here? The questions continued with no end until Jacky's aunt, the only relative they had living close by, suddenly appeared at the hospital and began talking to him about staying with her. His fears were confirmed; his dad was pushing him away, getting rid of him, keeping him from his mother. In a fit of fear and anger, he ran into the emergency room and searched around each of the curtained beds for his mother. He found her, frail and diminished, almost vanishing into the white sheets and lights shining on her pale skin. One look at her told him what he had been refusing to believe; she wasn't getting better, she was going to die.

He sat by her bed, talking, pleading, clinging to her thin hand as if holding her to life. She was tired and weak, but he kept talking, kept holding to her as a drowning man would hold onto a lifeline. He was fighting his own exhaustion; his own eyes burned with a need for sleep, but he kept talking to her, being her anchor. He lost track of time; he ran out of things to say. He didn't know how, but he fell asleep.

He woke with a start, the shock of realization when he opened his eyes. As he feared, she was gone. He was still holding her hand, but it was cold; her eyes were closed, but her face was blank. Her lips were partially open as if she was going to say something to him.

He let go of her hand and walked away from her. He felt the cold, empty feeling of death in his heart. The other Jacky, the foolishly trusting one, was dead, lying back there with his mother as he walked to his new life with his father, the stranger.

In another week, he had to suffer through the funeral. It was without a doubt the most depressing time he spent with a room full of strangers in his life. Jacky didn't understand the reason why he had to be there, sitting in a hot, scratchy, ill-fitting suit, pretending to be grateful as a hundred weeping strangers told him how sorry they were or stared at him with sad eyes. One of them had the nerve to say she was "in a better place." It took all his strength to avoid jumping up and screaming at the woman. He couldn't believe the nerve of some people.

The funeral and the gravesite service took most of the day. Jacky and his dad went out to have dinner that night but it was a quiet one, neither of them said much. Jacky had no idea what to expect once everything was done and there was nothing left but carry on without her. The house was empty when they got home; even though the two men in the family were living there, it seemed to be missing its spirit.

Father

It took time, a few weeks. Life eventually established a new routine as the two men of the family slipped back into the pattern of daily living without Jacky's mother. Jacky went back to school after the funeral. It made more sense than sitting around the house being depressed while his school work piled up. His dad followed suit and returned to work. After a few days, they got used to living with each other. There were challenges and misunderstandings in the process, a few arguments, and some laughs. Jacky had to learn how to cook dinner, and his dad tried harder to come home from work. This was a challenge as he was promoted to a senior position and had greater responsibilities. Some days Jacky ate alone. He was twelve; he figured he could handle things.

There were the good times, the moments where they enjoyed being together. Jacky and his dad went on vacation after school ended for the summer. They went to Disneyland. They went fishing, saw movies and played miniature golf. Those moments ignited feelings he only knew with his mother; love, trust, understanding. The question still itched in his mind, why did he try to keep Jacky away from his mother when she was dying? It never came up; Jacky avoided asking it. He liked this new relationship he had with his father; he wanted to keep it.

They agreed, after several months of avoiding the topic, to put his mother's things away and remove the ghost of her in the house. Since she died, they hadn't changed a single thing. The house looked like she left it, as if they were keeping it for her to return at any time. They put her clothes in boxes along with most of her odd collections of rocks, crafts, and knickknacks. They moved the furniture around in the living room and brought the television up from the basement, something she would never agree to.

It was a long and very emotional day, but it was also a relief. They could talk about her and remember the great times they had with her. Jacky's dad talked about how they met and the travelling they did before they got married and had Jacky. He had to imagine the two of them young, travelling around, dating. His dad was enjoying it; his mind was going back to those times, so long ago, and he smiled at his thoughts.

As they hauled the boxes downstairs, his dad tried to figure out the best way to move things in the storage room under the stairs so they could add the new boxes. The space was packed with archives of everything Jacky had played with or made in school with a backdrop of other boxes that ranged in age and colour, from new looking cardboard to very old, dark looking boxes. Some had mover's logos on them and some were so old they had to be taped shut to avoid tearing. Jacky pointed to them.

"Dad, what's in those?"

His dad looked back, brushing the dust from his pants, "Old picture albums, I think. That and books probably."

"Really? I don't think I've ever seen them. I mean, the boxes have been back there as long as I can remember, so I've looked inside them."

"Did you want to?" his dad said.

"Yeah, if they're of you and Mom."

That was the rest of the day, spent downstairs pulling old photo albums out of boxes and his dad explaining what they were. Jacky's excitement was hard to contain. These pictures showed an entire life he never knew. His parents as a young couple, travelling around Europe and England, the jungle in South America, in New York, New Orleans, and San Francisco. His mother was pretty, the same eyes and red hair, just a lot younger. His dad looked the same with more hair and a smug look of a guy who has the popular girl.

There were a thousand pictures of Jacky, from his first day alive to Christmas getting presents, to some things he remembered. Hanging out with Lenny, going to his first school. Winning his first basketball trophy. He opened an old box and pulled out an older album. This had pictures, old ones, of people he didn't recognize in places he didn't know. By the ocean, in older cars, strange houses. There were several pictures of a young boy who looked familiar but Jacky didn't know.

"That's me," his dad said, grinning. "Don't you recognize the family similarity? I was younger than you in those ones." He pointed out some of the people in the pictures, naming names Jacky wouldn't remember. There was a picture of his father as a young boy sitting at a picnic table with two people next to a car in a park. His dad looked at it and peeled it out of the album.

"That's your grandmother." He was pointing to the woman who was smiling at the camera with her arm on her son's shoulder. Jacky pointed to the man who was sitting next to them. He didn't smile but had a look like someone who was being forced to pose.

"Is that your father?" Jacky asked.

"Yup, wasn't one for having pictures taken." His dad was packing books back into boxes while Jacky continued to look through the album. It was great seeing those pictures of his dad. He could see him growing up gradually from a young boy to a teenager. Jacky turned the page and gasped. Unlike the other pictures in the book that were about four inches square and some six by four, this picture was a full-sized enlargement in bright full colour. It was of his dad at about Jacky's age, but he was dressed in a colourful Scottish outfit including a kilt, hat, dress shirt and jacket, and a black thing on his waist that looked like s cross between a purse and a small leather satchel. His legs were bare, but he had high socks and black dress shoes. It looked very formal and really different. The biggest surprise in the picture was that his dad was holding a set of bagpipes. Jacky heard of bagpipes and knew some songs played by them but he had never paid any attention to them. He assumed they were for old, Scottish people and military funerals. He never thought of himself as being Scottish; he was born in Canada as was everyone else in his family. He had to ask.

His father explained that their family came to Canada from Scotland in the mid-1800s. They mostly settled in Nova Scotia, but others, like him, moved out to other parts of the country and some moved to the United States. But they kept their traditions, including playing the pipes and wearing the tartan.

Jacky pointed to the bagpipes. "Do you know how to play the bagpipes?" Jacky asked.

"Sure, that and the guitar and the tin whistle, the essentials."

Jacky noticed something in his dad's voice as he looked at the picture of himself. Pride, maybe, certainly happiness at the memory of it. He saw the same thing in the younger image of his father, the same sort of pride. Bagpipes, who knew?

They finally finished putting everything away and ordered in pizza while they each showered the dust off and watched the movie *Alien*, which was a favourite of his dad's. Jacky liked it, too, especially the scary parts.

They were starting to form a new, closer relationship.

And then it ended.

Shortly after school started in the fall, Jacky ran into the same problems he had in grade seven. His dad's work was busier, and he was tired most of the time. Their conversations gradually became more about problems and arguments. Jacky had turned thirteen and was having his own emotional problems aside from the constant questions from his dad who seemed to think Jacky was always about to get into trouble. It was all garbage; his dad was watching too much TV and listening to the news. Jacky tried to ignore him and focus on his homework. He didn't have time to get into trouble. He had too much homework and studying to do; he rarely had time to spend online or playing games.

He wished they could stop and rewind, back to the summer when he and his dad got along. It felt like his dad hated him or something, like he wanted Jacky to fail, or he had no confidence in his own kid. Sitting alone at home, eating his dinner with nothing else to do but think, he remembered what his mother told him about his father. More specifically, the upsetting thing that his grandfather had done.

"Your father grew up in a boarding school. He never saw his father again," she had told him when he was asking about his grandparents. His grandmother had died in a car accident, and his grandfather dumped his only kid in a boarding school and took off. The similarities of the two situations startled him as he stopped eating, feeling sick to his stomach. His dad wouldn't do that to him, would he? His father wasn't the kind who would dump his kid off at a school and go away, except, he was always away at work. He was always losing his temper with Jacky, unfairly sometimes. His mother died. But still, did people do that? There were boarding schools in Canada. Maybe they do.

The fear of it, just the possibility of it became Jacky's nightmare; it was a real fear that wouldn't go away. It drove him to do something he never thought possible. He would prove himself, and earn his father's love so he could stay at home. The only way he could do that was to connect with something his father loved as well; he would have to learn to play the bagpipes.

7

Falling from the Sky

As soon as everyone saw the smaller plane sitting by itself out on the tarmac with its doors open and the wheeled stairs rolled up to it, the grumbling began. It was a skinny looking, propeller-driven airplane with its wings mounted on top of the body. It was leaning forward on its tiny front wheel, and its back wheels stuck out behind the engines. It was going to be cramped and noisy. Compared to the large, wide body jet they had flown in to Vancouver, this plane looked like riding a scooter after travelling most of the way in a limo.

They weren't going very far, not compared to some of the much larger planes moving around and lifting off the runways in the distance. They only had to skip over the mountains and head north. They would only be bunched into that golf cart with wings for an hour. Then they'd be hanging out with the Royal Family in a private resort, one of the perks of being the best in the world. Still it would be nicer to go there in a jet.

Jacky wasn't the only one standing at the big window looking witheringly out at their ride. Rick and Terry, two of the drummers, stood next to him staring at the plane. Terry had a sneer on his face, but Rick had an unmistakable look of fear in his eyes. Jacky could see the claustrophobia written on his face and thought about what would happen if his fear-fuelled, Hulk-like persona kicked in while they were in the air. Rick turned and saw Jacky looking at him and changed his expression. He snorted, "Oh look, Granny's Airline and Crop Duster

Service. I wonder how old that thing is." Terry sniggered and they walked back to the Starbucks kiosk.

"Great," Jacky grunted to himself. "We get to be locked up in a metal tube at 30,000 feet with a frightened sasquatch. What could possibly go wrong?" He was still looking down at the plane, watching them load the instruments and suitcases into the cargo hold. The weather had changed dramatically, and the baggage handlers were struggling with the strong winds blowing everything around. Jacky was glad he brought his warm clothes and gloves, even though he originally planned to leave them at home. Weather in British Columbia was supposed to be warmer, but not today. He hoped it would change when they got to the island.

The other band members were wandering around, bored and anxious, but mostly bored. The chaperones, Mr. Stewart and Mrs. Walford, who was also a nurse, were keeping track of everyone and not letting anyone wander too far from the gate. They were going to eat lunch on the plane and have dinner when they got to the island. Everyone was encouraged to load up on snacks and water if they wanted, and to use the washroom before heading down to the plane. Larry Walford wasn't happy about having his mother along to watch him, and the other guys enjoyed giving him a hard time about it.

Jacky was flicking through different screens on his iPad, thinking about his plans for the day. They should be on the ground and checked into their hotel within two hours. That gave him lots of time to upload his letters of recommendation and his application form and cover letter. He scanned his father's signature with his camera; something he knew was both illegal and unfair. His dad needed to know what Jacky was planning to do; he just wanted to tell him after he was accepted rather than ask permission beforehand. Time was the crucial element now, and he didn't want anything to delay his plans. He had to have all of the documents uploaded along with his application when the school's website portal opened. That was going to be one in the morning in British Columbia. Jacky still had to get up the next morning and play a concert; he was going to regret being up so late, but it would be worth it.

As long as the wifi in the hotel was working, that is. He hadn't considered that as a potential problem, but now he was thinking about it.

If he had to he could link his phone to the computer. That would be a huge amount of data, and his dad would definitely see that on the cell phone bill. He shrugged it off; that would have to be the worst case scenario, he figured. Probably wouldn't happen; everyone had wifi these days.

He would have given anything if this trip could have happened some other time, even a week later would be better. British Columbia was the farthest west and therefore the farthest away from the United Kingdom he could get. Timing was vital as the number of applications the school accepted was so limited, and an awful lot of people would be applying to get in. They opened the online applications once a year and only until the maximum number of applications was submitted, then it closed. No questions, no workaround. Getting in there was as hard as buying tickets online to a Taylor Swift concert.

"Passengers on the charter service to Graham Island please check in at the gate and be ready to board your flight," the lady standing at the desk announced. Mr. Stewart and Mrs. Walford were rounding up the band members. Once everyone was lined up, they opened the door and a cold blast of wind blew in. The metal walkway wound down and turned at the end with a door that opened to the tarmac. The plane was sitting back from the building far enough that they had to walk out onto the stairs, along a marked walkway while luggage carts and other machinery drove around them. Jet engines whined around them, and the wind blew mercilessly. A lady in a blue winter coat was standing at the doorway directing them into the plane. Jacky could smell the oily jet fuel and hear the roar of engines as jets took off on the runway.

The weather was bad, and the sky was socked in with clouds. The wind and drizzle froze them like a cold bath. It was suddenly a very long walk to the plane. The other planes and airport machines were so loud he had to yell to be heard.

"I thought Vancouver was warm," he yelled, but no one seemed to hear him or wanted to talk. The band members ran to the plane holding their bags against their coats or over their heads. Jacky could see dark mountains off at a distance and the ocean was just past the airport. Foam from the waves that were washing over the shore confirmed there was a serious storm coming. Not a great time to be flying in a bush plane.

As he climbed into the plane, Jacky could see just how different this plane would be from the larger jet. This one had a much lower ceiling with two cramped seats on either side of a narrow aisle. No video screens or headphones and one toilet up front by the cabin. The band members each had a carry-on bag and their instruments, except for the drums that were stored in the cargo section. There was enough room on the plane for everyone to sit by themselves. Jacky chose a seat to the right side of the plane, next to the propeller, and tucked his bag, which was his backpack from his camping days, under the seat and his bagpipes in the overhead bin. The backpack was stuffed with every form of electronic entertainment possible for one weekend plus some comic books, snacks and drinks. He didn't do water. He was planning to stay inside while they were there, playing *World of Warcraft*, after he got his application out.

An older man, balding, with a thick moustache of grey-and-white hair was walking down the aisle talking to everyone as they settled in. He was wearing a hat and jacket. Jacky assumed he was the pilot. He was friendly, shaking hands and laughing, so that was a good sign. Jacky was pulling out his various entertainment devices for the trip when the voice startled him.

"Hello, young fella. You seem to be equipped for a long stay. I don't think the flight's going to be long enough to use all of your electronics, there."

The pilot's face was cheerful, his eyes bright despite his age. Jacky grinned, "Just keeping my options open."

"Are you a piper or a drummer?" the man asked.

"Piper," Jacky answered, then, on a whim, he stuck out his hand. "Jacky Fraser, I'm the second piper in the group."

They shook hands. "Pleased to meet you, Jacky. This must be very exciting for you, to play for the prince and princess, I mean."

"Oh yeah, it's an honour." Jacky looked enthusiastic. "I hope it's warmer when we get there, though."

The pilot nodded. "It's supposed to be much nicer up there. This is a front blowing through, and I think we'll pass it on our way up. Don't worry. I'm excited to see you play as well. We're going to stay there and bring you back the next day, so I get to see you perform. I do love the pipes."

"Excellent," Jacky said, not able to think of anything else to say. The pilot smiled as he moved on to the next seat. Jacky turned on his iPad, checking through the latest posts before he lost the wifi at the airport.

A few minutes later, he heard doors thumping closed and the plane was suddenly quieter. The flight attendant, an older lady, who was moving back and forth up the aisle, making people put bags and coats away, getting them seated and telling everyone to take out their earphones until they were in the air and turn off their cell phones. Jacky put away the iPad and had his face buried in a comic book when he heard a different voice talking on the intercom. Jacky looked up and saw a tall man with dark silver hair and moustache similar to the pilot's giving instructions on the use of seat belts while the flight attendant did the physical demonstration. Jacky always ignored these, as if he needed instructions on how to use a seat belt or put on an oxygen mask. He kept reading.

"Excuse me," a voice said over his head. Jacky looked up and saw the same man looking at him with a cold stare. "I need you to pay attention."

What the—Jacky thought as he put down the comic and watched as the man returned to the microphone and read out the instructions. It was just like every other airline presentation on safety except the man delivered it in such a threatening manner Jacky figured they were flying to prison. Wear the seat belt at all times, okay to use electronic devices but do not transmit or make phone calls, check. Keep bags and belongings under the seats or in the overhead compartment. Man, this guy had some serious authoritarian issues. When the lecture ended with a curt "We may be experiencing some turbulence so please stay in your seats. Enjoy your flight," Jacky mumbled, "Aye, aye, Cap'n" and saluted. Someone near him sniggered.

The engines whined and the propellers began to spin. Not very fast initially as they had to be pushed out on to the runway by a small tractor. The plane turned and started moving on its own power, driving back and forth on an endless maze of runways, each marked with illuminated letters. Jacky heard Rick, who was sitting in the back, remark, "I guess we're driving there." Jacky laughed along with a few others. The plane turned again and stopped. It was in a line with other, larger planes waiting to take off. When their turn came, the sound of the engines rose to an almost deafening level and the plane itself, with all its plastic parts that held it together, were vibrating in harmony with the engines. There was no point in trying to listen to music or talk; no one could hear over that racket. The propellers became semi-transparent disks as the lights glinted off the fins of the propellers and reflected on the window. They were in the air and climbing fast before they knew it. The plane levelled off and the engines settled into a lower noise level, but the vibration continued. Jacky watched out the window. They weren't as high this time, which was nice because there was more to see. They were passing over the mountains and water heading for the coast. The view was fantastic, even without the sun.

They were supposed to be landing after two hours, but, a few minutes after takeoff, they started getting hit by turbulence. The pilot came on the speaker to say they had to fly around the cold front so it would take a little longer to get down. That wasn't what anyone wanted to hear. Jacky looked out the window and saw snow flying horizontally so thick that no sky or ground could be seen. He couldn't tell if it was day or night. He sighed and went back to his reading. The first hard jolt startled everyone and caused a few screams. The flight attendant was running back and forth checking on people. The pilot's voice came on the speakers again.

"Sorry about that, folks. Seems we didn't escape the weather completely. We're heading in to some more turbulence so please make sure your seat belts are fastened and any loose items you have are securely tucked into the seat pockets in front of you and under your seats. Thank you."

Some people were crawling under the seats trying to grab on to lost phones and other things that had fallen from their seats. Jacky had already stuffed his game and notebook into his backpack. He wanted to check it again to make sure it was secure. As he was bending down to grab the bag, the plane jolted harder and he whacked his head on the window. There was more screaming around him; some people hadn't got their seat belts done up in time, and the flight attendant was scurrying back and forth, helping people get secured. Another jolt hit the plane, and she fell hard. Jacky heard her cry out and was about to pull off his seat belt when Mr. Stewart and Mrs. Walford ran past him. They carefully helped her to a seat, and Mrs. Walford examined her arm. It sounded like she broke it or sprained it. Either way she was hurting bad as she moaned with the pain. She wasn't going to be able to do anything but ride out the storm with the rest of them. Mrs. Walford strapped in the seat next to her and Mr. Stewart worked his way back up the aisle to his seat.

The plane continued to jump and shake, but the raised voices had gone silent. The fear was measurable, with sniffling and whispers. People were holding onto their seats, staring out of the windows and waiting. Jacky heard the engines rise in pitch and the plane leaned upwards, climbing, but the snow and the shaking continued. They levelled off, and the co-pilot came running down the aisle to see how the flight attendant was doing. They talked quietly and he looked at her arm. He stood and said, "Okay, just stay put. We'll get someone to help at the other end," and ran back to the front. Mrs. Walford dug through her bag and gave the flight attendant some pills and a bottle of water. Jacky felt an urge to run to the toilet but he chose to ignore it. His eyes were glued to the window and the endless snow while bracing for another bout of hammering from the wind. His head still hurt where he had hit the window, but he said nothing. Mrs. Walford had her hands full already and she looked nervous herself. The shak-ing was making him sick with fear, like being on a roller coaster that wouldn't stop. The noise, the rattling of the plane, and all the loose bits rattling around him added to his fear and he worried his stomach was about to hurl.

Then something changed. Not the shaking or the noise around him, not the wind or the sound of the engines, but—no, it *was* the sound of the engines. They were still humming but at a different pitch, sounding lopsided like a stereo with a broken speaker. Jacky thought his ears might have popped, but the rest of the sounds were the same. It had to be. He felt a thick, icy ripple of fear running down his back as he looked out his window and saw the propeller spinning.

He shouldn't have been able to see it but he could. The fins were turning but gradually slowing. The engine had stopped, that's what was wrong with the sound. He watched in disbelief, the black propeller slowed until it snapped to a stop. The sound of the other engine rose in pitch as the voice of the pilot came on the speakers again.

"Ah, folks, we have developed a problem with one of our engines. I'm afraid we are going to have to retrace our steps and set down at another airport so we can sit out this storm. I'm very sorry about this; I know you're anxious to get to your destination. The forecasters hadn't predicted the cold front would move this way so quickly. The plane can fly just fine on one engine, but I don't want to take any more chances in this storm. We apologize for the delay."

The plane leaned to the side and went into a wide turn with the remaining engine working overtime. The turbulence continued, as did the snow. Jacky hoped there was an airport close by. He wanted off that plane more than anything. He looked out the window and his stomach sank. All there was to see were the mountains. Snow-covered peaks stretched out below them everywhere, and there was nothing that looked anything like a town or a landing strip. He leaned back and breathed slowly. The pilots knew what they were doing. The pilots know how to handle emergency situations; they're trained for this stuff. There are lots of places to land, and this is the twenty-first century; airplanes don't get lost in flight. Not now.

The remaining engine coughed, at least the sound cut out briefly, like a bad cell phone connection. It was still working so Jacky shook his head. Then it cut out again; this time everyone heard it as the nervous cries started up again. The co-pilot appeared at the front of the plane as he grabbed the mic. He looked worried but his voice was as clear and loud as before.

"Can I have your attention, please? We're having some trouble with the other engine and we're going to have to put down right away. Everyone, please make sure there is nothing loose that can fly around and hit you. Don't panic; everything is under control. Please make sure your seat belts are pulled tight and keep in your seats. Don't get up for any reason. We're going to land soon and we should be okay, but, in the unlikely event that there are problems, we need you to stay in your seats, keep your heads down, and brace yourselves."

He returned to the cabin and closed the door; everyone else on the plane was silent. The only sound remaining was the oscillating rise and fall of the struggling engine and the wind. Someone was praying, and someone else was crying and sniffling while another voice tried to be reassuring. The silence had become as loud as the engine humming through the plane. The engine's problems were more exaggerated in the tense silence. It would stop, then ramp up as if accelerating hard, the sound cutting in and out irregularly causing an audible gasp from the passengers. Then the engine stopped completely, and the propeller gradually slowed to a standstill. The silence was sickening, the absence of vibration in Jacky's legs felt more disturbing than anything. Every muscle in his body was tight and he had trouble breathing. He lifted his head to look around. Everyone was gripping the seat in front of them but staring out outside, eyes fixed on the stationary propellers. Jacky looked out his window and saw darkness. He thought they were still high up but, suddenly, there was a field of trees on a mountain side in his window. It was rushing straight toward them. There was a bright light reflecting off the flying snow that played tricks on his eyes, making everything else seem dark. He could see they were very close to the ground and travelling fast with no engines. The plane pitched downward and then levelled, leaving Jacky's stomach behind with every rise and fall. The plane leaned to one side and then levelled again. The ground was coming closer, and the flaps of the wings were moving up and down to control their descent. Of course, Jacky realized, they were gliding, the pilot was controlling the direction of the plane with the flaps. They were moving toward the trees that covered the side of a mountain; that was where they were going to land. Jacky stared at the back of the seat he was pushing against to brace himself, waiting. Was this what it was like to die?

He had flown often enough to memorize the process of landing. There was the manoeuvring over the runway, the dropping of the wheels, the slowing of the engines and that almost silent expectant pause before the tires hit the pavement and the engines rushed to life slowing the plane. The silence of falling slowly from the sky was like that, only painfully longer. He knew the ground was rushing up to them and the plane was gliding toward it with no power but gravity and momentum. He didn't know what would happen next. He realized the wheels hadn't come down so they were going to land on the plane's belly. They were very close to the trees and rocks. Would they smash and crumble when they hit the ground? Would the fuel catch fire? Were they about to be crushed? The plane tilted up slightly and Jacky looked up. Maybe they were—

There was a loud crashing as something hit the body of the plane. Then they hit the ground in an explosion of snow, and the force of the impact threw Jacky painfully up against the seat in front of him, even though his arms were pushing against the seat back. He bounced off the window then back into his seat. His head flopped around while the seat belt dug deeply into his abdomen. Everything was moving fast and out of control. The plane bounced up and hit the ground again, lifting him and driving him back into his seat. Although they were on the ground, they were still sliding fast along the snow with the lights from the plane lighting up the snow squalls around them like a blizzard. Had they landed on the ground only to be crushed by rocks and trees? Jacky was aware of people screaming and the noise of things falling, but his gaze was fixed on the movement outside the window and his hands were white knuckled on the seat in front of him. The plane was still barrelling through snow, out of control. Trees rushed by the window like power poles on a highway, illuminated by the plane's lights. The wings were missing them or sweeping over the smaller ones. In a flash, a large tree appeared in the light close to the plane and whacked the window next to him. Snow flew in the air past the windows and the sound of the plane grinding on the snow and rocks under them added to the madness. Only the propellers sat still and calm as the snow and trees flew past. The plane turned sharply and collided with something hard. It lurched hard to the left and there was a loud bang. Everyone screamed as the plane listed and then righted itself. People flopped around in their seats like rag dolls, unable to control their movements. The overhead bins finally gave up the fight and fell open as cases started spilling out on top of people. Everyone was screaming including, he was surprised to realize, Jacky himself. Something hard had become airborne in the collision, and Jacky was in its path as the projectile clipped him on the side of the head and he saw spots floating past his eyes. Everything slowed, sounds, movement, light, everything moved around in a weird dance as the world started to move away from him down a long, black tunnel.

"Jacky, Jacky, can you hear me?" The voice was familiar. He felt a rough movement like he was being shaken and yelled at. He opened his eyes slowly. It wasn't a dream; people were still in a panic, crying and moving around but in real time. It took less than a second for his mind to focus and another for his head to start splitting open.

"Owww, stop," he screamed at whomever was touching his head. Yelling only made it worse.

"Settle down, Jacky, and hold still." It was Mr. Stewart. Jacky felt the pressure on the side of his head and he saw blood on the front of his shirt.

"It's all right, now; it's over. Just hold still. You got whacked in the head pretty hard, and we need to make sure you're not going to slip away from us again." Mr. Stewart's voice was clear, but there was still so much commotion. People were crying and yelling and moving around. The only thing that was different was the plane wasn't moving anymore. They landed; the horror was finished. No, it wasn't.

There was another roaring, deeper and farther away. It started as a low rumble but quickly grew to a thunderous blast. It sounded like a train coming at them, closer and closer. As it hit, the plane shook, rocking hard side to side, and the world outside went dark. The inside of the plane was chaos and screaming. Jacky could hear Mr. Stewart speaking, chanting something quietly, through the rumble. He was pleading for it to stop. Please, don't hurt anyone.

"It's an avalanche," someone screamed. The plane rolled severely, almost completely sideways before rolling back, knocking everyone over each other. The noise and the movement seemed endless as tons of snow continued to fall on them. Jacky couldn't fight the panic as he started to scream.

Learning to Play

Jacky quickly discovered there was an enormous difference between deciding to play the bagpipes and being able to do it. The instrument is complicated, difficult to hold, and harder to play. It's a mechanism of wooden pipes and a multitude of reeds that require a strong force of air to play them, a recorder-like chanter that has finger holes to produce the melody, and a thick, stomach-shaped bag that must be simultaneously inflated by blowing into it and squeezed to push the air out of it in order to produce any sound at all. Playing the bagpipes requires strong lungs, mental focus, and a good memory for memorizing the music. These were not Jacky's strongest characteristics. Pipers usually march or stand and play. They don't have music stands and sheet music to play from. Jacky faced the extra challenge of getting a set of pipes to play and then finding someone to teach him.

Jacky eventually did find someone willing to teach him how to play and was able to borrow a set of pipes to learn on, but that solution only brought an additional problem. Jacky planned to do this project without his father's knowledge to make it a surprise, so he had to keep it secret. His lessons would be after school so he would have to lie, something he never wanted to do. But the other problem was his lessons were at the police station because his teacher was Sergeant MacGregor, the leader of the Police Department Pipe Band.

Since his mother died, Jacky's dad had been watching him doggedly for any sign of drugs or drinking or anything that "teenagers were into these days." Jacky was offended by his dad's suspicion but he didn't like the chances of being seen at the police station or what his father's reaction would be if he found out. Still, Jacky went ahead with it. Learning to play took hours of practice so he made arrangements with the school's music teacher to work on it after school on non-lesson days. His teacher was ecstatic; being British herself she loved the pipes. Playing was hard enough, but his homework was piling up at the same time. The whole plan came very close to falling apart when Jacky's dad would lose his temper and accuse Jacky of being irresponsible and not focusing on his homework. The fact that Jacky was trying to do something incredibly hard and getting in trouble for it made the situation more tense as Jacky's secrecy only inflamed his father's suspicions.

The arguments got worse over time, building to a point that became Jacky's worst possible nightmare. Both of them were tired and both lost their temper. They both said things that were hurtful and unfair. Jacky finally screamed, "I hate you," before running to his room and slamming the door. The next day they didn't see each other at all until later in the day. That wasn't unusual for them as his dad usually left for work before Jacky got up. The argument was an unpleasant memory, like most of the ones that happened before, and Jacky hoped the new day would wash away the bad feelings. It was only when Jacky came home and found his dad lying in bed, very sick and barely breathing that he understood something was seriously wrong.

"What can I do?" he was pleading to the 911 operator, "please send an ambulance."

"It's already on the way," she said in a calm voice. "Try and cool him down, take off any blankets and put a cold cloth on his head. Most of all, you have to stay calm."

Stay calm? How the heck was he going to do that? He remembered the argument they had the previous night, and what he said.

"I hate you," that was what he had said. It came back at him like an echo, winding around and slapping his face. He killed his own father.

The ambulance was there in minutes and, with unbelievable ease and speed, the paramedics loaded his dad onto the gurney and into the ambulance and drove away, siren wailing. The paramedic working on his dad asked a lot of questions but he was nice, explaining everything they were doing and reassuring Jacky that an argument wasn't going to kill his dad. It helped but didn't remove all the guilt from his mind. The two events were so closely connected.

Jacky almost told his dad his plans; he almost broke down and begged his forgiveness for scheming the whole thing behind his back. It was supposed to be a surprise, supposed to be nice, not a cause for fighting. He didn't do it; he didn't have to. His dad apologized to him.

"Jacky, I've been so scared of screwing up and making a mistake since your mom died that I let my fears get in the way of my better judgment. I know you're not getting in trouble and I'm sorry your school is stressful for you. We'll take care of all of that once I get out of here. Let's not talk about it anymore, and tell me you forgive me, okay?"

His dad's expression was so sad and intense that Jacky couldn't speak, couldn't explain anything. All he could do was hug his dad and surrender to the reality that he was going to have to stay with his aunt, his mother's sister, and his annoying cousin until his dad got out of hospital.

The sergeant wouldn't cancel the solo or let Jacky off from his lessons. They were too close to the day and they couldn't stop things now. That was Jacky's other problem. Aside from the fact that he had to take two buses to get to his lessons, and keep fighting off his aunt's offers to drive him to school, there was a chance he would have to do the performance without his dad there. There was no way of knowing when his dad would be out of hospital and when he'd be able to go out and see Jacky play. He still didn't know about Jacky's planned surprise and, unless he got out in time, he might not see it.

Jacky was sharing his cousin's room at his aunt's house. He had nothing to say to his relatives; he barely knew them at all. His aunt was overbearing and asked too many questions, and Jacky wasn't going to tell her anything about his scheme, either. His father was supposed to be out of the hospital in two weeks to a month, and Jacky was playing a solo for the first time in his life in front of thousands of people in three weeks. All he could do was watch the calendar, wait by the phone, and worry.

Two weeks before the event, Jacky took a bus after school to a store that sold Scottish clothing. He was dressed in full Scottish regalia. It was both strange and exciting to wear those clothes, a kilt, jacket, and hat with a sporran. When he saw himself in the mirror, he was shocked to see the image of his father looking back at him. He didn't realize how much like his dad he was starting to look, but the kid in the mirror looked just like the one he saw in that picture of his dad.

He hoped his dad got out of hospital in time. This was really important.

In Concert

For once, everything worked out right. His dad was home from the hospital after just over two weeks. He was on sick leave from work so he was uncharacteristically calm, walking around the house in his pyjamas, watching TV and in a good mood. He never questioned why Jacky stayed late after school and asked no questions about his school work.

Jacky did feel bad because he was out and lying to his dad now. It was for a good reason and all, but his dad seemed to trust him more when he lied than he did when Jacky was being honest.

Whatever, he thought, *everything will be over soon, and it will be worth it.*

The idea of playing the solo was more terrifying than doing it. He struggled with his emotions, and his stomach. He wanted to run, to quit, to back out. He didn't even know if his father was there. But he couldn't. He had to take control of his nerves and his doubts; he forced himself to march out on the field and started to play. Strangely, playing the solo was the easiest part. He'd practised it so often he didn't have to think, it just happened, his fingers knew where to go, the song played in his mind just as it played out to the audience. When the rest of the police band joined him, the sound flowed over him and the rest of the song just happened. His dad was there, looking shocked and pleased, and Jacky succeeded in doing something good, for the first time in his life. No matter what happened after that, he would never be a failure.

"There's something you need to understand, Jacky," his dad said, driving home after going out for dinner. They had been talking for hours after the concert, and it was getting late. Jacky was very tired after being up so early, so he just listened as his dad spoke. "The world, your life, my life, everything is going to keep changing. All we can do is decide what we're going to do with the changes that occur. Some of it will happen by choice, like you deciding to play the bagpipes in front of a million people. But a lot of it, like Mom getting sick, that stuff just happens and nothing you do will stop it. All you can do is handle those things as best you can and carry on. You've got a long life in front of you; you don't have to waste any of it worrying about the past."

Jacky looked at his dad, who was lost in his own thoughts.

"Don't you worry about forgetting things?" Jacky asked. His dad looked at him and shrugged.

"There are only two things I care about in my life, Jacky. You and your mother. I started to worry that I wasn't doing enough to try to save your mom and then I worried that I wasn't being a good enough parent for you. Look where that got me. No, I remember everything that I want to, the rest I'll just wait and see what happens. With you, of course."

That made sense. Jacky smiled to himself and watched the city pass by.

His performance at the Police Games got some media attention in the local TV news and newspapers and his picture was on the front of the police newsletter along with a beaming Sergeant MacGregor. He was also famous around the school for a day, at least with the teachers. Shortly afterwards, he started getting invitations from some of the local pipe bands, including the New Caledonians Pipe Band, one of the best bands in the country. Jacky knew that was Sergeant MacGregor's doing. Jacky had promised the sergeant he would continue to play the pipes, and it looked like he was going to make sure that happened. Jacky was accepted into the band and started going to weekly practices.

He discovered that his journey into piping was also remarkable in that most new pipers spend at least a year learning the basics on the chanter before they even get to blow into a set of pipes. The fact that he accomplished the feat in a few months was considered both remarkable and, by some, unorthodox and improper. Either way, it was high praise for Jacky and it raised his level of confidence significantly.

Jacky was also thrilled to be in an award-winning band. No one else he knew in school had even seen bagpipes never mind played them, so being able to play with other pipers his age was a different challenge. It also helped that his short time working with the sergeant was a lot more intense than the weekly practices and marching drills the band members were subject to. Jacky could march like a soldier and memorize most of the songs quickly. He rose up the ranks of players over a couple of years and became second piper after Larry Walford, the oldest and best player in the group.

The best part of being in the band was the travelling. The New Caledonians competed in all of the major piping competitions in Canada and the United States, but the ultimate was the World Pipe Band Competition at Glasgow, Scotland. In his second year, the band placed second in their division at the Worlds and first at the North American Championships at Glengarry in Ontario. During his years in the band, Jacky's Instagram feed became full of pictures from places like Canmore, Alberta; Kincardine, Ontario; Richmond, Virginia; and all around Scotland.

But after two years of playing, he was done. He spent most of his weekends working to raise money for the band and his summers travelling. After their win at Glasgow, Jacky decided that was the last one. You can't do better than Glasgow, and there were no more goals he wanted to reach. Not as a piper. He was into different things now; he wanted his weekends and nights back. He told his dad about his plans at the end of that summer, as he was about to return to high school to start grade eleven. There were more classes and harder courses, and he needed more time to do homework; the school was already sending out information on colleges and universities to go to after high school. His dad called him out; he wasn't buying it. Jacky's marks were good, and he had no trouble keeping up with the work in spite of being in the band.

"Why do you want to quit? You're so good at playing the pipes. I thought that's what you liked doing," his dad said.

"Not for the rest of my life, Dad. I have other interests, you know." Jacky was ready to read off a grand list of his hobbies, but his dad interrupted him.

"Yeah, I know about other interests, Jacky. I was a teenager, too. It's too late anyway, I've already paid for your membership for the year and the band has special plans next year. You're staying."

And that was it. End of discussion.

Solid Ground

The sound of the avalanche faded, and the panicked screaming calmed with it. Maybe the falling snow had stopped or they were buried so far down they couldn't hear it anymore. Either way, they were powerless to change anything. The cabin door opened in the front, and the co-pilot hurried out to Mrs. Walford and Mr. Stewart, who were sitting in the front seats. Mrs. Walford jumped up, grabbing her bag, and ran into the front cabin. The door slammed shut. A moment later the co-pilot returned and started calling out over the din of voices.

"Everyone please stay in your seats and stay calm. If you are hurt please identify yourselves, and we'll help you," Suddenly a bright green glow appeared at the front of the aisle, and the co-pilot's face shone in a green horror movie gloom. He was walking down the aisle handing out glow sticks to everyone.

"We've had to turn off the lights to preserve power. Once we know everyone is safe, we'll have to dig ourselves out from the snow." He handed a stick to Jacky and moved on. Jacky lifted the shining stick to the window. All he could see was packed snow. He got up from his seat and checked himself for injuries. As soon as he stood, he felt dizzy from the shock of hitting his head. He steadied himself against the seat and closed his eyes. He did a mental inventory of himself, feeling his arms, his head, and his legs with his hand. He was sore and bruised everywhere, and the dent on his head was very tender, but there was nothing broken or cut. He looked around in the green glow of the inside of the plane and saw a lot of dazed and frightened faces. He looked up front and saw Mr. Stewart talking to the co-pilot. He heard Rick sitting in the back complaining and wondered if the big guy's claustrophobia was going to kick in. Rick could calm himself with drugs but long trips were a problem for him, and they had never been buried under snow with him before. The co-pilot and Mr. Stewart were putting on their coats and gloves. They had a shovel and a bucket, and Jacky heard something behind him and looked to see Rick quickly putting on his coat and running to the front. He was shrugging off warnings from the co-pilot to stay put and insisted on helping. *Let him help*, Jacky thought, *or you'll wish you had.* The look of near panic in Rick's eyes as he walked past was obvious, and Jacky knew his fear was building.

Rick, the co-pilot, and Mr. Stewart started working on opening the door. This was their best option as the door in the front opened out and down, creating a staircase to climb to the ground. The emergency exits were by the seats and were designed for escape, not to be reused and closed again, assuming they would need to close the door to stay warm. The hard part was pushing the door outward into the snow. It was too hard packed to push away from the door. Jacky watched intently. Rick was larger and heavier than Mr. Stewart so he and the co-pilot did the heavy pushing. The door eventually inched outward, and snow started to fall inside the plane. There was a solid wall of snow showing through the opening, it was impossible to tell how badly they were buried. They heaved on the door and it slid outward. That was a good sign, Jacky realized. They wouldn't be able to do that if they were packed in tight. There must be enough air in the snow to allow them to push the door open. The co-pilot started shovelling the snow, and Mr. Stewart was putting the snow that fell in the plane into a bucket.

"Light," Rick yelled in an excited voice, almost desperate. "I can see light. Let me through." He pushed the co-pilot aside and dove into the snow in a hard run. Mr. Stewart and the co-pilot tried to stop him, and a few of the people in the plane cried out. It was an incredibly dumb thing for Rick to do, Jacky knew. Rick could have been buried again with no air and nowhere to run. He could fall off a cliff;

they didn't know where they were. He might just have committed suicide. But sunlight burst through the doorway, and Rick ran back in a moment later, panting and covered in snow. He had a maniacal smile on his face and was screaming unintelligibly. He crouched and breathed deeply to calm himself.

"It's not that bad," he said between breaths. "We're okay; it's solid ground out there." Cheering arose, and people were scrambling to get into coats and gloves. The co-pilot and Mr. Stewart had cleaned the doorway and stood outside the plane as the trapped passengers poured out into the daylight.

"Stay close to the plane and no loud noises," commanded the co-pilot. Jacky emerged through the door and looked around at the site. The sky was cloudy and snow was still falling, but the blizzard had stopped and there wasn't as much wind. It was very cold, and he hadn't bothered to put gloves on so he stamped his way around by the door with his hands in his pockets. Mrs. Walford ran outside and spoke with the co-pilot who jerked like he got a shock; he went back into the plane with her. This left Mr. Stewart to manage the group of excited kids wandering around the crash site.

"All right, everyone." He was their leader again. "Gather around. We are going to do our breathing exercises. We all need to calm down, especially Rick." Nervous laughter all around as everyone moved toward him. Breathing exercises was how they started each weekly practice session. It was strangely calming to do something so normal in such a strange situation. After the exercises were done, there was a lot of hugging. The wind was picking up, and the sun was going down. Mr. Stewart spoke up again.

"Everyone, please, quiet, thank you. We just lived through a hell of a scare. We're all alive and safe with the exception of a few bruises and cuts, and now we have something to tell our families when we get home. Unfortunately, Mrs. Fournier, our flight attendant, has suffered a broken arm, and our pilot, Captain Connelly, was badly injured in the collision so thank God we have Mrs. Walford along to look after him and the rest of us."

The group started cheering for Mrs. Walford. Mr. Stewart waited, smiled, and continued, "Exactly, thank you, Mrs. Walford, although I suspect she was hoping for a quiet holiday on this trip. Unfortunately that does look like it's going to happen, so please take it easy with Mrs. Walford; she's got a full plate already. We don't know how long it's going to take for the rescuers to get here so we'll have to set up camp in the meantime. That will be tomorrow. For now everyone please come back inside so we can close the door and keep out the cold. We're going to figure out our food and bathroom needs. We will have to ration the food. Hopefully that won't be a problem, but I would ask you to bring me anything you have to eat—snacks, chocolate bars, energy bars, what have you. Also, and this is from the co-pilot, please leave your phones turned off and keep them warm to save the batteries. We'll try to see if we can get a signal in the morning. Hopefully this snow will stop falling and we can figure out where we are. Okay, everyone inside please." He pointed to the door, and people started filing back into the plane.

Jacky was happy to be outside, away from the cramped seat and depressing darkness. Sleeping tonight was going to be interesting; he didn't sleep well on planes normally, so bunking out in a wreck should be a lot harder. He walked back a few paces to see the whole site. The plane was completely buried in a pile of snow that fell from the cornice overhead. Jacky looked up and saw a jagged section of snow was missing where the avalanche had originated. There was a lot more up there.

It hit him at that moment that they were not going to get out of there. The plane was hidden from view overhead by the snow, and the weather could keep searchers away. There was almost no chance he was going to be able to get his application for the school in on time. He wasn't going to make it. A sharp pain shot through his skull. It felt like a bullet or a bolt of lightning hit him, and he doubled over in agony. His stomach responded by violently hurling its contents up his throat. Jacky fell to his hands and knees, retching loud enough to bring others out after him. His head was spinning and nothing made sense. He heard voices and he felt like he was moving but in a detached, distant way. Sounds echoed down a long passageway, and images were only silhouettes against a dull filter of insensibility. Nothing made sense; nothing mattered.

11

Falling

Climbing through the tight stands of tree trunks growing out of the deep snow was difficult enough without the constant interference of shrubs and old roots that snagged and pulled on his boots as he worked his way toward the slope. Jacky felt like he was swimming against a strong current, but he could see daylight ahead, through the trees. He was sure of his destination but kept the rock wall beside him for guidance. He could still turn around and get back to the site if he had to. The snow covering the floor of the forest was about knee deep, so it kept his pants wet and his feet cold, but occasionally he would step into a deep rut and be over his waist in snow. The mountain seemed to be holding him back, but he pushed on toward the light and snatches of blue sky. He needed to find a clearing to get his bearings and head downhill. After about twenty minutes, he turned away from the safety of the rock wall and out toward the outer edge of the trees. He was confident of his progress, in spite of the drag on his feet from the snow and undergrowth. The trees opened for him, and he walked into daylight again. He smiled, pleased with himself as he began his descent.

He stepped up onto a fallen log and then down into a thick pile of snow-covered twigs and pine needles. It was identical to every other pile he had stepped into, which was usually supported by a log or twigs under the snow. Instead, his foot sank through where the ground should have been and, in spite of flailing his arms to try and right himself, he lost his balance and fell forward into the snow. He'd fallen a few times by then, laughed embarrassed and got back up. This time the snow and branches fell away easily, and he was slowly tumbling down into a large drift. This was really embarrassing; he almost laughed at the awkwardness of it. Just as suddenly as he had fallen, he was wrapped in darkness. The world was still moving around him, but he had no sense of up or down or how deep he was. Fear started burning through his body, and he grabbed blindly at anything solid he felt go by. He knew he could get buried out here and he could suffocate. They might not find him. Why was he still falling? He had no control of his actions, his arms and legs moving by impulse, searching for anything solid. He was literally drowning in snow in what felt like an endless vertical tunnel. He was focused on his breathing to avoid hyperventilating and passing out. A moment or several minutes later, he had no idea, his foot met with a rock, which stopped his fall but only for a moment as it slipped off again and he continued to descend. It gave him enough time to react. Jacky turned quickly and grabbed at the obstacle with his hands and held on. This stopped his fall, but the snow and debris continued to slide over him as it passed, hitting his head and upper body with hard bits of wood that hurt as it made contact. As he clung for life, he closed his eyes and his mouth to protect them and waited until the chaos ended. He wasn't falling through the snow, he was falling *with* it. He didn't want to think about what that meant. He lost any sense of time, the beautiful blue sky, or his goals of hiking down the mountain. He clung to his perch frozen in fear, begging for the downpour to stop.

Minutes passed. Jacky didn't know how long he had been clinging to his sanctuary, but he gradually became aware that the avalanche around him had stopped. The only sound he heard was his own rapid breathing. Slowly, he opened his eyes and relaxed his cramping muscles. He struggled to look around behind him to get a bearing on his location. Not only was he in bright daylight again, he was actually hanging from a tree that was sticking out of the ground at a ninety-degree angle. He looked down at his dangling feet and saw, with a cold jolt that ran up his body, there was nothing below him. Fighting back a wave of nausea, he pulled himself up on the tree and gradually brought his leg over to sit on the trunk. Slowly and cautiously he pushed himself backwards until he felt the solid earth behind him. Again he looked down past his feet and saw the wide expanse of a valley hundreds of feet below him. There was almost nothing past this point to stop him from falling to his death. His heart raced, and his breathing became fast and shallow as his panic returned. He wrapped his arms tightly around the tree. His stomach gave up trying to hold on to his lunch, and he retched as the vomit tumbled out of him. The stream of muck tumbled slowly through space as it fell, taking Jacky's hopes of escape with it. He was shaking uncontrollably and moaning to himself. He knew had to calm down otherwise he might faint and follow his lunch the rest of the way down. He closed his eyes and forced himself to slow his breathing and settle his nerves. He talked to himself in a slow, low tone.

Easy, calm down, everything's fine. Stay clear, don't panic. He started humming a song, no idea what, to distract his thoughts. His whole body was shaking with fear, but he was warm from the exertion. Slowly he felt his muscles start to relax. He took a deep breath and opened his eyes to look around and appraise his situation.

The tree trunk extended out a few feet past him. It seemed solid, not cracking or swaying under his weight. He looked up and saw his movements through the snow. He had actually stepped off the side of the mountain and the snow drift slowed his fall, otherwise he would have simply dropped hundreds of feet to his death. The realization made him momentarily dizzy, and he swayed dangerously before catching himself. The snow was powder, barely hanging on the side of the rock and tree roots, which created a mesh of vines. Jacky was almost certain he could dig through the soft snow to the actual rock wall and, hopefully, climb back up. He was aware that his life depended on the strength of the wood he was sitting on and he was careful not to move too quickly. Thankfully, it seemed this tree had been around long enough to resist the weight of the snow and the constant pull of gravity trying to tear it down. This was reassuring because he would have to turn himself around to face the wall before he could start climbing. Grabbing onto a root poking out from the snow, Jacky pulled his leg over the tree until he was sitting on his perch with his legs on one side and nothing preventing him from rolling over backwards off the tree. Carefully he changed hands and slowly turned himself toward the snowbank, lifting his other leg over the tree to hang over the other side. His fingers were full of slivers, but he felt nothing but waves of fear with every movement of the tree underneath him. Finally he was facing the wall and looking up at where he needed to go. He hadn't fallen to his death, so he was good so far.

Pushing the snow from the tree only brought more of it pouring down on top of him. Some of it melted and trickled down his back; some got in his ears and mouth. He shook his head and spit out the dirt. The warmth he felt earlier was gone, and he was shivering again as the melting snow brought down his body temperature. He paused to breathe on his hands and slap them together to keep the blood flowing in his fingers. He pulled on the roots sticking out from the ground and they held. Carefully, he stood on the tree and reached for another stiff root to hold on to. The wall had many smaller roots and rocks sticking out far enough to serve as a foothold. Jacky climbed the wall one foot at a time, clinging to the tree roots. The sharp ends scratched his face and threatened to tear his coat, and the footing on the rocks and larger branches was anything but certain. Several times he put his weight on a rock to lift himself only to have it slip off as he scrambled to find something to hang on to. The snow and debris that continued to rain down on him was maddening, and dangerous. As he looked up to reach for another branch, a large drift fell away overhead and blinded him with inches of snow covering his face. He held onto his branch and swayed dangerously in the falling snow. Once he felt sure of his hold, he yelled out his irritation as loud as he could and shook his face to get rid of the snow. His hands were busy, and he could only turn his head and blink to clear his eyes, rubbing his face on his wet sleeve. When he could focus again, he saw he wasn't far from the top. The edge had become exposed after the snow slide, and he could almost reach it. Except he couldn't; there was at least three feet of clay and short, scrubby branches between him and the top. Nothing to hang on to. He was so close yet he was still in danger. His bare hands were numb, and his legs were getting weak from exertion. He looked around, determined, anxious, pushing snow away and searching for another anchor. His fear and frustration boiled up inside. He focused his energy on his legs and pushed up, jumping and grabbing at the roots sticking out at the top edge of the cliff. He connected and grabbed with his frozen fingers, but the roots were weak and pulled down easily. Jacky slid sideways and dangled dangerously, holding the branches with his hands but nothing under his feet.

"I don't want to die today," he screamed. His voice was surprisingly strong and it echoed off the rocks around him. Then he heard a sound overhead, a shuffling noise, and then a small amount of snow tumbled down past him. He turned away to let it pass then looked up again. He saw the top of a hat he didn't recognize and a hand reaching down to him.

"Take my hand," said a familiar voice. Jacky reached up with one arm to try to reach the hand but inches separated them. He clutched the roots and rooted around to get a footing. He was swinging over the abyss by his hands and he didn't want to let go.

"Lower, I can't reach you," he yelled. The hand pulled back, more shuffling overhead, more snow falling, and then the hand came lower toward him.

He pulled himself up with the roots, swung his left arm around, and made contact with the hand. They gripped together like a train coupling. His mystery hero had a strong grip and Jacky reached higher with his other hand to grab at another branch. He was still dangling dangerously with only the hand and some small roots keeping him from disaster. He didn't know for sure but he might have screamed. He was blinded by fear and grabbing madly at anything he could reach. The hand gripped tighter, crushing his fingers, and another hand joined it, pulling on his arm. Jacky scrabbled frantically for a footing and found the edge of a stone. He pushed up and felt himself being pulled higher; his confidence and strength returned and he pulled. As he rose up he found stronger branches and roots to pull on until, with a final tug by his rescuer, he sailed over the edge and landed face first in the snow. He was covered with it and freezing but he didn't care. The release of fear took away his grip on all of his emotions as he cried and laughed, shaking his entire body. The ground was solid beneath him and he wasn't falling anymore. He owed thanks to someone and he had to know who it was. He pushed himself up out of the snow and stared. He was looking at the stern, worried face of Nadine Fassbender, the girl who had saved him from Rick and the last person he expected to see out there. She was staring back at him, still covered in snow and secured to a tree with a rope. He regarded the rope with envy and surprise. Why didn't he think to bring that?

"Nadine?"

"Yeah?" she answered, brushing herself off. "Not who you were expecting?" She untied the rope around her waist.

Jacky opened his mouth to say something, but his brain froze. He didn't know what to say. He had only rarely spoken to Nadine. Hardly anyone spoke to Nadine; she was a bit of a loner. She was loud and very opinionated. She had something to say about almost everything, and it was usually the opposite of what everyone else thought. She had short, cropped hair and wore drab looking clothes. She was usually ignored by the others in the band, including Jacky, and now he owed her his life.

"You're really strong," he said, flexing his aching hand.

She looped the rope and put it in her backpack and frowned at him. "That's what you want to say to me? Yeah, I can bench press two ten. And you're either an idiot or you picked a bad time to go mountain climbing," she said. She walked toward him and held out a hand to help him up. He took it and lifted himself awkwardly to his feet. "You're welcome, by the way."

He felt his face going red. "I was getting to that. Thank you for—for—"

"For rescuing you - again?" she interrupted him, "It's okay, Jacky. I was in the neighbourhood. You wanna tell me what you're doing out here?"

He avoided looking at her but he knew she was staring at him. He wanted to think up a line to avoid the truth, but his brain wasn't keeping up. He sighed.

"I was trying to get away. I wanted to get out of here." He was looking at his feet.

"I guessed that," Nadine said. "Why? You know it's dangerous. Why chance falling off a cliff when they're coming to rescue us?"

"It'll take too long," he blurted out, then immediately regretted it. He said too much, and Nadine was going to keep asking him until he explained himself. He searched his mind for something to say. He stopped and faced her.

"You know how long we were flying around looking for a place to land. You know we were off course. They don't know where to start searching. Look around, Nadine, those mountains are huge, and we're so small. We could be up here for days before they find us." He turned and started walking away. Nadine ran to catch up with him.

"So you were just going to walk down the mountain and call for help?" she asked.

"Something like that," he said.

"How? You think they have pay phones out in the wilderness?" she persisted. Jacky pulled his phone from his pocket.

"There's cell service everywhere, Nadine. Everywhere but up here, but once I was down low enough they could have found my signal and found where we were."

"What are you so afraid of, Jacky? We're all safe, we have food, and we know they're searching for us."

It may have been the adrenalin still coursing through his blood, or it may have been the cold, but Jacky lost control of his temper. He stopped and faced Nadine. "I don't want to be here, okay? I never wanted to come on this trip and I don't want to play in this pipe band anymore, do you understand? We were supposed to fly there, play, and then I was going to quit. That's why I don't want to be stuck up here on the top of a stinking mountain, Nadine." His voice was getting gradually louder. When he stopped, still staring at her shocked face, he heard his voice echoing off the rocks and gradually fading off into the distance. Then he realized what he said and turned away. "I'm sorry, Nadine, I shouldn't have yelled at you."

"So you want to quit?" she repeated with a quavering voice and a loud swallow. "I thought you like the band; you're one of our best pipers. I'll be sorry to see you go." She walked away quickly, sniffing. Jacky followed her.

"Nadine, I'm sorry, I just—" He just what? He caught up to her and walked in silence for a moment, then he stepped in front of her. "What I said, that was just frustration and fear—and hunger. I'm starving and cold. Please don't tell Mr. Stewart what I said."

She crossed her arms and frowned. "But you're still planning on quitting?"

"Yeah, maybe, I'm not sure. There's something else I want to do," he said, avoiding her eyes.

"What?"

Jacky grimaced. "Ah, Nadine, look, I can't tell you. I'm sorry."

"Hmm, you can apologize to me a million times but you obviously can't trust me with your huge secret, even though I saved your life," she snorted and walked past him. "It doesn't matter anyway, Jacky," she said over her shoulder as he tried to catch up, "you're stuck with us whether you like it or not. C'mon, Mr. Stewart is looking for you."

"How did you find me?" he asked, following her.

"They noticed you were gone, and I remembered seeing you walk around the back of the plane. It wasn't hard to figure that you'd snuck off to do something stupid like this, but I wanted to save you the trouble of getting caught. I followed your footsteps to the place where you fell off the cliff and I thought you were dead. I was terrified for you until I heard you crying so I thought I'd give you a hand."

Jacky walked in silence for a moment. The only sound was the crunch of snow under their feet. "I wasn't crying," he mumbled.

Nadine turned and laughed at him. "You were so crying. I'm surprised everyone else couldn't hear you. 'I don't want to die, waaaa.'" She turned and trudged on ahead.

Jacky's face was burning. "Fine, you don't have to rub it in. It was scary as hell out there." Why, out of everyone on the plane, did it have to be Nadine who found him?

"Jacky, what the hell are you doing out there?" the voice startled him. Jacky looked up and saw Mr. Stewart staring at him from ten feet away. He was standing at the edge of the trees with a look of terror on his face. Jacky shrugged and walked toward him. His feelings were still smarting from Nadine's mocking, but his fear had passed.

"I was looking for a way down," he said as casually as possible. There was no point lying about it; Nadine would probably tell them anyway if he lied about it. He pointed to the trail behind him. "But we can't get out that way." He smiled at the band manager as he passed. "I guess we're stuck up here."

Mr. Stewart stared in the direction of the trees, at Nadine and Jacky as they walked past, then chased after them. He wasn't finished.

"Jesus, Jacky, what the hell were you thinking? It's all I need, to have you wandering off and falling off the damn mountain. You scared the bejesus out of me, out of all of us."

"I'm sorry, Mr. Stewart, I just wanted to get help," Jacky called back as they walked to the site. The adrenalin rush of surviving a second near-death experience in two days was wearing off and being replaced with a resigned acceptance that they were helplessly stuck. That meant he was also hopelessly stuck in his own life.

When they walked back into the full view of the site, Jacky saw that he really had been missed as a small crowd formed around him. The co-pilot was staring at Jacky from the back of the group with an open glare of disapproval. Jacky figured the guy wouldn't have minded if he had taken a tumble off the side of the mountain. Then he could have lectured everyone about safety and saying "I told you so" as often as possible. Mrs. Walford stepped forward and started checking Jacky over, looking at his hands and opening up his coat to look at the scratches on his neck. The rest of the band members were staring at him, and Jacky felt the heat of his embarrassment running up his face.

"I'm okay, Mrs. Walford," he protested, but she ignored him.

"Your hands are frozen, and you're soaking wet," she said. "Those scratches need to be disinfected. You might have frostbite and you could get sick from whatever you ingested out there. Go inside now and change out of these clothes and try to get warm. I'll come and see you in a few minutes. I really wish we could have a fire." The last words were directed over her shoulder. Jacky followed her voice and looked at the co-pilot, who had moved in closer to the group.

"It's too dangerous, I told you." The co-pilot returned his gaze. "If everyone would just stay close to the plane like I said, this wouldn't happen." He snorted loudly and walked away. Jacky looked around at the faces of the others as they began to break away from the group, some looking at him with derision; others, like Rick and Terry, looked disappointed. Jacky suspected they really wanted him to find a way out of there, and his failure meant they couldn't do the same.

Jacky found his seat on the plane, pulled off his coat and dug through the pile of clothes and things he had taken out of his backpack for some dry jeans. He changed quickly, replacing his wet socks for dry ones. He hung the wet pants and socks over the edge of the luggage compartment doors, which had all sprung open after their rough landing. He wrapped his sweat shirts and everything else he could find around himself and lay across the seat. Even curled up as he was he knew that he wasn't going to get warm but he lay there shivering anyway. He wasn't going back outside now for anything.

"Here," a blanket suddenly appeared and covered his field of vision. He knew the voice and considered refusing it but not for long. He reached for it and wrapped it around his legs.

"Thank you," he said. Nadine stared at him in silence with her arms crossed. Jacky closed his eyes, trying to ignore her but surrendered, "I said thank you, Nadine. Thanks for—everything."

"I'm just lending it to you. I want it back tonight," she said.

"I understand." He closed his eyes again, hoping she would take the hint, but Nadine stood her ground. The silence hung for a minute until she spoke again.

"I thought about what you said and I want you to know," she paused, "it upset me, but I doubt that matters very much. But I will agree not to tell anyone about it."

"Thanks, I appreciate that," he said, keeping his eyes closed.

"On one condition," she continued. Jacky groaned. "That you promise me you won't try anything like this again. You will stay close to the plane and help out here like everyone else. And you don't tell anyone else what you told me, especially not Mr. Stewart. It will hurt him to think you want to abandon the group. That's the deal." Jacky opened his eyes and looked at her. She stood in place, red faced and upset but unmoving. He was prepared to tell her to leave him alone and not give him rules but he saw the intensity in her eyes. They were drilling through him with a kind of anger, maybe disappointment, but her face was close to tears. Then he understood that he was wrong about Nadine; she wasn't the unpopular girl in the group but the one who cared the most about everyone in it. He got the message. He raised his hand.

"I swear, Nadine. I won't say or do anything to upset Mr. Stewart or the band members in any way. Thank you for the blanket and, you know, the other stuff." She relaxed her gaze and nodded. He sighed and lay his head down again. The blanket was so comfortable and warm, he was asleep in seconds.

12

Stuck in Transit

That night the wind started blowing harder and bringing colder weather and snow with it. They had to close the plane door to keep out the cold. Without lights for reading, and with most of the phones, laptops and tablets running out of battery power, the inside of the plane was dark. There was an emergency flashlight by the door for anyone who had a midnight nature call. The toilet inside the plane was frozen—and full—so they had to put up two makeshift outhouses in the back by the tail. The guys in the group didn't care; most of them simply wandered into the bush and let fly. It was cold enough that no one ventured out for too long, and Mr. Stewart made sure to know who was going out and when they came back. Jacky figured the band manager hadn't slept since they landed on this hilltop. He wrapped himself in his coat and curled up as much as he could. He'd given back the blanket to Nadine as promised, and she was snoring away in her chair, warm and irritating.

It was a long night. Jacky spent most of it remembering the argument he had with his dad about coming on this trip.

"I don't understand why you're not excited about going on this trip. You'll be playing for the Prince of Wales, the future king. It is a huge honour, Jacky, you should want to go." His dad was incredulous, almost laughing in disbelief.

"Because, Dad, we've played for lots of 'important people' (he used air quotes as he spoke) and it's no different than playing for anyone else. Just because they're in the audience doesn't change anything. It's not like the guy is going to come over and shake my hand and say hi, Dad. It's just a concert. It won't matter if I'm there or not." Jacky was forcing himself to speak calmly and not raise his voice. His dad wasn't doing the same.

"That's insane, Jacky. This is a once-in-a-lifetime opportunity, and you will never have this chance again. You are going on this trip and you are going to play as well as you played in Glasgow. That's what got you that award and that's why you're flying up to meet the prince. Trust me, you would regret not going, when you're older and can think straight. It will be great, you'll see."

"Yeah, good idea, Dad," Jacky mumbled to himself as he lay, shivering, on the cold plane seat. The wind was blowing outside, and he could hear snow skittering against the window next to his head.

The sun rose the next day several hours before Jacky woke. When he stepped outside the plane he saw the wind had managed to undo most of their work from yesterday. People were once again brushing snow off the plane but with far less enthusiasm. It didn't serve any real purpose other than killing off time. Jacky trotted to the back of the site to use the facilities. That was the only time he was grateful for the cold. You could freeze your ass off but at least it didn't smell back there.

Hours later, Jacky sat on the wing of the plane, seeking out the highest perch available to watch the sky. Except for a few random clouds, the sky remained frustratingly empty. The sun shining on the wings generated a bit of heat, but a quick gust of wind was all it took to take any warmth away. Still, he sat and stared. He was mentally willing a helicopter or airplane to appear with no luck.

Everyone had their own way of spending the empty hours as they ticked slowly by. Some of the band members had iPods and Kindles that still worked. Jacky's phone had given up the last of its charge by the time he crawled in to sleep. He cursed himself for forgetting to turn it off before he passed out from exhaustion. All of the entertainment he had packed was electronic, which was what most of them had brought. Phones, pads, portable gaming units, laptops; all of them needed power to recharge and most of them needed Internet access to work. As a result of the boredom, the magazines that were on the plane had been rifled through and anyone who had cards or any kind of board games became very popular.

"You should probably come down and move around a bit, Jacky." Mr. Stewart was below the wing looking up at him. "You don't need to keep watch; when they get here, we'll know." He stood back and waited for Jacky to climb down. Jacky sighed and stood up stiffly. Mr. Stewart was right; he needed to move, and he slid off the wing with a thump.

"You look frozen," said Mr. Stewart. "C'mon, walk with me for a minute."

Jacky stuffed his gloved hands in his coat pockets and fell in with Mr. Stewart as he walked away from the plane. They approached the edge of the cliff and looked out over the steep drop.

"It's a long way down," Mr. Stewart said, looking down.

"Yeah," agreed Jacky.

Mr. Stewart straightened and scanned the horizon. "That was quite the hike you took yesterday," he said, not looking at Jacky. "I imagine you were pretty nervous out there."

Jacky looked at him, waiting for some clue of where the conversation was going. "Not really, not until I fell off the edge. Before that I wasn't scared. I thought I might have made it."

Mr. Stewart continued to look outward, as if talking to the air. "Did you have an opportunity to look around before you set out on your hike?" He looked at Jacky directly then, his face was serious. "I mean you didn't have a choice of trails to try out there?"

Then the question was clear; Jacky understood what Mr. Stewart wanted to know. "No sir, there was no other way down. Not that I saw."

Mr. Stewart nodded and looked at him. "All right, then, thank you." He inhaled deeply and breathed out slowly. "It's a big place, Jacky, but they're coming for us, you know it. Stop worrying so much."

Jacky thought of saying the same thing to Mr. Stewart, except he wasn't worried about getting rescued, he was impatient. Obviously Mr. Stewart was thinking about it, along with everything else, he assumed.

The manager was responsible for all of them; he put them on that plane and would have to answer if anyone got hurt. Yet he was asking Jacky if there was a way out of here. Was Mr. Stewart thinking they wouldn't be found? That didn't help; it only made things worse. He walked back to the plane in silence. There wasn't any way to ask the questions that Jacky had in his mind, and it wouldn't make any difference to talk about things. They weren't going anywhere, regardless.

Then a different thought occurred to him. "Mr. Stewart, do you have any books to read?"

Mr. Stewart raised his eyebrows and looked at him.

"My phone's dead, and I didn't bring anything else to read," Jacky said. "I was hoping you might have something I could borrow."

Mr. Stewart's face brightened. "Yes, as a matter of fact I do, but I'm not sure if you would like them. I've been reading the classics lately, trying to refresh my memory with some old books I haven't read in a while. Mostly Joyce, Hemingway, Conrad, that sort of thing, probably nothing you'd be interested in. But you're welcome to read them if you want."

Jacky didn't know any of the stories, but he had heard of them. He wouldn't bother even trying to read anything that old but, then again, beggars can't really choose. "Yeah, that would be great, thanks," Jacky said.

Mr. Stewart smiled, "Okay, then, come over to my office."

His office was his seat at the front of the plane, filled with his luggage, a blanket, and a pillow. Mr. Stewart zipped open his black plastic suitcase and pulled out a Kindle. He offered it to Jacky.

"It's one of those new e-readers," said Mr. Stewart. "My wife got me this one so I could bring all of my books with me without bringing another suitcase. Go ahead, you can read it."

Jacky held the device in his hand. It was the size of a comic book with a screen like his iPad. He'd heard of them but never actually used one. He never needed to. He flicked the switch and the screen came to life with a listing of books stored on the unit. There was nothing he knew, just a collection of old books. Jacky had heard of some of the titles; *The Sun Also Rises*, *Heart of Darkness*, *Portrait of an Artist as a Young Man*.

"It's pretty incredible," Mr. Stewart said. "The battery lasts for weeks, but it's best if you keep it warm and turn it off when you're done with it."

Jacky smiled and turned the unit off. "I will. Thanks, Mr. Stewart."

Mr. Stewart closed the suitcase. "Enjoy, Jacky."

They ate half sub sandwiches again with packages of Oreo cookies with water for dinner. Almost everyone was nestled into their seats to keep warm. It was getting cold outside again, and the co-pilot closed the plane door to keep out the wind. Jacky finished eating quickly and leaned back against the wall to read his borrowed ebook. The unit was a screen with words on it and no back-lighting. Probably why the battery lasted so long. It needed lighting to read, but fortunately there was daylight and Jacky made sure his window was clear.

He began with Hemingway's *The Old Man and the Sea*. The story was a little heavy for him, at least at the start. An old man, Santiago, was a fisherman who hadn't caught anything for a long time and he was thin and weak. His closest friend was a boy who seemed very wise for being so young. It felt like the book should be *The Old Man and the Boy*. After a while, Jacky closed the unit down and rubbed his sore eyes. The light was getting too low to read anyway; clouds were rolling in and blocking the sun. He wrapped his airline blanket around his feet and rolled up his coat to use as a pillow. He lay uncomfortably on the seat staring out at the gloom filling the window. He wasn't looking forward to waiting through another night of cold silence in the plane. The emptiness only amplified the questions that were screaming for attention in his brain.

What happened? He thought things were going so well with his dad. Why was he being so unreasonable?

13

Nova Scotia

Home life reformed itself for Jacky after his performance at the Police Games. His relationship with his father was changed for the better, and it felt like a wall that stood between them was gone. Understanding was the new normal; asking questions with no filters was easier when there was trust between them. That took some getting used to, but over time it became normal for them to talk frankly about school and work and any problems they had. All the cards were on the table; there was no more need for secrecy.

The real benefit of their new relationship was that Jacky's confidence had started to reignite. Before, when his mother was still around, Jacky was always more sure of himself. But losing her reassuring presence, and facing his dad's lack of trust, made him doubt himself. Failure was easy when you expect the worst. It was only after he realized he could take control of his own life that he regained his courage. With confidence came curiosity. Once he lost his fear of failure he quested for knowledge. His marks returned to their previous A's and B's, and he had no trouble mastering his workload. His temporary fame bought him some goodwill from his teachers, and they let him rewrite some of his work to bring his marks up. It was like a space opened in his brain, and Jacky longed to fill it with knowledge. He couldn't get enough new information about things.

Then school ended. It was summer and the warm days and late nights stretched on into the immediate future. Jacky had no plans; he was too young to get a job and he had nothing else to do but sleep in and play video games. Life was sweet. Right until the first Saturday of summer holidays when Jacky got up and was enjoying a bowl of Honey Nut Cheerios covered with sliced bananas and strawberry yogurt. His dad walked in, poured a coffee and dropped two airline tickets on the table. Jacky picked them up and read; return flights to Halifax, Nova Scotia. He looked at his dad who sat across the table with his newspaper and a plate of scrambled eggs.

"What do you think?" his dad asked, digging into the steaming pile of food.

"Cool," Jacky said. "What's in Halifax?"

"Lots of stuff, but we're not just going to Halifax. Do you remember when we were looking at those old pictures after your mom died?" his dad said, not waiting for an answer. "Of course you do, that's what started your whole bagpipes thing." He paused to take a long drink of coffee. "I told you then we would go back sometime so you can see where my family, your family comes from. That's where we're going."

The memory of that day came back into Jacky's mind. They spent the whole day and night digging through old boxes of pictures. That was Jacky's first glimpse of his parents when they were younger, and the first time he saw his grandparents. Then there was that big, colour picture of his dad, at age fifteen, holding a set of bagpipes that started Jacky playing, and ultimately led to him perform in front of five thousand people.

"Awesome," Jacky said.

Two weeks later, they were on a plane flying to Halifax. The WestJet flight was long and fully booked, and with so many people on board talking and at least two babies crying behind them, it was impossible to have any kind of conversation. It didn't matter because his dad was snoring in his seat right after they took off. Jacky spent most of the flight staring out the window or flipping through the PC Gaming magazine he bought at the airport. He brought his Nintendo 3DS to play on the flight, but it was in his carry-on bag and that was in the overhead bin three seats back because some jerk had taken the space over their seat. All he could do was wait, and think.

He wondered why his dad chose to go there. Jacky wasn't against coming out to the east coast, but it wasn't his first choice for a holiday; he hoped they could go to Europe or someplace different. Still, this was the first time he'd ever been to the east coast, so technically it was different. Who were they going to meet, and what would they do in Nova Scotia? His grandparents were both dead, and his dad didn't have sisters or brothers. He hadn't mentioned any other family.

They arrived in the afternoon, retrieved their bags, and rented a car at the airport. Jacky had seen the ocean from the plane as they were landing and he was looking forward to seeing it up close, but the drive from the airport was just endless miles of farmland and trees everywhere with the occasional lake going by but no vast body of water with ships in it. Eventually they drove into the city. The streets were lined with large trees and rows of houses that were mostly old and had strings of long, black power lines running between them on wooden poles going down the street. It felt like they were driving through an old TV show.

"Is this Halifax, Dad?" Jacky was looking past the houses, trying to see the ocean. His dad was driving slowly, looking at the houses as they passed.

"No, this is Dartmouth. Halifax is over that way. I'm looking for something; it will be just a minute." Jacky followed his father's gaze as they drove down the road. They slowed in front of a house that was old, like the others, but had been fixed up recently with new windows, fresh paint and a massive wooden door in front. His dad stopped the car and stared at the house. Jacky didn't know what to say; his dad's far away expression didn't give him any clues. His dad said nothing but he was thinking about something, intensely judging from the look in his eyes. He made a deep grunting sound and shook his head. They got out of the car and walked to the door; his dad paused to look at the yard, and then rang the doorbell. Someone inside pulled a curtain open to see them. A moment later, the front door opened and a man about his dad's age walked out. The man's face didn't show any sign of recognition.

"Help you?" he said, glancing at both of them. Jacky felt awkward standing on the step with nothing to say. His dad took a deep breath.

"I used to have family who lived here," he said. That surprised Jacky and he looked at the other man to see his reaction.

"That so?" the man answered, no friendlier than before. "It's been in my family all along, so we must be related." He lifted his hand to shake, "Grant Fraser."

They shook hands. Jacky's dad gave him a dry smile and said, "Murray Fraser, from Inverness."

The man nodded, and he seemed to connect something in his memory. "Hmm, I see. We must have met before, back then after—" He paused, clearing his throat and glancing at Jacky. "Makes us second cousins, I guess. This your boy, then?"

His dad smiled for the first time and put his hand on Jacky's shoulder as he introduced him. Jacky shook hands with Grant Fraser, the first member of his dad's family he ever met.

"I'd invite you in but the place isn't really ready for company. We're still renovating," Grant said.

"That's fine, we're just passing," his dad answered.

"Looks really nice, what you've done," Jacky chimed in. Grant smiled and looked back at the house.

"Thank you. Of course it ought to, it's costing enough. The wife wanted to sell it and buy something new, but I'd prefer to keep it in the family." He was talking to Jacky's dad. "What brings you here?"

Jacky interjected. "My dad's taking me to his hometown to show me where he grew up."

Grant looked from Jacky to his dad. "That so? You're going up to Inverness, then?"

His dad pointed to Jacky. "Yeah, he's never been. I figured it was probably time."

Grant smiled and nodded in agreement. His expression changed as he spoke, "He never came back here, you know. We never saw or heard from him again after—afterwards."

"Yeah, I figured that." Jacky's dad shrugged. "Probably for the best." Jacky looked from one to the other for some explanation of who they were talking about and what "afterwards" meant, but neither of them were talking. It was obvious from their expressions that whatever happened was pretty bad. He would ask his dad about it later.

"I don't remember too much other than everyone in the family was really upset about it," Grant said. "By the time I learned about it the whole thing was over and done with. I'm just real sorry, is all."

You're sorry, thought Jacky, his curiosity growing, *at least you know what happened.*

Jacky's dad nodded and forced a smile. "Thank you, it's best left in the past. I just wanted to see the place once more while we were here. Good meeting you, Grant," he said as they shook hands again.

"You, too," Grant said and turned to Jacky, offering his hand. "Good to meet you, Jacky. Take care of your dad and have a good time in Inverness. It's a nice place." They shook hands. Jacky didn't know what to say after what he'd heard and not heard. He followed his dad to the car and got in, still hoping for some explanation of what they were talking about. He snapped on his seat belt and looked to his dad who was staring at the house with an indescribable look of sadness on his face. His eyes said he was in a faraway place. They sat in silence for a long moment before his dad snapped out of it. He smiled at Jacky as he started the car and drove away from the house.

"Sorry about the detour," his dad said after a few minutes. "Let's get to Halifax and unpack. We're having lobster tonight; it's going to be the best food you've ever eaten. I guarantee it."

Jacky felt like he missed something, as if he switched channels halfway through a movie.

"Dad, what was that all about? What happened at that house?" he had to ask.

His dad glanced sideways at him. "I stayed in that house for a while when my mother—after my parents were in an accident. They sent her down here to the hospital. My father put me up with relatives— there, to wait until she got out. That's all. It wasn't a good memory for me, son. I haven't been back since then but I wanted to see the place while we were here."

"That wasn't the place we were coming here to see?" Jacky asked, relieved.

His dad gave a dry, humourless laugh. "No, Jacky. That isn't why we came here. You're going to meet some special people and have fun. Trust me."

Halifax

They drove past a large shopping centre and then on to a long bridge. The city burst out around them. Jacky knew Halifax was an old city; he studied that in Canadian history. But the city looked anything but old. Shining glass buildings lined the edge of the waterfront and boats of all types were sailing in and out of the harbour. It seemed to be alive with activity. Driving over the bridge, Jacky could see every kind of ship by the docks, including grey navy ships, huge white cruise ships, fishing boats and ferries that were packed with people slipping past them on the water.

"Here we are." His dad's voice was completely different, more enthusiastic. "Now you can see the city. There's Citadel, that hill over there. Those are the Royal Canadian Navy ships, and over there is where the Halifax explosion happened." He was pointing out the window on Jacky's side. "Blew away that whole section of the city."

Jacky stared through the passing girders of the bridge trying to see where the blast happened. He read about the whole thing in school. A century ago, it was the largest man-made explosion in history before the invention of the hydrogen bomb. He'd written an essay about it. He knew things would have been rebuilt since then but he was a little disappointed not to see some remnants of the destruction. Everything was new and undamaged.

"Dad?"

His father glanced over. "Yeah?"

"I'm really excited about this trip."

"Yeah, me, too. I've been meaning to bring you for a long time but, you know, life happens. Anyway here we are, finally. Let's have fun."

They drove down the hill that took them into the downtown. They passed the waterfront, which was alive with crowds of people doing all kinds of activities. Music and food were everywhere. They drove past restaurants and stores and eventually down streets full of very old, elegant houses. They pulled up in front of one large, grand looking one with a green and gold lettered Bed and Breakfast sign on the gate. Another small blue plaque by the front door said it was over 150 years old and was originally owned by . . . bla bla bla . . . Jacky didn't care; he wanted to get back outside and check out the waterfront. Walking in the front door he took in the large open area; the wide, carpeted stairway with carved, wooden banisters; and the long hallway panelled entirely with dark wood and old-fashioned wallpaper. Thick-framed, faded pictures of serious looking people hung every few feet down the hallway.

The lady who ran the place greeted them cheerfully. She was a tiny person with snow white hair and a British accent that reminded Jacky of Mrs. Miller, his music teacher in middle school. She was very talkative, with lots of questions about where they were from and what their plans were. She rattled off a long list of suggestions on where to go and things to do in Halifax, talking constantly as she filled in forms, processed the credit card payment, and handed them a key to the room. She led them up the grand staircase to their room on the top floor. Like the rest of the house, the bedroom felt like it existed in another time with the wooden floors and panelling on the walls, the old furniture, and the large, framed pictures of ships at sea. It felt like they had slipped back to the nineteenth century. The only exceptions were the black power outlets on the wall and the small, flat panel TV set on the bureau. They dumped their bags on the floor, not even bothering to unpack, and walked back to the docks to check out the sights.

It was a festival atmosphere by the water. There were fiddlers, singers, and bagpipers playing along the waterfront and kids screaming and running around the clowns and jugglers who kept the action wildly frenetic. There was so much to see and hear; Jacky felt his brain start to overload. All he could do was keep walking while the sounds and smells ran through him. They ate dinner in a restaurant on an old ship where they ate lobster and scallops and potatoes and apple pie until Jacky's stomach hurt. When they stepped back outside it was dark and the tinging of ship masts and the groaning of ropes binding the boats to the docks replaced the sound of children playing along the waterfront with the occasional splash of waves coming in with the tide. Jacky looked out into the night, the blackness broken by the lights of the houses on the far shore and the ships anchored out on the water. He looked up at the city as it rose above them and saw the giant clock on Citadel Hill. He surprised himself when he started to say something but instead his mouth sprung open with a monstrous yawn. His dad chuckled.

"Well, either you were trying to suck in a wave or you're very tired. C'mon, let's get back to the house so you can go to bed."

'Uh huh," Jacky surrendered; every part of him was exhausted. "This is great. Thanks for bringing me here, Dad."

"You're welcome, Jacky. I'm glad you like it. Of course, this is just the start, so you better get a good night's sleep."

They walked in silence back to the bed and breakfast as sleep gradually took over Jacky's brain. The walk back, climbing the stairs of the old house, and falling into bed happened in a haze of half-sleep and muscle memory. When he woke the next morning, he couldn't remember going to bed.

The morning sun poured into the room and hit his eyes like a flood light. He sat up, turning away from the window and rubbed his eyes to ease the transition from sleep. He heard the hiss of the shower. His dad was always more of a morning person than he could ever be. He walked to the window and looked out at the city. Their room was high enough to see over the trees and most of the houses around them. He could see the water and some of the pier they walked on the previous day.

"Good morning, sleepyhead," his dad said, stepping out of the bathroom wearing a towel and rubbing his hair. "You were pretty tired last night so I let you sleep. You won't be able to do that again while we're here. They get up pretty early on the east coast."

"I really have to go to the bathroom," Jacky said, feeling the call of nature. "And I need a shower to wake up."

"Go for it," his dad said, waving toward the bathroom door. "The room is yours."

They packed before going down to breakfast.

"What are we doing today?" Jacky asked, stuffing his clothes in the suitcase.

"We're going to check out some stuff here in Halifax. The Maritime Museum and the Citadel, then we'll hit the road. We should be in Inverness by dinner."

"Inverness? That's where we're going?"

"Yes," his dad said, zipping his case shut.

"Where's that?"

"That way," his dad grinned, pointing north.

"You're real helpful."

"Doesn't matter where it is," his dad said. "You'll see it for yourself in a while. Now let's go." Jacky grabbed his suitcase and followed his dad downstairs. They ate a quick breakfast, said goodbye to the landlady, and drove back into the city.

What separated Halifax from other cities in the county was its history. There was so much of it there. So many people came there from other countries, so many things happened in the past that brought them there. The Maritime Museum was full of stories and pictures from the Halifax Explosion in 1917, when two ships collided in the harbour and one, which was full of ammunition for Europe and the war, drifted as it burned. It reached the other side of the harbour, closest to the homes of working people before it exploded. That was the destruction Jacky was looking to see from the bridge. The pictures were terrible to look at, and yet, they were all taken after the fact, after the damage was done and a heavy snow fell to cover the burned city. The people in the pictures looked at the camera with empty, dull looks. As far as they were concerned, the world had ended and there was nothing else left. And yet, a hundred years later, these pictures are all that was left of the devastation.

They wandered through the section on the sinking of the *Titanic*. Jacky had forgotten that many of the people who died, and many who were rescued, ended up in Halifax afterwards. All the things he was seeing—the hard life of fishermen, the death and tragedy on the sea, and all the fighting and wars—was a contradiction. That city, with all its life and activity, was built on a history of destruction and hardship. The whole thing was getting depressing.

"Dad, do you think we could—" He wasn't sure how to say it politely. His dad looked and nodded.

"Yeah, it's too much tragedy to start the day. Let's go."

Driving out of Halifax, they passed shipping yards where thousands of containers were piled up next to monster ships with Chinese and Korean names painted on them. They drove past more large houses, parks, and a few smaller marinas with many boats tied up or sitting at anchor. Eventually they were on the highway, driving away from the water and the city.

Driving on the highway anywhere looked much the same to Jacky. Endless stretches of fields, trees, and occasional towns zipping past. In the quiet, Jacky found himself thinking of his mother again. After his concert, he and his dad had stood in the park and watched as city workers installed a plaque on a bench that his dad had ordered in her memory. It was where she used to sit after a long walk and watch children playing and people enjoying their day. It was a nice moment, one that she wouldn't be around to enjoy.

"Did you ever come here with Mom?" Jacky's voice broke the silence that had settled in the car. The suddenness of it startled his dad out of his thoughts.

"What made you think of Mom?" his dad asked, not answering the question.

"I don't know, I guess I was thinking how great it would be if she could be here, too," Jacky said, looking out at the unfamiliar scenery.

"Hmm, yeah, you're right. It would have been." His dad thought for a moment then shook his head. "No, your mom never saw this place. I met her when we were at university together in Toronto. We travelled all over the place, but I never brought her to Nova Scotia." His voice was very matter-of-fact.

"I guess that's what bothers me the most," Jacky said. "It's not fair. She's missed so much—my concert, Disneyland, travelling here. I wish she could have seen it all."

"That's the thing about life, Jacky," his dad said. "You never know what's going to happen. I miss your mom every day, but we still have to carry on living. That's one of the reasons I brought you here, to meet other people in your family. Besides, if you think of it, you might not have learned the bagpipes if your mom was alive. Everything that happens changes part of our lives, and you don't know what might have been if things were different. I'm pretty sure your mom would have said that, too, although she would have loved to see you play the bagpipes. She liked them, too."

They stopped in Pictou for a break. They spent a few minutes looking at the *History of New Scotland* display by the replica of the *Hector*, the ship that brought many Scots to Canada. They were removed from their land by the British in the late 1700s. It was hard to believe that people could be that cruel to each other.

"This is how we came to Canada," Jacky's dad said while they were walking on the deck of the ship. The statement puzzled Jacky until he realized—duh—of course it had to be. His family came from Scotland, probably on a ship like this one. This was where it all started for them; he still couldn't imagine what it would be like to be kicked out of your own home.

Then they were back on the road driving inland, away from the water. They passed Stellerton and Antigonish. They rode up a narrow causeway, passing a sign welcoming them to Cape Breton. *Finally*, Jacky thought. His butt was getting sore, and they could see water. He wished his dad had rented a nicer car; this one was hot and cheap. They were driving past small towns and fishing ports with names like Creignish, Craigmore, and Mabou. There was no question that these people were Scots. There were so many Scottish flags, around and many of the town signs had Gaelic translations as well. Jacky glanced across the car at his dad. Was he happy to be here? His expression was impossible to read; his jaw was set, and he stared straight out the window, not speaking. Jacky knew his dad well enough to recognize when he was deep in thought. What was he thinking about? What would they find in Inverness, he wondered.

Inverness

The answers weren't any clearer when they finally arrived at Inverness, a small town by the water that looked like every other town they had passed. The place used to be a mining town and used to be a lot bigger and more prosperous from what Jacky could see. The town itself snuck up on them as they drove in. There was a house or two on the highway, but then suddenly they were surrounded. Houses and stores were scattered along the main road with big gaps of space between them. The buildings were either very old or made to look that way. They drove past streets with names like Old Mill Road and Old Deepdale Road, and Jacky wondered how old this place was. Was there anything new here? Did they have Internet access? He hoped they were driving to a hotel so he could get out of the car and stretch, but they seemed to be wandering randomly down various streets. His dad still hadn't said anything but, since arriving in town, he was clearly looking for something. Jacky was anxious to know why they had come here. What was here that was so important? Who was here? Were they lost in this tiny town? That would be embarrassing.

They drove down another street, past a garage, a school, and a huge white church. The road got narrower, but they kept moving on. There seemed to be some purpose, but it was a mystery. Then the road just ended. His dad stopped and turned off the car. Jacky looked around; there were a few houses, some trees, a field, and a fence. He looked back at his dad who was staring out ahead.

"We're here," his dad said, pointing with his chin.

Jacky looked out again and frowned. "Here?" Then he saw that it wasn't a field. There was a sign he hadn't seen the first time: Stella Maris Parish Cemetery.

"I said we were coming here so you could learn about your family. This is where we start," his dad said, opening the door.

Jacky got out of the car and followed him through the gate. His dad was walking up the rows looking at the stones, pausing, backtracking, reading each name. Jacky stayed back, looking at the stones at the edge. Some were newer and easy to read, others were worn and faded. He read names like MacMaster, McFarlane, Sheehan, MacTavish, Donald. They meant nothing to him. Where were the Frasers? He assumed they came from here if his dad did. Then his father called him from the other end of the cemetery. Jacky walked over and looked at the name carved in the stone his dad was pointing to: *Mulreall (Molly) Fraser (nee Corbett) B-1946 D-1979.*

Followed with:

Lift up your hearts and share with me
God wants me now, he set me free

This was not a name he knew. The words on the stone seemed strange, sort of awkward, like something you'd say if you were unhappy with living and were glad to be done with it. It wasn't the usual *Much Loved and Missed,* or *Lives with God,* something joyful and happy. He glanced back at his dad's face and saw the beginning of tears starting to fall, even though his face showed no real emotion. Jacky realized this was probably the first time his dad had been here for a while. He did the math in his head and figured she had died very young, younger than his own mother was.

"How did she die?" he asked, his voice breaking the quiet that was filled by the wind in the leaves and the distant screaming of seagulls. His dad didn't move; he just stared at the stone.

"There was an accident," he said after a long pause, his voice cracking. "They were driving home in a storm and they might have hit some black ice. The car went into the water." His father's gaze never left the words on the stone. Jacky felt awkward; he couldn't think of anything to say so he said nothing. He looked around at the gravestones on either side of them. There were no other Frasers that he could see, but there were several Corbetts close by.

"Are these other Corbetts related? I don't see any Frasers around. Isn't your father here?" His dad sighed loudly, wiped his eyes and looked up, clearing his throat.

"My father was from Dartmouth; his people didn't live here. He moved us to Inverness to be close to my mother's people. I think it's what she wanted." He pointed to a stone close by. "That's her mother and father, and there's her aunt. Pretty well her whole family is around here. My father is buried out in Alberta."

That told Jacky much more than he expected, but it also added more questions. When his dad said they were coming out here to see family, he assumed it would be Frasers he was coming to see. He didn't even know his grandmother's maiden name until now. The fact of that brief, uncomfortable meeting with his cousin in Dartmouth and the way his dad had blown off talking about his father told Jacky everything about how close that family was. It was sad, but it made Jacky more curious about what happened between them.

He knew his grandfather worked for the railroad and was away from home a lot, so it made sense that they moved closer to his mother's family. But then why did his grandfather leave his only son in a boarding school when his mother died? Why did his dad stay at school if he had family out here? Who are they? He looked up at his dad, but he was in another place, staring at his mother's gravestone. Jacky let it go; he'd have to wait. The questions in his brain didn't stop. The family Jacky was learning about weren't close, or happy by the sounds of things. Yet the pictures he'd seen last year were of a family that looked happy. They did things together; they travelled and went on picnics. Those two versions of his grandparents didn't match. The unknowns were adding up and making him feel queasy. They hadn't come all this way to talk about sad things and unhappy times, but that was all he was seeing so far.

His dad's voice startled him out of his thoughts. "Hey, Bud, sorry. I haven't been here for a while and I didn't expect it to hit me quite so hard. I miss her, just like you miss your mom. C'mon, we have to eat, and there's people I want you to meet."

They returned to the car and drove back up Central Avenue to the main part of town. Jacky was looking forward to eating something. He didn't notice how hungry he was until his dad mentioned it. Now he was starved and sore. Driving all day was as hard on him as walking.

The restaurant was an old building surrounded by other old buildings, down the block from a newer looking Co-op store. As they walked in the front door, Jacky was deluged with the odours of cooking, fish and wood smoke. Sunlight beamed into the room through greasy windows, but it seemed dark after coming in from the sunlight outside. When his eyes adjusted to the light he was aware that everyone in the room was staring at them. No one was speaking either; the only sounds came from the kitchen and an old radio in the corner. Going into strange places and being sized up by people made Jacky uncomfortable. Wanting to move away from the doorway and everyone's cold stare, Jacky started toward the counter to order some food. His hunger was ignited by the smell coming from the kitchen. His dad's hand clapped on to his shoulder.

"Hold on a sec, I'm looking for someone." He was scanning the room. A moment later a voice called out from the far wall, a large, dark form rising slowly from a chair. The window lit the man in a silhouette, but Jacky could see he was massive, thick, and tall and his voice was deep as he called his dad's name.

"Murray Fraser, you son of a bitch, get over here."

16

Angus

The change in the restaurant was immediate. Jacky followed his dad as he walked across the room toward the man. As they passed, others rose to greet his dad, calling him by name and slapping him on the back. Surprise stacked on confusion for Jacky; one second they were strangers and suddenly his dad is so popular he couldn't get across the floor without stopping to shake everyone's hand. Everyone in the restaurant was talking again; the noise level was so high Jacky couldn't call out. He had to weave through the people and around the tables to catch up to his dad who was already at the back of the room talking to the tall man who called him. Just before Jacky got there, the men hugged each other and Jacky stopped. He'd never seen his dad hug anyone, other than him and that was only once. He was never the hugging type, but his dad looked different, happier. His face was beaming. Obviously this guy must be a long lost friend. But, judging from the reactions of the other people in the room when they heard his name, Jacky's dad was still well known to a lot of people in this town, even though he'd been away for so long. The two men sat down at the table and were deep in conversation. Like everyone else in the room, they were oblivious to Jacky's presence. He stood within eyeshot of his dad, waiting to be introduced for an awkward moment and decided it wasn't going to happen. He walked to the table and his dad pulled out a chair for him.

"There you are, Jacky, sit down." He wasn't even speaking with his normal voice. He was talking with the same dialect as the others in the restaurant, with long A sounds and ending each sentence with a question. His dad smiled at him and gestured toward the tall, heavily bearded man seated across from him. "Jacky, this is my cousin, Angus Corbett. Angus, this is my son, Jacky."

Angus, who was well over six feet tall, was wearing a large jacket over several layers of shirts and a baseball cap that was so worn Jacky couldn't read the logo on it. He had a beard that covered the lower part of his face, down to his chest, and his eyes were shaded by the brim of the hat so Jacky couldn't tell what they looked like. He held out a big meaty hand and said with a voice that sounded like a truck engine idling, "Hey, Jacky, I've heard a lot about you. How's she going, eh?"

Jacky had no idea what to say. He shook the big man's hand and said hi. Jacky's dad chuckled and asked him what he wanted to eat. Jacky looked for a menu, and his dad laughed again.

"They don't have menus here, son. They wait to see what comes in," he said.

"Why don't you have the special," Angus said. "I caught it myself." He pointed to a chalk board on the wall with a list of fish dishes written in barely decipherable handwriting. It said the special was cod. Jacky didn't know one fish from the other, but it came with fries so he figured that would be okay. Besides, he was hungry enough to eat anything. He nodded.

Angus stood and walked to the kitchen window and called, "Margaret, these young fellows and me are going to have specials, with two beers and—" he looked at Jacky, "a milkshake?"

Jacky jumped at the suggestion, "Yes, chocolate, please."

Angus called to the kitchen, "A chocolate shake."

A loud woman's voice called back from the kitchen, "We have staff here, Angus. You don't need to be standing there, yellin' at me."

Angus laughed, "I know you do, but Lucy here is pretty busy with 'er other customers and I want to make sure you serve my cod and not that frozen garbage you get from Halifax."

A metal spoon flew out of the kitchen window, just missing Angus's head and crashing on the wall. "I don't serve frozen fish, Angus. Now go sit down or I'll feed your lunch to the cats," the voice yelled from the kitchen to a collective laugh from the rest of the customers. Angus smiled and walked back to the table.

The drinks came out first. Jacky couldn't remember the last milk-shake he had but it couldn't have been anywhere as good as this. The tall glass and metal container holding a second helping looked like something out of the 1960s. It was so cool he took a picture with his phone.

"Just drink it, Jacky," his dad said. "You won't need a picture. I promise you won't forget that shake for a long time."

Jacky took a long drink and fell in love. Angus laughed.

"I used to drink those here when I was a kid," he said. "So did your dad. I don't think either of us will ever forget how good they were. Probably what caused me to have high blood pressure—but don't tell Margaret I said that. She's in a mood."

The food arrived, and Jacky's mouth watered as he started on his fish without waiting for the others. He forced himself to eat slowly, taking in the aroma and flavour of his new favourite food while the two men talked.

Angus watched him eat. "You like it?" he asked.

Jacky's eyes widened, and he swallowed and wiped his mouth. "I've never tasted anything this good in my life." He wanted to keep eating, but his dad gave him the eye and angling his head toward Angus, a hint for him to talk. Jacky put down his fork, reluctantly, to join the conversation.

"Your dad says you're pretty good on the pipes," Angus said.

"He took it on himself to learn," his dad interrupted, "then he marched out and played in front of about ten thousand people. I couldn't have been prouder."

Jacky groaned, "Dad, don't exaggerate. It was only about five thousand, and they were there for the games, not just to see me."

Angus laughed. "Folks in this family don't do things halfway. Go big or go home, eh?"

Jacky nodded, remembering how he had almost gone home instead of playing the concert. He almost let fear ruin his life but then he went for it. Angus's words settled in his mind and gave him a new feeling of satisfaction. He was part of a bigger family. He finished eating while his dad and Angus had started arguing about something.

"You can't stay in a hotel. My wife will kill me if I don't bring you home. She's already made plans," Angus said.

Jacky's dad shook his head. "We're not sleeping at your house, Angus. I appreciate the offer; I know she told you to make it but I've had all the family reunions I can handle today. Besides, we like our freedom and don't want to intrude. Tell Natalie we aren't going to miss anything she has planned."

"What plans?" Jacky asked. His dad cocked his head toward Angus.

"Angus's planned a big party for us, inviting every member of the family he could find in a fifty-mile radius."

"Everybody wants to meet you and your dad," Angus defended himself. "Isn't very often we get to see him, with you guys being so far away and all."

"I didn't know we had other family here," Jacky said. "I thought it was just Angus."

Angus laughed. "Oh no, your grandmother's family spread out over a big chunk of Cape Breton. It's going to be a pretty big party, fair warning."

"Which is why we want to be able to be by ourselves in the meantime," his dad added.

"As you wish," Angus said. "But do you think young Jacky, here, would like to go out on my boat in the morning?" He was looking sideways at Jacky, watching for his reaction. Jacky's eyes flared at the invitation. On a boat, on the ocean? This holiday was getting better by the minute.

"Yes," Jacky answered emphatically, not waiting to discuss it. "Yes, I really want to do that."

Angus nodded. "All right, then, it's decided. I'll be shipping out at—let's say eight o'clock to give you drylanders time to eat breakfast before we go."

This really was turning out to be the best part of the summer. Angus said goodbye and left the restaurant, his boots thumping the wood floor hard enough to shake the glasses on the tables.

They checked in at a motel off the main road. It was a basic, two-storey building that exists in every town on any highway, except this place came with a real ocean as a background. The room had two beds, a bathroom, and a TV, a new one but an old connection so the picture was stretched to fit the wide screen. Jacky dragged himself up the stairs to the room, had a shower, and climbed into bed. His muscles ached for sleep, but his head was still working through all he had seen so far. He had expectations coming into this trip but, as soon as they stopped at that house in Dartmouth, he lost track of what they were. Now he had no idea what to expect, other than they were going on Angus's boat in the morning and he had eaten the best food of his life. His mind was ticking through the list while his drooping eyes were watching a rerun of *The Big Bang Theory* on TV. The characters looked distorted and the sound was off so he could just watch without being committed to following the story. His dad stepped out of the bathroom and put on his coat.

"Are you going out?" Jacky asked, yawning, his eyes fighting to stay open.

"Yep, I'm going for a walk to clear my head. Have a good sleep. We've got a big day tomorrow," his dad said, opening the door.

"'Night," Jacky mumbled. The door closed and he turned off the TV. "Big day, mmmm."

17

Desperate Moves

The mumbling from the back of the plane was impossible to ignore, but Jacky tried anyway. He was engrossed in his book and he didn't want any distractions. The old man in Hemingway's story had caught his large fish and was trying to tire it out before bringing it in. The fish was a greater score than Santiago had counted on, so big that it wouldn't fit in his boat. That was one problem. The other was the fish was still alive and running out to the open sea, dragging Santiago with him. Be careful what you wish for, Jacky thought. Santiago was about to face down the fish and either kill it or die trying. *For being such a short story, it had a lot of action*, Jacky thought. Hemingway was a pretty good writer.

But Jacky couldn't ignore the whispers behind him. The plane was too small and he knew the voices of every player in the group. He knew who was back there and that they were probably plotting something. He was getting irritated, having to read the page over repeatedly. Rick and Terry, the two oldest and biggest players in the band, both drummers, had been complaining about the situation since the accident and getting on everyone's nerves. Asking if the radio was working, where the searcher teams were, could they light a fire to get attention? Everyone knew Rick was claustrophobic and hyperactive, and Terry just liked to complain. There had already been several blowups about their persistent irritations between those two guys and Mr. Stewart. If they weren't such solid drummers Jacky was sure they both would have been gone long ago. He didn't know what they were cooking up then and he didn't want to. He was trying to read.

Santiago just killed his prize fish and was preparing to bring it home but he is so far out at sea, he's worried he might not make it back.

"Jacky," Nadine was standing by his seat looking worried.

"Nadine?" he kept reading, glancing up at her briefly.

"They're planning on climbing down the mountain," she said in a frantic whisper. She was pointing toward the back. "I heard them talking." She shot a worried look to the back. "They'll get killed, Jacky, you have to talk to them."

No one but Nadine and Mr. Stewart knew of Jacky's failed attempt to escape down the hill. He stopped reading and looked up at Nadine, "I have to tell them? Since when? Go get Mr. Stewart."

Nadine leaned in closer, "If I tell Mr. Stewart they'll get in trouble and probably get kicked out of the band. They'll listen to you, Jacky, you've been there." She was staring at him with a "you owe me" look on her face.

Jacky was considering arguing the point that they would listen to anyone, but she had him at a disadvantage. He grunted, put down the e-reader, and swung his feet off the seat. He stretched his back to work out cramps and walked back to confront them with Nadine following. The guys were in the last seats in the back on opposite sides of the plane.

"I'm guessing three, four hours max—" Rick stopped talking when he saw Jacky and Nadine staring at them.

"What?" Terry swallowed and stared. Both looked guilty and defiant together.

"You know what," Jacky said flatly. "We can hear you at the other end of the plane," a slight exaggeration intended to let Nadine off the hook. "And you can forget your great escape plan. It's not going to work."

"What plan?" Terry tried to say but Jacky gave him a cold look to shut him up, then continued to talk to Rick.

"You can't just walk down the mountain in your Nikes. You'll freeze to death, or get eaten."

Rick's smug face dropped, and he looked around the seats. "Shud-dup, Fraser," he whisper yelled, then took a breath, then lowered his voice. "It's only a couple of miles and the compass on my watch works fine. Unlike you, I've climbed lots of times; we'll be fine."

"Yeah," Terry piped in.

"You're crazy," Jacky said, not quietly. "And wrong."

Rick's face went bright red and he clenched his fist. "Dude, don't call me crazy."

Jacky was unimpressed and not intimidated. Threats were mean-ingless there. He crossed his arms and smirked. "Just so you know, I don't care if you guys want to die out there in the snow but everyone else here, including Nadine and Mr. Stewart, would be worried about you. They'd have to look for your bodies after the rest of us are all home and safe." Jacky was making it up as he went. The expression of the boys' faces changed from confident to worried.

"You don't know that. What do you know about mountain climb-ing?" Rick demanded. "I've done this height a hundred times; it's nothing. You don't know anything."

"I know about hyperthermia and gravity. I know you don't have the right equipment with you and that you will fall to your death twenty steps off this ledge." He could have listed off many more reasons, except the best one; he'd already tried it once himself and he was lucky to be alive. And these two idiots were trying to tell him that a climb down the mountain was a weekend hike. It was obvious they were not going to listen to him.

"Actually, I do know, for a fact," Jacky said, straight faced, forcing the fear he felt warming up in his stomach back down. He took a deep breath and kept his eyes on Rick. Terry wouldn't do anything by himself so he wasn't the one who needed persuading. "I know because I tried."

Rick's smug face fell, then he sneered, "Bullshit, you never did. I would have heard about it."

"You didn't, though, did you," said Jacky. "It was the first day after we landed here. Mr. Stewart made me promise not to tell anyone because I almost died. I'm telling you now because, you know, I like to brag about killing myself. Not for your benefit."

"You did, really?" asked Terry, impressed. "What happened?"

Jacky smiled. "I figured it was maybe a couple of miles downhill, what's the worst that could happen? It turns out the north face of this mountain is a sheer cliff. I was hanging by a single branch over a drop of a few hundred feet before Nadine, here, found me and pulled me up. She saved my life." Both Rick and Terry looked at Nadine with surprised gapes. "She's the reason I'm here talking sense to you now, otherwise I wouldn't say anything," Jacky continued. He looked at them for a moment, reading their faces. He made a decision and acted on it before he had a chance to rethink it and maybe regret his actions.

"There's something else you need to know." Jacky spoke quietly, waving the others closer, "Something else I promised not to tell anyone."

A few minutes later Jacky walked back to his seat, leaving Terry and Rick looking pale. Nadine ran after him and confronted him at his seat. Jacky was already leaning back against the wall of the plane and reading.

"What did you tell them that for?" She was furious, barely restraining her voice.

Jacky put down his e-book. "You can only threaten someone's life so many times when they are already afraid of dying. At some point, they think they have nothing to lose. I had to appeal to their strengths as well. We need them to help the morale around here. Don't think they're the only ones who want to run away from here."

"You told them what Mr. Stewart said to you, in confidence. He trusted you." Nadine was straining her voice, whispering with so much rage.

Jacky leaned forward. "I told them the truth. And what happened when I told them? They changed their minds. Suddenly they're important. Mr. Stewart needs that more than a burning secret."

"I'm telling him what you did, Jacky." Nadine started to move. Jacky reached out and took her arm.

"Nadine, wait. The last thing we need right now is for you to start a panic. You'll only make things worse for Mr. Stewart. Those two are onside now and we, you and I, are the best support Mr. Stewart's got. Please, keep it to yourself. If anything goes wrong, I will tell Mr. Stewart myself. I promise."

She stared at him for a long moment, appraising him. Then her shoulders dropped and she nodded. Turning away, she went back to her seat. Jacky watched her go then leaned back and picked up the e-reader.

One disaster averted, but it wouldn't be the last one. He was certain.

More than anything, he desperately wanted to get off this mountain.

18

Capsized

He was standing on a wooden deck as the world around him was rocking and swaying with the sound of the ocean lashing at the ship. Even though it was dark, there seemed to be noise and movement all around him. He was holding on to a mast, waiting for instructions from someone, for some direction of what to do. He wasn't a sailor; he had no knowledge of ships. The wind roared like a beast; the ship dipped its bow under the water, then shot up spraying water over everything. The full sails billowed out with the wind and pushed hard to one side, threatening to capsize the ship. He looked up at the riggings as they waved back and forth in a crazy circus routine. There were no men climbing the ropes, tying up the sails. Why? Where were they? He started to climb but was snagged hopelessly in the ropes. He looked back at the deck and saw the wheel spinning uncontrolled; no one was steering the ship. They would crash. He was on the deck, running back to the wheel to change course, but it wasn't there. He was standing on deck at the back of the ship as it rocked heavily from side to side. He called for help, thrashing around on the deck in the madness. There was a light shining out of the cabin window. He could see that the room was full of people, including his dad. They seemed to be having a great time, talking and laughing. They even hugged each other and drank beer, oblivious to the ship's imminent destruction. He yelled for his dad through the noise of the wind and waves. He banged on the window until his father turned and looked at him.

"Jacky," he called, his voice unnaturally loud and clear. "Wake up, Jacky."

His eyes cracked open, and the dream evaporated. The sun shone in through the open window, and the sound of waves and seagulls filled the room. His dad was wearing a towel and drying his hair briskly.

"You better get up if you want to ride on Angus's boat. He won't wait for us." He walked back into the bathroom and closed the door.

The sheets had imprisoned him. His rolling and kicking had wrapped them so tightly he had to unravel them off his legs. He stumbled into the shower after his father finished and tried to wash away the last of the fog that refused to clear from his head. His dad was on the phone when he came out of the bathroom. He put on two extra shirts, remembering how Angus was dressed when they saw him the day before.

"Is this all right?" Jacky asked as his dad looked him over.

"You're probably going to get overheated with that many layers, but you can peel them off. Angus has a slicker for you to wear, but your shoes are going to get soaked."

Jacky looked at his red sneakers. They were his everyday shoes but they were on their way out. His toes were pushing the outer seams and he would have to buy another size before fall. He shrugged, grabbed his cell phone off the charger and dropped it in his pocket.

They ate a quick, greasy breakfast at the motel restaurant, disappointing compared to the fabulous food they had the day before. They got in the car and were at the docks at MacIsaac's Pond in minutes. Angus was there, loading supplies on board. The boat was massive, over sixty feet long and painted bright red with white stripes. The cabin was in the front section with a large flat area on the main deck. The top of the boat had all kinds of metal towers, radar and radio antennae. From up on the road, the boats tied up to the docks looked like small fishing boats, wheel house in front and flat deck in back. But up close they were large and complex, with more electronics and digital equipment than Jacky had ever seen. He had a lot to learn about fishing.

Angus was Jacky's idea of the quintessential fisherman. He was tall and broad across the shoulders, probably stronger than most guys. He wore similar clothes to what he had on the day before, including the same hat, but Jacky could see more of his face in the sunshine. He had streaks of grey in his thick, dark beard, like his hair. His voice was very deep and raspy. He probably smoked.

"Mornin', slowpokes," Angus said, picking up a thermal mug of coffee and sipping. He handed one to Jacky's dad and offered another to Jacky. "If you want to know what it's like to be a fisherman then you have to learn how we manage to wake up early on a cold morning."

Jacky took the thermos cautiously, looking at his dad who was drinking it with a satisfied look on his face. "I haven't tasted this stuff in years, which is probably a good thing," he said, smiling. "I see you're still mixing it with gravel and diesel fuel for that first-thing-in-the-morning kick," he chuckled and winked at Jacky. "It's very hot and pretty strong, too. You'll want to drink it slowly and don't drink too much."

That sounded like a challenge. Jacky took a big mouthful and immediately winced as it burned his tongue, then rolled into his stomach and burned there, too. The coffee was stronger and thicker than he thought possible. Still, he was taking the challenge so he tipped back a couple more mouthfuls.

"Ah, that's good," he said. His dad laughed.

Angus was climbing onto the boat. "All right, let's cast off."

Jacky's dad untied the lines holding the boat at the stern and directed Jacky to handle the one at the bow. The engine was running, idling with a deep rumble below them as they climbed onboard. When Angus pushed the throttle, it roared to life, and Jacky realized just how big the boat really was. It lifted as the bow cut through the water. They left a wake behind them that would have upset smaller boats. Several gulls flew away and screamed in protest. Jacky's dad handed him a life jacket and snapped one on himself.

They navigated through the inlet that was Inverness Harbour and out to the Northumberland Strait, which eventually flowed to the Atlantic Ocean. Once they were in open water, Angus opened the throttle and the ship's engines sang at a higher pitch and the world slipped past them in a stream of spray. Jacky felt a thrill, a mix of excitement and fear; it was like riding a massive roller coaster or fly-ing in a plane. You know it's safe, but the basic action of the thing is against all rules of nature. He closed his eyes and inhaled deeply the salty, cool wind blowing into his face.

Life was great.

His dad tapped him on the shoulder. "We have to go put on slick-ers; otherwise, we're going to get drenched." Jacky noticed that Angus had already put on his shiny yellow outfit.

They climbed below deck to the living quarters. Jacky didn't expect that. He assumed the below decks were all engine and storage for the fish, but this was almost spacious, like a camper. There was a sitting area with a kitchen, a bathroom, and several bunks.

"Why does he need all this space?" Jacky asked.

His dad was pulling out the rain gear from the storage locker. He paused and looked at his son with a smirk.

"Angus doesn't do this by himself, Jacky. Normally he has a crew, four or five people working shifts twenty-four hours a day. They're out on the water for weeks at a time. Today is just a cruise for your benefit. Angus wants to show off his boat, and you're the new guy to show it to."

Jacky blinked. "Weeks? You mean they live in here while they fish?"

"Sure," his dad said. "This is how they make their living. It's hard work. Twenty-four-hour days, storms, and sometimes they don't find the fish so they have to drive around looking for them. They only have a short time on the water but they have to earn enough for the whole year. It's a tough life. I even did this for a while."

Jacky was halfway into his yellow jacket. He stopped and stared at his dad. "You were a fisherman?"

"Don't look so surprised," his dad snorted. "I am from here and people here either mine or fish or both. Angus and I worked for his dad before Angus took it over. You'll meet most of the family tonight. They're holding a *céilidh* for us. That's what they call a party, Jacky."

"I know what *céilidh* means, Dad." Jacky finished dressing and climbed back on deck. He was still enjoying the fact that he actually had a newly discovered family. He was looking forward to experienc-ing something incredible.

As they entered the wheel house, Angus looked back and flicked a lever. The boat slowed, and the engine calmed to a low rumble.

"You want to take the wheel, Jacky?" he asked.

Jacky looked back at his dad, but he waved him on.

"Yes," Jacky wasn't expecting that. He almost tripped running up the last of the stairs. Angus stepped back and pointed to the console.

"Get up here, then, take the helm."

Jacky sat in the seat and took in the complex controls of the ship. Angus pointed as he explained, "That's your throttle, there's your speed. Keep it at about ten knots. That's the wheel and that's your compass. See our bearing? Keep to that, don't let it wonder and keep your eyes on the horizon. There's your front monitor, your rear, that's radar, which I'm not going to explain right now, and that's all you need to know. The ship is yours." He backed away.

Jacky reviewed everything he was just told, put his hand on the throttle and pushed. The motors rose up in response with a harmony of deep notes, and the world slipped past them again. He pulled back on the controls when he passed his speed and held the wheel on course. He was in control. He could hear his father and Angus talking behind him but all that mattered was in front of him, on the horizon. He could almost feel his heart fill as his spirit lifted. His world had been slowly evolving, growing and improving, and this was the moment for its great unveiling. His life was finally interesting, exciting, and real.

"How's it going, Captain?" Jacky started. He didn't realize that Angus was standing next to him.

"Fantastic," Jacky said, glancing sideways for a moment. "I'm charting a course for England."

"We'll need a lot more fuel for that," Angus said. "Throttle down to five knots, we're going to stop a bit over there." He pointed to a cove off to the starboard side. Jacky felt a thrill when the big boat slowed down and calmed from a roar to a low hum, responding to his control. This was so much better than playing video games. Angus pointed to the right.

"You see the two buoys over there by that cove? You think you can put this boat between them?"

Adrenalin mixed with fear zinged through him like electricity, "Um, yes, sir," he clung to the wheel and turned it slowly. The world slid to the right and he oversteered, heading toward the rocks. He turned back, overcompensating again and missing the mark. Thankfully he was well back of the bouys.

"Steady, there," said Angus, sounding calm. "She takes a while to respond. Move the wheel a bit to the right and give her a moment. That's it, slow and easy."

Jacky lined up the bow between the bobbing buoys and held the wheel straight as they approached. They slipped past the markers and the rocks into the small inlet by a rocky coastline. They were coasting slowly, but his hands were gripping the wheel so tight his arm was cramping.

"Okay now, bring her around. We want to be facing outward toward the open water." Angus's instructions were calm and patient, which helped control the nervousness Jacky felt in steering the massive boat. He recalled thinking it was small when he saw it from the highway but now, under his control, it felt like he was piloting an oil tanker. It seemed immense from his perch on top of the boat. He turned the wheel and idled the engines. The boat gradually turned around and settled facing just slightly toward a huge rock outcropping, but in the vicinity of the buoys. Angus killed the engines and clapped Jacky on the back.

"Good job, we'll make a fisherman of you yet."

Jacky peeled his fingers off the wheel and stood, rubbing his hands, and felt his back muscles ache. He was more tense than he thought as his calves were knotted as well. He limped around the deck to loosen up. He lost track of time while he was driving and was surprised when he saw his dad bringing out sandwiches and drinks for lunch. Had it been that long? Angus was still in the wheel house checking things, and Jacky climbed back up.

"Was my dad a fisherman, too?" Jacky asked.

"Oh yeah, he loved it out on the water, your dad," Angus said.

"That's strange," Jacky was thinking out loud.

Angus looked at him. "What's strange?"

"Why did my grandfather take my dad away to stay at a boarding school if he could have lived here?" Jacky asked.

Angus paused for a moment, still looking at him. "What makes you think boarding school was your grandfather's idea?"

Jacky wasn't expecting the question; he stopped and swallowed. What did he just do?

"Uh, but I thought—" What did he think? What did he actually know? Angus leaned against the wheel and crossed his arms.

"Who said he was put in school by his father?" Angus asked again, waiting for an answer.

Grandfather Fraser

Jacky scoured his memory to think of what his mother said, but his mind was rudderless. He never actually asked his dad about why he went to boarding school; he was sure she said that his father put him there. Now he wasn't. He felt his joy draining away and replaced with embarrassment. "I don't remember," he said, wishing he could vanish on the spot.

"Don't remember what?" His dad's voice came behind him. Jacky gasped, turning to look. His dad was smiling but his eyes were on Jacky with a questioning look.

"Jacky, here, is under the impression that you were left at school by your dad," Angus said, as casual as if he was talking about the weather. Jacky cringed; he was still trying to think of where he got that idea. He didn't want to start anything, which was too late. Keep your mouth shut, he ordered himself.

His dad's eyebrows jumped, "Well, I never told him that." His smile dropped and he jerked his head sideways. "Lunch is ready in the galley. Let's eat before it gets cold." He disappeared back down the stairs. Jacky glanced up at Angus, not knowing what to say or ask. Angus shrugged and walked to the doorway.

"I assumed you wanted an answer to your question," he said as he walked down the stairs. Jacky remained alone on deck, breathing slowly to calm his fast-beating heart and rubbing his palms together to stem some of his nervousness. Yes, he did want an answer, but not if it ruined their holiday. Things were going so well, why did he bring it up?

When Jacky stepped into the galley, his dad and Angus were at the table, eating and making small talk. They looked at Jacky as he entered, and Angus pushed a chair out for him with his foot. Jacky walked into the room hesitantly. His dad didn't look angry but old fears never die. He didn't know why but he felt bad about bringing the subject up. He sat, staring down at the hot soup in front of him. Angus broke the tense silence.

"You may not be aware, but this isn't the first time the discussion about going to school has come up. I assume from your question, Jacky, you've never talked about this with your dad."

Jacky's dad spoke. "No he hasn't, and neither have I. Frankly, I don't know why we're talking about it now. That was in the past, Angus. Let it go."

"It was Jacky who brought it up," Angus said. "Seems to be on his mind. What do you know about it, Jacky?" All eyes were on him.

"Mom told me that you went to boarding school after your mother died. I can't remember exactly what she said but I thought you were left there. I mean, why would anyone want to go to boarding school?"

His dad didn't answer. He leaned back and exhaled loudly, rubbing his face and crossing his arms while he stared at the ceiling. Angus looked between them silently, then he thumped his large fist against the table. Jacky jumped, spilling his soup.

"For God's sake, Murray, the man's dead, your son's sitting right there. Just explain things to him. You can see it's bothering him," he commanded, his loud voice filling the room.

Jacky's dad frowned, leaning his elbows on the table. "I don't want to talk about him. I want it all to stay in the past and never think about my father again, to be honest."

"Looks like that ship has sailed," said Angus, calmer as he got up to grab a towel to clean the table. "Why not talk it out, clear the air and then put it back in the chest and leave it there? Okay, Jacky?" He was looking at Jacky, who nodded and stared at his dad. This was both troubling and intriguing. What happened with his grandfather? His dad was fidgeting with his bottle of beer, lost in thought. The food sat uneaten and getting cold. His dad took a deep breath, letting it out slowly, and looked at Jacky.

"My father preferred his job to his family. There was never a point that he ever wanted to punch out and come home. He'd sooner stay at work or go drinking with the guys after his shift than come home to my mother and me. He got married and had a kid because that's what you were expected to do, but then he'd be on the rails for weeks, doing double shifts, anything to avoid coming home. Of course my mother tried very hard to make things seem normal for me and for everyone else who liked to gossip behind her back. It was hard for her, doing the work of both parents and keeping everything going at home. He wasn't very generous with money, either; he'd spend it or just forget to send anything home to us to pay rent or buy food. She still found ways of keeping the lights on and food on the table. I'll never forgive him for that. A man looks after his family, not himself."

He took a drink of his beer and scowled. The room was silent except for the groaning of the boat as it rocked slowly in the water. The sound of the distant surf washing up on the island shore drifted down through the open doorway as the three of them sat waiting for someone to break the silence. Jacky's chest felt heavy; it always did when he knew his dad was angry about something. He wanted to tell his dad to forget about it, but he really did want to hear about his grandfather. His dad was thinking quietly until, without warning, he burst into tears. Jacky started and looked at Angus who shook his head but didn't move. He seemed to be expecting that reaction. Jacky sat back and waited, fighting the urge to comfort his dad.

"He killed my mother and all he cared about was himself," his dad bawled, his face a deep red as tears and snot ran down his face. He dropped his face into his hands. Jacky was silently cursing himself. His wanted to tell Angus to forget it. Nothing was that important. But he held back, taking his cue from Angus who sat unmoved, watching and waiting.

Then Angus spoke, "Tell Jacky what happened, about the accident." Jacky's dad sniffed and shook his head. Angus sighed and looked at Jacky.

"No one's accusing anyone of anything, but it's important that you understand what happened," Angus said, his deep voice vibrating the table and Jacky's nerves as he braced for the worst. Angus glanced at his dad. "Everyone here knows this story, in one version or another, so it's just as well you hear it from me, if you're not going to hear it from your dad. Your grandmother was very well liked around here; everyone knew her and they supported her." He directed the last part toward Jacky's dad, raising his voice to make the point. "But she always stood by your grandfather, no matter what kind of man he was. She was a good wife and a good mother. That day, she managed to talk your grandfather into going for dinner in Cheticamp to celebrate their anniversary once he got off work. Not sure how she did that; some think she made a bit of money doing some babysitting and odd jobs. He'd been away for a long stretch, and she wanted to celebrate while he was home. Your dad stayed with us while they went out. We know that they had dinner there, but then it was another hour's drive home. An early winter storm set in and they never made it back."

Jacky felt his stomach twist. He looked at his dad who was staring at his hands, which were flat on the table. Angus took a drink, wiped his whiskers, and continued.

"When they realized something was wrong the folks here set out to find them. It was dark and raining and there was a lot of ground to cover. They eventually found the car in the water; it was mostly submerged. There was a turn in the road, might have been some black ice, looked like he drove off the road anyway. Thing was, when they climbed down the bank they found your grandfather sitting on the shore, soaked to the bone and shaking with the cold. He was holding Molly in his arms and rocking back and forth begging forgiveness. This is what I was told. I don't know if he was begging Molly or God. Both of them were hurt pretty bad, and they were rushed to hospital. The new hospital in Inverness hadn't been built yet and the old place wasn't able to help your grandmother so they flew her to Halifax."

Jacky looked at his dad again. "That's when you stayed at the house in Dartmouth, with your cousins?"

His dad still hadn't spoken, his gaze unmoved from his hands. Jacky wondered what he was thinking. Angus continued.

"Not right away. Your grandmother was in a coma, but it was even odds as to whether she was going to pull through. Your grandfather had a fever and a touch of pneumonia but he was out in a few days. He drove to Halifax and took your dad with him. Members of his family put them up, but your grandfather stayed at the hospital with Molly. Sadly, she didn't make it. The last time I saw your grandfather after that was at the funeral." Angus looked at Jacky's dad. "That's as much as I've got, Murray. You gotta finish it or leave it there."

"I never saw her." Jacky's dad blurted the words at the table, not looking up. "He was supposed to take me to see her, but she died that night and he left me at the house so he could sit with her until they took her away. He never let me see her again." The last words jolted Jacky. He remembered the night his mother died. He was angry at his dad for leaving him in the waiting room. No, he corrected himself, he tried to send Jacky to his aunt's house. He felt a hot flash in remembering. His own father had done the exact same thing to him? Maybe his dad didn't see it, yet he felt the same way.

His dad's face was red, tear streaked, and angry. He sniffed and looked up at them. "The police came to talk to him in Halifax, before the funeral. They were investigating the crash. He said it was an accident, there was black ice. I could hear them talking. They said there wasn't any ice on the patch of road he was on. It could have melted. They asked if he'd been drinking 'cause he smelled of it, which he denied; he said they only had a bottle of wine at the restaurant. They asked if he was tired from working a double shift and going out for dinner and drinks. Any chance he maybe fell asleep at the wheel? He denied everything, and they couldn't prove anything other than the facts of the accident so they closed the case."

He looked at Jacky. "He wasn't charged with anything but he knew everyone blamed him for my mother's death. He packed up as fast as he could and ran away. He was madder than hell when I said I wouldn't go with him. He figured I should stand by him no matter what, but I wasn't going to." His anger at the memory was rising; Jacky could hear it in his voice. "The only time he remembered he had a son was when he needed me to defend him because he was my father. I wasn't going to stay with that murderer, no bloody way."

The room was silent; Jacky was having trouble breathing as he was aware that tears were running down his face.

"You hated your dad?" Jacky's voice cracked with a squeak so "hate" came out in a high-pitched chirp. Jacky grabbed the bottle of water on the table and swallowed a mouthful. His dad shrugged, silent.

"But why boarding school?" Jacky asked. "Why not stay with relatives, like Angus?"

His dad shook his head. "My mother was from here and everyone missed her. I would have reminded them of her so I couldn't stay. Besides, I was ready to move on. I'm not a fisherman, or a miner or a farmer for that matter. I liked math and wanted to work with numbers, what good was that to people around here? I picked a school I liked, and Angus's uncle helped convince my father to pay for it."

Angus cleared his throat. "He's a lawyer, not a fighter. In case that's what you're thinking."

His dad sighed, took a drink, and continued. "I did stay with Angus and his parents during the summers. I'd earn money fishing, but I was never going to make a career of it."

"Didn't you miss anyone?" Jacky asked. "I mean, living by yourself in school sounds kinda rough."

"Not really. School was nice, and I made a lot of friends. Boarding school isn't like a Dickens novel, Jacky. They don't flog you and strap you to the treadmill, at least not anymore." He grinned. "I liked it there. I was still close enough to this place I could visit when I wanted. Mostly I liked the freedom to be who I wanted to be."

There it was; Jacky had the whole story. It was still impossible to imagine hating your own father so much you would sooner live at school than at home, but it happened. He heard it firsthand. They sat in silence for a while; the only sound was the water splashing against the side of the boat and the constant screaming of gulls.

"Your lunch is cold," Angus said. He picked up the bowls of soup and put each in the microwave to warm. The smell of warm chowder filled the room again and Jacky's appetite returned.

"That tastes great," he said as he swallowed his first mouthful. He followed it with a second bowl and lost track of how many sandwiches he ate.

"I didn't know that I like seafood so much," Jacky said when he finally finished eating, leaning back to give his stomach more room.

"Of course you wouldn't have thought that if you ate that frozen garbage you have back home. Fresh from the sea is the only way to enjoy it," Angus said.

"For those who can," added Jacky's dad. "Most of us don't have the luxury of owning our own fishing boat."

"If you think this is luxury, you pencil pushing drylander, you should try owning one for a while. It's no picnic, I'll tell you that," Angus was preaching.

"You're doing okay by it," said Jacky's dad, waving him away like a fly. "And this is all you would ever do. If you had a million bucks tomorrow you'd still be running this boat and complaining about the hard life being a fisherman. I know you, Angus, and I knew your dad. You come by it honestly."

Angus laughed, "It's true."

His dad laughed, too, a comforting sound to hear. "You know, if it wasn't for Jacky, here, I probably wouldn't have come back at all. I wanted him to see where he comes from."

Angus smiled at Jacky and raised his beer bottle, "Here's to Jacky, then, for bringing our favourite son home."

Jacky didn't know what that meant but that seemed to be the end of that conversation, so he joined in the toast and stayed silent. They cleaned up the lunch dishes and trash, stowed everything, and climbed back upstairs to turn the boat back to port.

In High School

When Jacky started in middle school he wanted nothing more than to fit in. For everyone in the school to know who he was and like him for it. During his three years there, he saw plenty of evidence to show that wasn't possible. People gravitated to their groups, their comfort zones, while others were ridiculed and harassed for being who they were, no matter how much they tried to fit in. By the time he started in high school, he'd had enough. He didn't want to fit in with anyone, he wanted to be different. That part was easy, he played bagpipes.

Things were so much different for him then. He no longer feared what he didn't know and he no longer worried about what others liked. He never lacked for friends or a social life; people were always drawn to someone who had character, who weren't afraid of rejection. But who he considered to be a friend was someone whom he could trust but who knew when to give him his space. The last real friendship he had was with Lenny and that didn't survive middle school. Jacky realized friendship was all in the mind and not really all that important. He was happy to be living his own life without the unnecessary involvement of friends, girlfriends, and cliques.

Jacky had become obsessed with one subject: science. That was all he wanted to focus on in his life, but the requirements to graduate high school meant he spent countless hours doing other, less important and distracting subjects, like phys ed, English literature, social studies, and art. Jacky was good at math and sciences, those were logical and made sense, but having to write endless essays about books and poems was frustrating. Abstract thinking about words and pictures was a waste of his time. He liked music; he had been playing instruments since grade seven and he played in the pipe band. Besides, music was similar to math; it made sense, it was logical. Everything else was energy lost.

The discovery of his fascination for science came, ironically, as a gift from his mother. When she was diagnosed with cancer and after she had surgery, they began giving her radiation treatments. Jacky came along to give her emotional support. As he sat in the control room watching the procedure through the large window, he asked questions to the radiologist about the technology. Fortunately for him, the guy loved his work and was happy to explain the whole process of how the system worked. It was amazing to see it in action. He began reading about the science behind radiation therapy, then about the uses of radiation itself.

This was his introduction to physics. The fact that everything in nature could be changed and made to suit specific needs with experimentation and observation became incredibly fascinating. A rock could be utilized to treat cancer or destroy whole cities; water could be made to cut through stone or propel a spaceship; carbon particles, smaller than the eye can see, could make thin sheets that were stronger than steel. Jacky hungrily dove into books to learn, to cram as much knowledge as possible. There was no end to what he wanted to know because there was no limit to what science could do. There was so much to know and nothing, literally nothing, was what it seemed.

He was fortunate enough, in his last year of middle school, to have a science teacher who was generous with his time. In class, they wrote their own computer code and they took field trips to the nanotechnology lab at the university and the government observatory. They studied cell biology and dissected virtual human corpses. Some students complained and quit the class, but Jacky was right into it; he couldn't get enough. He would talk to his teacher after class ended and brought his own experiments to ask questions about them. The teacher was impressed enough that he put Jacky in touch with a professor at the university. They were starting an outreach program for high school students interested in science as a career. Jacky was still in grade nine so he would have to wait until the following year to join, but it gave him something to look forward to.

Once he was actually in high school, Jacky knew he wanted to be a scientist. There was no question in his mind, but he had three years to wait before he would graduate. All he could do for the duration was to make sure his marks were high enough to qualify for admission to a university where he could focus on physics full time. The competition to get into any of those specialized schools was fierce. He needed to stay focused, no time for friends or girlfriends.

"Hi, Jacky." He was walking to math class when a voice spoke from behind, startling him out of his thoughts. He turned around and saw a guy with curly hair that stuck up on the top of his head. He was shorter than Jacky and wore black-framed glasses. It took a minute, but Jacky eventually placed him. He was one of the guys from the University Science Faculty open house he had gone to. He was trying to remember the guy's name. It had something to do with math, it was . . .

"Miles," he said, anticipating the question. "My name is Miles. I figured that's what you were trying to remember so I saved you the trouble. It's okay, no one remembers my name; I'm used to it. We're both signed up for the Science Outreach program at the university."

"Yeah, no, I remembered that," Jacky said. "I just—" Just what? Why bother explaining?

"I was hoping I'd meet up with you today," Miles continued. "I wanted to ask if you'd be interested in working with me in AP Science. I got the textbook during the summer and read over all the material we have to cover this year." He pulled out a Samsung tablet and started rapidly flipping through pages of notes and diagrams. "I already started on some of the projects we're going to do and I figure, maybe we can work on some of the optional projects for extra credits."

"You what?" Jacky was way behind, still staring at the screen. He suddenly liked this guy—Miles—he liked Miles a lot. "You mean you spent your whole summer doing school work?"

Miles shrugged. "My parents were off travelling, and my sister was working. I had nothing else to do. They got me this new tablet, and

I wrote some apps to help figure out the answers for the chemistry questions." He smiled at Jacky. "I could send them to you."

Jacky had found his new best friend, just when he decided he didn't need one. He hadn't counted on Miles, who was more advanced in physics, chemistry, and math than he was. Miles was a lot more introverted than Jacky; he just wanted a friend who shared his interests. Miles could write code for almost any device and he had a freakishly complicated knowledge of math. Jacky understood math; he had no trouble working on it but he found it boring, except when it came to applied physics. Jacky liked the unrestricted and creative world of physics, but Miles preferred the logical world of math and chemistry.

Miles didn't have any other outside interests. His parents made him take piano lessons as a kid but he quit the moment they let him. He had no interest in music, preferring to listen to podcasts of lectures rather than songs on his phone. Jacky thought Miles might be a bit obsessive compulsive; he definitely didn't know how to have fun, other than getting excited about writing a new app or completing a math challenge. It wasn't until he met Miles's family that he understood him.

Miles's parents ran a successful business and split their energies between promoting themselves and travelling. Their house, their cars, everything about them oozed success and they didn't really care that Miles wanted to be a great scientist. They measured achievement in dollars; his brothers and sisters were all in the family business and sharing their parents' goals. Being a scientist or an academic with a bunch of degrees was not their idea of career success. It didn't make much money. As a result, Miles had a lot of freedom to do what he wanted, as long as he didn't get in trouble or interfere with their busy lives. This made Miles very independent, a little reclusive and anti-social. Jacky began to understand how hard it was for Miles to approach him at school.

Miles was a survivor, at home and especially at school. He avoided getting bullied by offering to help the biggest guys with their homework and writing their assignments for them as a guarantee of personal safety. He was using his superior intelligence to survive. He had to, his parents refused to help. By the time Jacky met him, Miles was apathetic toward his family and was waiting, literally counting the days, until he could move away from them. Jacky was glad he didn't have that kind of relationship with his dad. Even though his dad was often busy at work, Jacky never felt apart or less important to him. They had a great relationship and Jacky could never see that changing. It couldn't; they were too close.

Right?

21

Dry Land

Instead of driving back to the motel, they turned north and headed up the coastline. Jacky had time to think, to recall all that had happened in the last few days.

"Dad?"

"Yeah?"

"Why did you stop by that house when we first got here?"

"That was where my grandparents lived. My father grew up there. I wanted to see if it was still the way I remembered it. That guy we met, Grant Fraser, is my second cousin, which means his father was my father's cousin."

"He seemed to know what happened," Jacky said.

"Everyone knew what happened, Jacky. It affected everyone in the family."

Jacky fell quiet, he might have pushed too far. Then his dad sighed loudly.

"It's a hell of a thing to say you hate your father," he said, staring at the road. "It happens all the time for lots of different reasons, but it's not natural. Part of you can't let go of the fact that he's your father. No matter what he did, you're supposed to forgive him. But I couldn't do that, there was no way."

He paused then looked at Jacky. "You told me that once and it nearly killed me."

That was unexpected, but Jacky remembered saying it. The guilt he felt then flared up in his head again.

"Dad, I—"

"Wait a minute, Jacky, let me finish. I know you didn't mean it, not the way I did anyway. But it got me thinking about what happened and how things ended up between my father and me. I never wanted to be like that to you, demanding and expecting obedience but not sharing anything. Love and respect should be earned and not just expected. We both learned that lesson, I think. The big difference is that I couldn't talk to my dad. I hated him, and he just shut me out. Then he died and I lost any chance of ever clearing the air. I want you to be able to talk to me, to ask me anything. If I don't want to answer right away, that's fine, too, but we will talk about it. I never want you to feel shut out and I would never wish you to have the guilt that I have had to deal with since then."

"Guilt?" Jacky asked, looking at him.

"He could have been telling the truth. He might have been unjustly accused, I don't know," his dad said. "He might have been a good person behind that crusty shell. I don't know that because he wouldn't open up me. My father expected obedience and respect, probably because that's what his father expected from him. I'm trying to break that chain, Jacky. I know I have some of his habits, like working too much and not being more open about your mom's illness, I know that now. For all of my faults, I'm trying to be a better father for you."

"I understand, Dad. I do," Jacky said. He didn't feel like talking about his mom anymore; he wanted to move on. His dad smiled and nodded. They drove on in silence watching the lives of ocean shore villages play out before them. The whale watching boats filled with tourists hoping to get a glance of the huge mammals were moving out to sea past the fishing boats and smaller motor boats that zipped back and forth on the water.

"So, you never heard from him again after that?" Jacky asked.

His dad shook his head. "Nope, he moved out to Alberta. He bought some land outside the foothills in a town called Hinton. They called me when he died, told me to go out and take care of his things. That was the closest I ever got to him after he left." He cleared his throat and sniffed. "That's probably the main reason why I never came back here, and one of the things I wish I could change."

"What do you want to change?" Jacky asked. "I don't understand."

"One of the things you will experience tonight, I'm sure, will be the endless stories told by relatives. Everyone has these wonderful stories to share that get passed on down the generations. Most of them have been handed down so many times I'm not sure how accurate they'll be, but it's part of who they are, who we are as a family. Everyone but you and me, that is. I have no stories of my family, no tales of my father that I can share with you. History is alive and well out here, Jacky, but I'm not part of it. I miss that, after growing up around these people and listening to them my whole life, I can't share that with you. That's what I mean. I hope you get some of that tonight. I hope you enjoy yourself."

"I will, Dad. I'm looking forward to it," Jacky said, a small zing of anticipation running through his chest. It sounded like it was going to be fun.

They got back to the hotel in time to change, wash off the smell of the sea and fish, and get ready for the party.

22

Family

The *ceilidh* that night was at Angus's house. Angus had told Jacky it was "just a small place off the highway." In reality the house was like a mansion on several acres of land a few miles from Inverness. They had a yard large enough for a small farm with livestock and still have a room for a few hundred people to drop by for a party. Jacky couldn't believe that Angus, a rough and worn-around-the-edges fisherman, owned such a beautiful home. The party was in a large rented tent they set up by the side of the house. There were already hundreds of people when they arrived, talking, drinking and dancing. Fire pits cooking meat smoked off to the side, and the smell of food hung over the yard like a fog. The sound of fiddlers and guitars playing and people talking drifted from the tent.

Jacky and his dad drove up to the house on time, but the party was already teeming with people and music. When they entered the tent, the music stopped and more than two hundred people looked at them and cheered. Jacky was stunned by the size of the group. How was it possible that all of these people were related to him? The crowd quickly surrounded them and ushered them in to the snacks and drinks table. Jacky was introduced to so many people and said hello so many times his voice was raw and his hand sore from shaking. He gave up trying to remember names to faces.

A half hour later, everyone was seated at long tables eating fish, sea-food, chicken, potatoes, and salad. The talking continued at virtually the same volume through dinner. After the meal was finished and cleared, the speeches began. Jacky knew this was his dad's least favourite part of things. They were sitting at the head table with Angus, who was dressed better, and Natalie his wife with a few others Jacky didn't remember. He watched as his dad stood at the microphone and fumbled through some words about coming home and great being there. Then he pointed to Jacky and everyone applauded. *Not fair, Dad*, he thought as he stood and waved, *this is your job. You're the one who came back*. Then Angus started talking on the mic. The sound of a hundred conversations in the room started overtaking Angus's speech so Jacky stopped trying to understand what he said and just watched. Angus whistled an ear-piercing trill, then gestured with his arms as he looked at Jacky with a big smile. A few others at the table looked as well, all were smiling at him.

Great, he thought, *now what?*

Then the sound of bagpipes started in the far corner of the room. Startled, Jacky looked over and saw a girl, younger than him but tall with a definite Angus family resemblance. She was stepping slowly to the centre of the room playing the "Skye Boat Song" on her pipes. She stood in front of the main table, playing a set of songs. Jacky was tapping his feet along with her playing. She was pretty and she knew her stuff, but it was the pipes themselves that caught his attention. He watched them closely as she played. The pipes were old and they had a clear, full sound that was typical of mature wooden pipes. When she ended her set, Jacky applauded with everyone as she curtsied and sat at the end of the table, a few seats down from him.

The formal part of the dinner ended, the speeches were over, and everyone went back to talking loudly. Jacky took advantage of the break to walk over to talk to his cousin.

"Hi," he said. "I'm Jacky."

"I know," she said. "I'm Emily."

"Thank you, I honestly could not hear what Angus was saying through the noise. You're his daughter?"

"Yeah," she said. "Makes us cousins, right?"

"Guess so," Jacky said. "You play very well."

"Thank you," she said, looking up at him, "I understand you do, too."

"Sure, I guess. Could I see your pipes for a second?" he asked. She got up and pulled out the case, putting it on the table and opening it. She handed the pipes to him.

"My dad gave them to me. Do you want to play them?" she asked.

"No, these are yours. I'm just curious about them. Thanks." He held them in his hands and looked at the wood and the bag. He had seen them before, but . . . He looked at his dad who was watching him. His dad met his eye and nodded. Of course, they were the pipes in the picture Jacky had seen of his father three years ago. Those were the bagpipes that were handed down to his father, then eventually down to Angus's daughter. The family tradition continued.

"I gotta get going," Emily said, pointing to the door, "if you're done with them."

"Sure, of course," he said, handing them back. "They're sure old, eh? They sound great."

"Yeah." She put them in the case, snapped it shut, and turned to go. She stopped and looked back. "It was nice to meet you, Jacky. Have a good trip."

"Thanks."

As the party was winding down, Angus found Jacky at the drinks table. He put his arm over Jacky's shoulder.

"Had a good time?" he asked, sipping on his beer.

"Yeah, this was—wow, what a blast." Jacky fumbled for words. He knew what he wanted to say, but he wasn't sure how to say it. He looked up at Angus. "That was pretty great, what you did for my dad today. You helped him a lot," he said.

Angus grinned, "Did it for you, too, you know. You're part of this family, even if most of us haven't met you before today. I always knew you were out there. Just had to wait for you to come out to see us."

"But I never knew about any of this," Jacky was waving at the people in the room, a hall full of strangers that were all related to him. "My whole life, I never knew this place existed. I didn't know I could be connected to so many different people."

"Everybody has lots of family, Jacky. You just have to look around. Your dad felt he had to get away from everyone here including his father's people, but, as you can see, we never forgot him."

It was true. Jacky saw his dad talking with lots of people that night, laughing and having a great time. Whatever he was afraid of, it clearly wasn't this. Jacky was grateful to his dad for bringing him out here. The party trickled to an end, with the last few stragglers wandering out with a handshake and a "don't be a stranger." They stayed behind to help Angus and Natalie clean up and talk some more. Finally, the final hugs and goodbyes shared, they drove back to the motel and slept their last night in Inverness. They left the next morning after joining Angus for breakfast at Margaret's restaurant and a final goodbye.

They were on a plane, flying home before the sun went down. The world was different for Jacky now and he liked it.

The Pilot

Someone nudged Jacky awake. Sleeping was what he did most of the time now; there was nothing else to do. Three days had passed so far without a sound coming from the sky. Jacky finished *The Old Man and the Sea*, a cautionary tale of being careful what you wish for, and some of *Howards End*, a book about rich women and poor men, but he gave up on it after a few chapters. He was halfway through *Heart of Darkness*, a tale of war and survival and the horrible things people do to each other. The book wasn't helping his mood at all. There were no more options; they had no way of escaping, and getting worried about it only upset everyone. He no longer cared if it was day or night; he was just cold and bored. He had drifted off while reading when he was startled out of sleep. As the fog lifted, he saw it was Mr. Stewart looking at him with an unreadable expression.

"C'mon, Jacky, we have an announcement." He cocked his head in the direction of the door and walked away, tapping other people in their seats and pointing to the door. Obviously something was happening, and it didn't look like good news. What else could go wrong? Jacky rubbed his eyes, grabbed his coat, and stumbled out toward the door. One look at the faces of the people gathered outside the plane told Jacky that everyone else was probably wondering the same thing. The co-pilot was standing next to Mr. Stewart, watching everyone with his usually quiet, cold stare, but his face was uncharacteristically drawn down. The flight attendant, her arm in a sling, stood next to him sobbing into her good hand. Mrs. Walford was comforting her, but her face was mournful as well. Mr. Stewart stood before the group and held his hat in his hand.

"I am sorry to have to tell you that Captain Connelly, our pilot, has died. As you all know, Mrs. Walford has been taking care of him since the accident. The captain sustained severe head injuries in the crash and has been unconscious since then. He passed away in his sleep last night."

Several in the group reacted with cries and moans, but Jacky kept silent as he looked around at the others reacting. The one thing that no one had said out loud just happened. They could actually die up there. He swallowed that thought and listened, holding his hands inside his coat. He had only met Captain Connelly once, when they were boarding the plane in Vancouver. Jacky remembered he was a really nice guy, older but very friendly—a complete opposite of the co-pilot, who was a miserable hard ass. The pilot said he liked the bagpipes and was impressed that they were playing for royalty. He reassured Jacky that the weather would be nicer when they got up to the islands. Jacky wished he had spoken more to Captain Connelly when they met, rather than rushing to his seat and bitching about the weather.

Mr. Stewart continued talking. "We all want to express our heartfelt sorrow to our co-pilot, Mr. Connelly. He is the captain's son." Mr. Stewart was facing the co-pilot who was going very red in the face. Jacky started, speechless. No wonder the guy was so angry; he had to watch his father die. Instantly, every wisecrack Jacky had made about the crash, the plane, the conditions, everything he complained about since they boarded in Vancouver, was hurtful. *Great*, he thought, *now I'm a jerk.*

The co-pilot took out a handkerchief and wiped his eyes, then cleared his throat. The group shuffled uncomfortably; no one wanted to look at him in the eye, least of all Jacky.

"My father," he began, his voice quivering, "loved to fly. He spent over thirty years in the air force and then in search and rescue. He was an excellent pilot; there was no plane that he couldn't fly. Watching him, I wanted nothing more than to follow and be a pilot. I flew for airlines for many years but, when my father retired, I jumped at the chance to start this company with him. This has been his dream, and—"

Then the big man broke down. He cried into his handkerchief, blew his nose, and stood silent for a moment while everyone watched. The whole situation was very tense.

"I want everyone here to know," the co-pilot slowly regained his composure and his voice had a tinge of urgency, "my father tried desperately to avoid this." He waved his hand in the direction of the site. "He was a great pilot and bringing it down here with no loss of life other than . . ." He paused and took a breath, "bringing the plane down here safely was his last act and it was one of tremendous bravery. I want you all to understand that." He was scanning the group and making eye contact with everyone, pausing for a painfully long moment on Jacky. "This was an unavoidable situation," he continued emphatically, "and not a mistake."

Mr. Stewart stepped in, putting a hand on the co-pilot's shoulder. "John, no one here thinks for a second that your father was anything but a professional. We owe him our lives and we are all very sorry for his passing." He turned to the group. "We all come from different backgrounds and religions but we all know how to respect the spirit of those who have left us. Let us all pause and pray and just send our thoughts to Captain Connelly. Let us thank him for his sacrifice. We are alive, thank him for that." He bowed his head, and everyone in the group followed suit, some whispering prayers while most, like Jacky, were silent.

He had no idea what to say. He hadn't even thought about how things could have been worse than they were. They could have died in a fiery crash. He mumbled "thank you" quietly. Then, behind him, someone suddenly started singing. Jacky blinked and looked over. Of course it was Nadine, with her hands in the air, shaking her head and wailing "Amazing Grace" like she was in some revival meeting. He couldn't believe her, using someone's death as an excuse to show off your religion. He was about to walk over and tell her when others started joining in. Soon most of the group were singing. Jacky shook his head; he looked at the co-pilot and tried to figure what he was thinking. He knew how it felt to lose someone close, instantly remembering how desperately he clung to his mother's hand to try and keep her from going. There was no fix for the pain of loss. At least Jacky still had his father and, hopefully, he would go home again.

"You see," said a voice beside him. "We should have tried to climb down the mountain, like I said." Jacky looked at Rick who was staring at him. He knew Rick was having trouble controlling his own fears, but Jacky didn't care about Rick then.

He stared back for a second, and then snorted, "Then go ahead, Rick, do it. If you think it's so easy then you're as stupid as you are crazy."

Rick's eyes flared as Jacky shook his head and walked away. While the singing continued, the co-pilot turned from the group and started walking toward the trees behind the plane. He probably wanted to be alone, but Jacky realized there was something he wanted to say to him. He followed the co-pilot around the back. The snow was deeper there. Jacky stumbled a few times and got snow in his boots. He wished the guy would stop but he only kept walking deeper into the woods. Eventually Jacky lost sight of him all together and had to follow his footprints. He finally found him sitting on a fallen tree with his head in his hands. Jacky tried to approach quietly but he stepped on a twig that snapped and the co-pilot started. He looked at Jacky and then turned away.

"Jesus, kid, can't you just leave me alone?" his voice was quieter than normal.

"I want to apologize," Jacky was struggling to stand straight in the snow, fighting his own emotions. "I was angry about being stuck up here. I didn't even want to be on this trip and all I've done is complain since we landed here." No response. Jacky moved a little closer. "I'm sorry about the way I acted, but I never thought this was your fault, or your dad's. I always assumed he landed here like this because that's what you do in that situation, as a pilot I mean. Like turning with a skid when you're driving."

The co-pilot raised his hand, his back still toward Jacky. "You're forgiven, now please go away."

Jacky walked around slowly to face the co-pilot. He had something to say that wasn't going to be ignored, even if it seemed like he was being rude or insensitive.

"My mother died a little while ago. She was sick for a long time, but it got worse all of a sudden and she just—went. I was never able to say to her what I wanted before she was gone. I've been trying to deal with it ever since."

The co-pilot wiped his eyes and looked up at Jacky. His face was red and his eyes were bloodshot. Jacky knew he was hurting but the coldness he usually saw in the man's eyes was not there. The co-pilot sniffed, "And why exactly are you telling me this?"

"Because I think you might be having the same problem. You've been so busy keeping us safe, and he never woke up after the accident, so I figure you probably had a lot you wanted to say to him." Jacky waited for a response. The man was either going to punch his lights out or agree with him. He did neither; he just stared at his hands. "I'm really sorry, about your dad. I just wanted you to know." Jacky started to walk away when the co-pilot spoke.

"What would you say?"

"Sorry?" Jacky turned.

"Your mother, what would you have said to her?" The co-pilot was looking at him, waiting for an answer.

Jacky's mind was blank; he'd never asked himself that question. What would he have said if he had the chance?

"I would have said I'm sorry."

The co-pilot squinted, "Sorry? What for?"

Jacky kicked the snow. "Sorry for being such a selfish, do nothing kid who took everything, including her, for granted. Sorry that she wouldn't get the chance to enjoy any of the good things that have happened after she died. I wished she could see it all now."

He felt tears working up in his eyes. He wiped them away and sniffed. The co-pilot just sat where he was, unmoving. Had he heard any of it? Did Jacky say it out loud, or was it all in his head? "I can't stop missing her," he said out loud.

The co-pilot looked at his hands, "Yeah, there's that."

Jacky walked. He needed to get away from there; the man wanted to be alone.

As Jacky trudged through the snow back to the plane he was suddenly knocked into a drift from behind. He was face down in the snow and branches before he knew what had happened. Still winded, he tried to rise but a huge weight landed on his back, pushing him further into the snow. The branches scratched his face, and the weight on his lungs was suffocating. Jacky was still confused and struggling for air when a fist clubbed him in the side of the head. The hit was clumsy and softened with a glove, the knee pushing into his back was more painful. He knew instantly what was going on.

"Rick, get off of me," he yelled, pushing up and blowing snow from his face. Another gloved fist to the head was his answer and another faceful of snow.

"Help," Jacky screamed. He didn't like pleading; it made him look weak. Normally he would have stood up to a tough guy like Rick, but this wasn't a fair fight. Jacky was pinned down and he didn't want to be injured on the top of a mountain. The punching continued.

Then Jacky heard a grunt, and the weight was lifted off his back. He scrambled to his feet, brushing off the snow and ready to take a swing back at Rick. The co-pilot was holding Rick by the back of his coat and Mr. Stewart was running from the plane, he was livid.

"What happened, here?" he demanded, looking from Rick to Jacky.

Rick was red faced and breathing fast. He pointed at Jacky, "He called me crazy. I'm not crazy."

"You're off your meds," Jacky yelled back at him, his own temper flaring.

"Jacky!" Mr. Stewart stared at him. "We're trying to keep things calm around here and you start name calling?"

"When I got here, he was the one doing the punching from behind," the co-pilot said, still holding the struggling Rick. "I don't care who started it; this boy has a problem with anger management. If he pulls another stunt like this I'll have him strapped to a chair." He let Rick go, and no one spoke or moved for a painfully long moment. Mr. Stewart broke the silence.

"You heard Mr. Connelly. Go back to the plane, both of you, and don't say a word."

Jacky turned, still burning with indignation. He pulled down the zipper on his coat and dug the snow out of his neck and sweater. He was so mad he didn't feel the cold. Once inside the plane he pulled the coat and sweater off, kicked off his boots, and crawled into the seat. He wanted to be far away from everyone right then, away from this crazy place. He was suffering from hypothermia, shaking uncontrollably, rubbing his arms for warmth.

"Move over." Nadine was standing beside his seat.

"What? Why?" Jacky said through chattering teeth.

"Because you're cold and I don't want you to get sick," she said as she sat on the seat, leaning against him. She wrapped her blanket around both of them and leaned closer. Her body heat warmed him, and he gradually stopped shaking. It was awkward; he was grateful for her kindness, but he was frustrated with his own helplessness. He didn't like to be looked after. She nudged him to turn sideways and snuggled behind him.

"Thank you," he whispered. The warmth flowing through him was healing.

"Mm hmm."

"You sing very well," he whispered.

"I know," she said.

"You're very warm."

No answer.

"I feel much better now," he said.

"That's good."

"Does this mean we have to get married?"

"Shut up," she said as she pulled off the blanket and carried it back to her own seat.

The next day they held a makeshift funeral for the captain after wrapping him in his coat and blanket and burying him under a temporary cairn, which was basically a snow pile with a cross made of tree branches stuck in the top. The co-pilot was silent for the whole event, not wanting to speak. Mr. Stewart was talking but Jacky felt a sickening sense of déjà vu and didn't want to be there. Memories of his mother's funeral were coming back to him. He walked into the plane and put in his earphones to block out the sound. He was trying to read *The Sun Also Rises*, but it was a waste of time. Nothing was making any sense.

The food they brought on the flight had run out, and they were rationing out the collection of snacks, energy bars, and drinks they collected before, but even those were running low. Everyone, even the adults, was getting moody, worried and angry. Several of them, not just Rick and Terry, talked openly about hiking down the mountain. Mr. Stewart led the group carefully to the back field where Jacky had fallen through the snow. That shut them up for a while.

It was cold all the time. Some mornings the sun was behind a thick layer of clouds, and it snowed sporadically. No one wanted to chance lighting a fire near the plane; there was no way of starting one anyway. The snow was too deep and would simply melt and drown out any fire they did start. They were still using water from the plane's tank, but it was also getting dangerously low. Jacky felt like he was in a bad version of *Lost*, one of the few shows his dad liked to watch. Jacky wanted more than anything to talk to his dad.

He looked longingly up to the sky. It was partially cloudy with a light wind and no chance of helicopters.

24

Five Days Out

By the fifth day, everyone was getting short tempered, hungry, and impatient waiting for something to happen. Boredom and fear were a bad mix, but added the fact that their food was running out, a blowout was bound to happen eventually.

"It's been too long, we have to do something," Mrs. Walford demanded.

"The only thing we can do is stay put and wait; there is no other choice," said the co-pilot.

"John, these children are my responsibility. We can't sit and do nothing indefinitely. We need to consider a—other options," Mr. Stewart was nearly begging. His face was lined with worry, which was exaggerated by the salt and pepper beard he was growing. Everyone in the band stood around them; there were no private meetings here, not anymore. The co-pilot was unmovable; unreasonable in Jacky's mind.

"Why can't we put together a party of the tallest members and hike down the mountain? It's only a couple of miles," said Terry.

"Because you'll fall down a crevice or over a cliff. There's a reason people aren't up here hiking and cross country skiing," the co-pilot said. He pointed to Jacky, "Your friend here discovered that."

"What's taking them so long?" asked a girl named Kelly. "They must be able to track us somehow, can't they?" The rest of the group were murmuring and nodding in agreement. The co-pilot didn't answer but looked away, which seemed strange to Jacky. He always had an answer for everything. There was something he wasn't saying. His knowledge of physics and chemistry told Jacky the effects that extreme cold had on things. Oh no—he didn't want to believe it, but nothing else made sense. He thought he would be sick again.

"What if—" he started to say, but stopped himself from going any further. Too late, everyone heard and was staring at him. One of the guys, maybe it was Rick, answered.

"What if what, Jacky?"

There was no going back. He blurted out what he was thinking, "What if they can't find us? What if they don't know where we are?"

Everyone stared at him; some went white faced. The co-pilot looked angry, and Mr. Stewart shook his head.

"Jacky, that doesn't help the situation. Of course they can find us," the manager said.

"The batteries are dead," Jacky interrupted, looking at the co-pilot. "Aren't they?" The co-pilot scowled at him but didn't speak. Jacky stood and approached him.

"I saw in the plane, all the lights were out including the exit lights. These planes use batteries that can last for years under normal operation, but in this cold and without the engines keeping them charged, it would be like leaving your car lights on." He waited for a response from the pilot. "Isn't that right?" The group was staring, waiting for an answer. The grumbling started quickly, rising in pitch.

Mr. Stewart looked at him and said, "John, I think you better say something."

The co-pilot blew out his breath between his pursed lips, "Smart-assed kid. We got a day or so from the batteries and I had hoped that Search and Rescue would have picked up our signal. I don't know if they did. The storm probably grounded them on that first night."

Tension rolled through the crowd, and the chatter became louder. The co-pilot yelled over the noise, "Nothing will be accomplished by panicking. They know what direction we were headed and they will find us. They are out there now looking. Settle down before someone gets hurt."

Rick was larger than the others, over six feet tall and maybe two hundred pounds. No one would ever, in their right mind, challenge him to a fight. He was a show-off but, as the group discovered during a long bus ride a few years before, he was also claustrophobic. Everyone knew he was taking pills to control his anxiety. Jacky guessed he was running out or else they weren't working anymore. Before anyone realized, Rick was standing and yelling in an angry, panicked voice.

"You mean they're looking for us with no idea where we are? We're here on a huge snowbank with a white plane half buried in snow and you think they're going to see us? We have to do something, Mr. Stewart, we could die up here."

Another loud burst of complaining from the group. Mr. Stewart was telling everyone to calm down as the co-pilot watched and frowned. The look on Mr. Stewart's face was as worried as everyone else there but he had to be the calm one. Jacky's mind was racing. This had become as much a challenge as a threat. Rick was right; they had to do something. The co-pilot was also sure that search and rescue teams were out looking for them. All that was needed was a way to get their attention. Cell phones were useless because they couldn't reach the towers; fire was impossible, and they couldn't yell loud enough. But . . .

"Wait a minute," he yelled with no effect. He took a big breath and whistled with all the lung capacity he had. "Hey, listen."

It worked. Everyone stopped and stared at him. The co-pilot laughed.

"Oh great, now what do you have to say? You started this panic in the first place," he said.

Jacky stood and faced him, "I told the truth." He was red faced, heat building under his coat. He wanted nothing more than to stop and cool down, but the fight was started and the co-pilot wasn't backing away.

"To what purpose?" the man said, "You got everyone here worried sick and it's changed nothing. We're in the same exact position as before except now everyone's giving up hope. That's your fault." The co-pilot pointed at him.

Jacky took a step toward him. "You would have had us do nothing but sit and wait while we run out of food and freeze to death."

The co-pilot waved his hands toward the sky, "There's nothing else we can do," his voice reaching a higher pitch and losing any sense of control. "You know that yourself. You damn near fell off a cliff trying to get away. Take a look around, young man, you'll see there is nothing else we can do."

"Yes, there is," Jacky said holding his ground.

The reaction was shocked silence; everyone was staring at Jacky. Mr. Stewart rose slowly, "Jacky, what are you talking about?"

"We can use the bagpipes," Jacky said calmly, looking at him.

"What do you mean, 'use the bagpipes'?" Mr. Stewart was standing next to Jacky, either to silence him or protect him from the co-pilot.

Jacky turned to face the rest of the group. He had their attention and he wasn't going to let this idea go. He'd worked this out in his mind, it seemed crazy at first but now it was probably their only real chance to save themselves.

"It's an instrument of war. Clans used them to warn their enemies that they were coming to battle. The sound carries for miles and you can't confuse them with any thing else. If we use all the pipes and drums we have there is no way they won't hear us if they're anywhere near here." He stopped and let them absorb what he said.

Murmurs, excited chatter started in the group, only this time it was positive. Jacky knew he had them. He had won. Then the co-pilot stood up and cleared his throat.

"There is one problem with that plan." The co-pilot had regained his military composure. "You will all recall the avalanche that we triggered when we landed here."

Jacky remembered it vividly. It was like a second collision, one that might have pushed them all the way off the mountaintop. It took them more than a day to dig themselves out from it.

"That, my friends, was a small one. The warm weather has severely destabilized the snowbanks and cornices up there." He pointed in the direction of the snow pile over their heads. With the exception of a gap where the first slide had broken away to fall on them, the snow looked pretty well banked straight across the rock face. All they could see up there was white snow and blue sky. Jacky hadn't considered that more snow could fall on them.

"Just so you understand me," the co-pilot continued, "I want to get off this mountain as much as any of you but that much noise could cause the rest of that snow to give way and fall on us. In other words, even if they hear you, we may not be here to get rescued. It's a good idea in theory, but the danger is far too great." He looked at Jacky. "And that, mister scientist, is the way it is."

Truth stared Jacky in the face, and he felt the last of his energy and hope melt out of him. He looked up again at the snow cornice looming high above them like gargoyles, hanging precariously, just waiting to fall. A good shake would be all they need to rain down on the group and kill them all. Checkmate, nature wins.

Fresh snow was starting to fall. There was no wind, no storm, no hint of a change in the weather; just the sudden appearance of snow falling as if to represent the shattering of their hopes of escape from this frozen prison. There was a new chill in the air as well, but not from the snow or the weather. Everyone transmitted it by looking at each other. Jacky felt it, too, the horrifying realization that they were really trapped and there was nothing they could do about it. They could actually die up here.

The wind picked up. Winter was coming back. The conversations stopped as the group gravitated back into the airplane. They closed the door to block out the wind. No doubt another storm was coming. Jacky headed back to his seat-nest passing small groups talking anxiously together; some sat alone crying and others complained. He passed Nadine and heard her praying in a frantic whisper. The doom and gloom in the plane was palpable. The only light was the dimming daylight coming through the windows. They had long ago run out of glow sticks. Jacky slid into his bunk and pulled out his notebook. He flipped through the pages until he found a blank one, then he started writing:

Dear Dad . . .
I don't know if I will ever see you again.
I'm sorry
I'm angry
I'm confused
"I'm what?" he said to the page.
The words wouldn't come.

The next day dawned like the others. This time no one bothered getting up to sweep the snow or clear the ground. There was no routine anymore. No meal times, no Kumbayah singalongs. They were losing hope; everyone could feel it. No one looked up to the sky anymore. Depression was setting in; it was sad, even for Jacky. He wished his plan would have worked, he was certain that everyone else agreed. At least then there would be something to hope for. Maybe a fast death from being crushed under a mountain of snow would be better than sitting there watching people's spirits die slowly. He could be pretty morbid sometimes, he realized.

With the lack of things to do or any kind of order, people mostly slept. A few determined types had started journaling their adventure. Others took to art, pencil drawing mostly because paint and ink froze quickly. People swapped books and there were impromptu groups that got together and talked about things, anything. The co-pilot spent most of his time in the cabin of the airplane, coming out occasionally to patrol the grounds. But basically nothing happened and everything was quiet.

Jacky was rereading *Heart of Darkness*, looking for a distraction. Conrad's story of a man searching for truth matched his mood that day. He had spent the previous night struggling to write something in his book, a letter to his dad explaining how he felt. He stared at the blank page for so long he fell asleep on it. He woke to find the note-book folded under him. He tried again, struggling to find the words, even walking around the site several times thinking and talking to himself, with no success.

Jacky felt conflicted, unable to resolve his own arguments. He loved his dad; they had a special bond that took a lot of time to create, and a solo performance in front of thousands of people, to seal the deal. He and his dad had been so close since then. He thought his dad was happy with the relationship; he was successful at work, so the only thing he was missing was a girlfriend. That was fine; Jacky wasn't against the idea of a girlfriend, but not if she suddenly took over everything in their lives. Not if Jacky was being pushed aside like an unwanted dog and only walked and petted when they felt generous. He wanted his dad to be happy but not at the loss of their relationship.

His dad could have said something if he was unhappy. He could have brought it up. They were both being busy and selfish, both looking out for their own interests. Still, Jacky was the one being replaced by a girl-friend. That's what hurt. The letter to his dad remained unfinished.

He was going to get off this stupid mountain if he had to jump. Gradually, another day petered out into night.

25

The Girlfriend

Jacky should have known something was going on; all the signs were there. They just weren't as obvious at first as they seemed after the fact. The worst part of it was that Jacky approved of the whole thing at first.

He knew his dad had started dating. He didn't mind that his dad was seeing other people. Who doesn't want their father to be happy? But there are limits, especially considering how much it ruined Jacky's life. And how it destroyed his relationship with his father.

The first sign of trouble appeared when Jacky came home from school on a Monday, which was usually the one day of the week that nothing happened. Sometimes his dad worked late and Jacky made dinner for himself. Other times, if it was the end of a long weekend, they would have pizza and watch a movie on TV. But on that Monday, his dad was already home, even though it was only four o'clock. Jacky could hear him upstairs taking a shower. The water hissed through the door and Jacky could hear him singing.

Jacky dumped his school work and lay on his bed. He pulled his iPad out of the overstuffed backpack and started flipping through Instagram and Facebook posts. The shower stopped, and his dad stepped out of the bathroom with a cloud of steam rolling out after him like dry ice fog at a rock concert. He was walking across to his bedroom, wrapped in a towel and drying his hair. He was humming something Jacky didn't recognize. That was usually a sign he was in a good mood. Jacky decided to wait until his dad finished dressing to ask what was going on. That ended up taking a while. His dad was still singing his song as he walked across the hall, making noises for the drum and guitar parts in a horrible wailing voice. He saw Jacky on the bed.

"Hey, Jacky. Why don't you grab a shower and find some nice clothes to put on? We're going out for dinner," he said in an uncharacteristically cheerful voice.

What? Shower, dressing up, eating out? *You've got to be kidding, it's Monday*, Jacky thought. "I have math homework, Dad, and midterms coming up. Can't you go by yourself?" He was laying it on thick to get out of whatever was going on, but his dad wasn't listening anyway.

"You can finish your homework later, I want you to meet someone." He held up his arm to check his watch. "Dinner's in an hour and a half so shake a leg, okay?" He strolled downstairs, half singing, half humming his song again.

Jacky punched the power button on his iPad and tossed it on the bed. "Crap," he grumbled as he shuffled to the bathroom. Shake a leg? What year is it?

His suit jacket was too small; Jacky hadn't worn it since his "graduation" from middle school, which was a lame excuse to get dressed and eat out. *Just like tonight*, Jacky thought as he tried to squeeze into his only pair of dress shoes. The difference was that they were both having a good time back then. Whatever was going on now with his dad was becoming annoying, and Jacky didn't like being in the dark. He settled for dress pants and a nice shirt, which needed ironing. He wore his sneakers because they were the only shoes that fit. They met in the hall, and his dad looked him up and down.

"Looks okay, except the sneakers. Don't you have shoes?" his dad asked.

"No, these are all I've got," Jacky said.

His dad thought for a moment then held up his hand. "Okay, just a sec," he said, as he ducked back in his room and came out with a pair of dress shoes.

"Seriously, Dad? These won't fit me," Jacky said, staring at the shoes.

"What, too big?" his dad asked.

"Too small. I wear eleven and a half," Jacky said.

"Oh, that's only one size off. You can wear them this once. Here, this will help," he handed Jacky a pair of dress socks. "If you were these instead of your thick sweat socks, you'll be more comfortable. Now let's go."

Jacky grumbled as he pulled off his shoes and socks and put his father's stuff on. He looked ridiculous and he felt like he looked it. He just needed the bright red nose and a whoopee whistle. Whatever this was about better be worth it. He stomped down the stairs to the front door.

The restaurant was posh, with bare brick walls and white covered tables arranged over the narrow floor. Jacky knew it was expensive as soon as they walked in; he was suddenly self-conscious about his appearance, his stupid looking clothes, and his dad's shoes. He fell in behind his dad as they walked through the maze of tables, following a woman in a tight, black dress. Fortunately, no one looked up at them as they passed, winding through the restaurant to the back where a woman sat alone in a half-circle booth looking at her phone. She was attractive, tall with blonde hair, and she looked oddly familiar, but he didn't know from where. When she saw them she smiled and stood and, to Jacky's surprise, embraced his dad and gave him a very long kiss. Jacky stared at them, his blood turning a little cold. He'd seen people kiss often enough but, what the heck, this strange woman, who wasn't his mother, was practically making out with his dad in front of him. He felt an urge to leave, but he resisted. His dad grinned at her and then at him.

"Jacky, this is Kerry. Kerry, this is Jacky, my son," his dad motioned with his hand. He had a grin on his face like a boy on his first date.

"Hi, Jacky," Kerry said as she extended her hand to shake. Jacky shook it while doing a quick appraisal. She had expensive tastes judging from the looks of the jewellery, her clothes, and the monster purse next to her with PRADA stamped on a metal plate. Jacky didn't know fashion from junk but you can't go to high school and not learn about brands and status symbols. It wasn't just the girls who fed into that craze; there were a lot of guys parading around in Le Bron shoes and Beats headphones. Jacky didn't buy into fashion and expensive brands; his mother would never go for any of that.

He surprised himself by how fast his mother came to mind. She had been dead for three years, but Jacky had no trouble remembering her. It was a shock to see his dad with another woman; it never occurred to Jacky that would happen. But that wasn't fair, his dad deserved to have a girlfriend—maybe. Except they were well past the first date by the looks of things. His dad was probably out with her rather than working late some nights. That added an extra burn to Jacky's flicker of disapproval. How long had this been going on? How serious were they? From the look on his dad's face, Jacky assumed the answer was "very." Well, he didn't care about her, she wasn't anything to him. He was just along for show, an accessory like a pet dog, there to impress the girlfriend. Jacky's stomach hurt. It was bad enough to be dressed up and dragged out here against his will but being forced to sit and be nice to this woman while he got to be the third wheel on his dad's date was the limit. He picked up the menu and looked for the most expensive thing listed.

"Hi, folks. I'm Ryan and I'll be your server tonight. Can I get you some drinks before dinner?" Ryan was one of those guys who dressed hipster style with oversized, black-rimmed glasses, slicked his hair up like a pop star and had a ghost of a beard. Jacky's dad ordered wine for both of them, and Jacky asked for sparkling water. That was probably a safer bet in a place like this than a Dr. Pepper.

"We have Voss Water," helpful Ryan suggested. Jacky nodded rather than ask what the hell Voss Water was. Ryan vanished and returned in a minute with bottles. It turned out Voss was bottled water from Norway.

Cool. Hopefully it was expensive.

"So, Jacky, your dad has told me absolutely nothing about you," Kerry turned to Jacky and began the inevitable get-to-know-you conversation, "which is probably fair because I assume you know nothing about me."

"Yes, that's right," Jacky said, sipping on his bubbly Voss Water.

"Okay then," she paused, "I'll go first. I used to work in television news for many years. I was on CBC for a while then Global." That was where he knew her from. Jacky never watched the news on TV, but it was always on. He'd seen Kerry on screen many times. He kept his face unchanged, listening politely. "Then I worked for the government but now I run my own consulting firm so I can tell others what to do." She laughed, and Jacky ignored it. "I met your dad at a conference that I was speaking at and now here we are. So that's my story; tell me about yourself."

"Well, um, I'm sixteen, in grade eleven. I like science and basketball and music. I play guitar and the bagpipes." He did that on purpose, and she reacted as he expected. She tilted her head to the side and raised her eyebrows.

"Bagpipes? That's interesting. Why did you choose that?" she asked. His dad interrupted.

"There's a family history. I played them when I was young, just for a short time and not very well. Jacky decided to learn them and show me how they are supposed to be played. He was in the news last year." He pulled out his phone and brought up the newspaper story of Jacky playing at the Police Games in about a second. Kerry took the phone and read the article. Then she handed the phone back.

"Very impressive. I'm afraid I'm one of those horrid people who never appreciated the bagpipes. I always just associated them with funerals or memorials, like Remembrance Day. I know that's not right, and I have a lot to learn, obviously."

"They're an instrument of war," Jacky said, bolder than he expected. He backed off a bit, "They were played in many countries, but the Scots used them to warn their enemies that they were coming, and to motivate the soldiers into fighting. They've been around for over five hundred years."

Kerry smiled, "See what I mean? I'm smarter already. You like science, too, you said."

"Yeah, I do," Jacky said. She was expecting him to talk, and he wasn't going to just open up for her. He didn't feel like being best friends.

Ryan appeared again, saving Jacky from further questions. "So do you know what you'd like for dinner this evening?"

Jacky flipped over the dinner menu and almost choked. A meal here was as much as groceries for a week. Were they eating there to impress Kerry? Okay, then, something on the expensive side, seeing that his dad was being so generous.

Frustratingly, his dad didn't even flinch when Jacky ordered the steak and crab, with salad and dessert. He was seriously in love with this woman, and Jacky knew he was going to have to get used to seeing Kerry around. She wasn't horrible or anything, but that wasn't the point.

They made a promise and now his dad was breaking it.

26

Betrayal

The second semester at school started after the Christmas holidays. Jacky was ecstatic to be back at school around people he knew. The holidays were all about gifts and Kerry, dinner and Kerry, staying home alone because his dad and Kerry had gone skiing. Two weeks away from school and being around Kerry was thirteen days longer than Jacky could stand. His friend, Miles Shapiro and his family didn't celebrate Christmas, they were Jewish, but they gave each other gifts and went to Florida every year to stay with relatives and get away from the cold. Jacky had no choice but sit at home and wait for the holidays to pass. When Monday arrived, Jacky was at school an hour early. He was now officially halfway through high school, but the end was still far away.

He walked down the hallways lined with couples wrapped around each other with their sickening, egocentric displays of affection. Everyone was showing off their latest swag and advertising their relationships. It was all garbage to Jacky; love, sex, popularity, possession. It was all a waste of time when you had so much more to look forward to. High school relationships were pointless the minute you graduated from school. It also didn't help that Jacky had to put up with the same stuff at home whenever Kerry showed up. Not quite the same, but Jacky was getting tired of playing second to Kerry all the time. He arrived at his locker to find Miles waiting for him.

"Hey, Jacky, what's happening?" Miles asked.

"Hey, Miles," Jacky said. "You have fun in Florida?"

"You've got to be kidding me. Are you really asking me that?" Miles grumbled. Complaining was his favourite thing to do.

"Nope," said Jacky, "Just small talk. I didn't do much either."

"Did you get anything for Christmas?" Miles asked.

"Nope," said Jacky. "Just gift cards."

"That sucks." Miles looked up. "They should just give you cash. Now you have to buy things with it."

Jacky shrugged, "I know but my dad has this thing against giving cash. He thinks it shows that he put some effort into picking a present if he gives me a card. I might get a new laptop."

Miles started walking. He snorted, "Whatever. My parents transferred money into my account electronically at 12:01 a.m. That's personal for them."

"Hmm," Jacky laughed dryly, falling in step.

They walked in silence down the hall toward the stairs to go up to math, the first period of the day. When they reached the top of the stairs, Miles stopped again and beckoned Jacky to the far wall.

"There is something I need to talk to you about. Have you heard of the Overseas Student Study Program in the UK?"

"No."

Miles looked around to make sure no one was listening, "It's a high school program in England that focuses specially on science. They take in a few overseas students every year. It's like a dream come true."

"Why are you telling me about this?" Jacky asked, sighing. Miles seemed to forget that he didn't have rich parents.

"Because I want to go there, and you should, too." Miles was trying to mask the enthusiasm in his voice by whisper yelling, which was heard by everyone down the hall, along with his fidgeting dance. Other kids were looking at them and laughing. Miles didn't see them.

"It would be better if we both go. I mean, graduating from that program almost guarantees you a spot at a place like MIT or Bern," he continued, his face not hiding his excitement.

Jacky sighed, "That sounds great, but you know I couldn't afford that. You can, obviously, so go for it." Jacky had a hard time hiding his disappointment. This was why he didn't want to have friends;

they always moved away. The same thing happened in middle school with his best friend Lenny. Now Miles was doing the same thing. He started walking.

"We're going to be late for math," he said. He stepped into the classroom and opened his books before Miles could say another word.

Miles wasn't going to stop, either. He cornered Jacky after class.

"I'm going to send you a link to the site. They have a limited number of scholarships for out of country students but they do the application online. It's like getting tickets to ComicCon, but you should try to get in. Really." Miles was practically begging.

Jacky already knew he didn't stand a chance against all the AP Science students in North America going online in one day. He'd tried to buy Springsteen tickets for his dad as a present but they sold out in less than a minute. And that was just local. Then he had to be approved for a scholarship, which was not going to happen. His marks were good but not that good.

"Yeah, whatever, sure. Send me the link and I'll check it out," he said. Miles grinned.

"Great, see you later." He was gone. Jacky opened his locker and changed his books for social studies. It's always easier for people like Miles; privileged and wealthy people don't worry about getting what they want. They just do. Jacky didn't care about the school so much. He'd get in to a university on his own without having to go to any place special. It would be nice, though, studying in another country, focusing on science. He would just have to do it the normal way.

"Whatever," he said as he slammed the door shut and snapped the lock in place. At least he was halfway done with high school.

As he promised, Jacky continued playing the bagpipes, and the New Caledonians Pipe Band were doing great in the annual competitions. During the previous summer's Worlds Competition in Glasgow, the band came in first in their division, and also earned top place at the Nationals, putting them at the top in Canada. The celebrations were great when they got back. They got their pictures in the paper and on TV and they had a huge party. That was when Jacky decided that he wanted to quit, to leave the band. He had fulfilled his promise and stuck with it long enough. He wanted more time to spend on his science projects with Miles. He told his dad what he was planning to do, but the idea was trashed immediately. His father demanded Jacky stay on for another year, at least. The argument was heated, but Jacky finally agreed, with full intentions of quitting at the end of the current year.

The practice sessions restarted after the Christmas holidays. At the end of that first session of the new year, Mr. Stewart called everyone together to share some news. He could barely control his excitement.

They probably won another award, thought Jacky.

Mr. Stewart spoke slowly, and his voice was barely controlled. "Because of our division wins at the Worlds and the Nationals last year, we—you, I mean—have all been invited to perform for the Prince and Princess of Wales and their guests at a special event in the Haida Gwaii Islands in British Columbia this April."

There had been an announcement of a royal visit to Canada in the spring and part of that tour was a stay at an exclusive resort on one of the small islands off the coast of British Columbia. The New Caledonians, being world champions, were invited to perform for the members of the Royal Family as an acknowledgement of their success. The band members, and the parents who were at the meeting, were ecstatic. Mr. Stewart was busy passing out information sheets and permission forms to take home. Jacky put his forms in his case and grabbed his coat.

He thought about the timing of the trip. April was close enough to summer that he could go, put on a good show, and then tell Mr. Stewart he was done. That way his dad wouldn't be able to sabotage him again. Yeah, that could work. He'd get a break from school just after the Easter holidays, and then he would have his whole summer to himself before his last year of high school.

Life is sweet sometimes, especially when things work out.

When Jacky arrived home, he saw Kerry's car parked outside. Again. He let himself in and heard them talking outside in the backyard. Jacky didn't call or say anything. He was just going to grab a drink and go up to his room unnoticed. Any chance of avoiding another awkward conversation with the lovers was worth taking. She was his dad's girlfriend and she was successful, but Jacky didn't have to like her. As he opened the fridge, he caught some of their conversation through the open window.

"I'm tired of being alone, Kerry. I don't do well by myself," his dad said. Kerry said something Jacky couldn't make out. His dad answered, the pitch of his voice was lower.

"I haven't felt the way I feel with you for a long time. This is a kind of happiness I almost forgot existed." His dad was getting sickly romantic. Kerry spoke quietly, and then his dad answered, "Will you at least consider moving in here? I want to be with you all the time."

Hot anger welled up in Jacky's body. Tired of being alone? Happier with her? His hands shook as he stared into the refrigerator; he felt hot in spite of the cold air around him. Not happy—with me? Tired of being alone—with me? All Jacky's angry thoughts circled in his head, giving him a searing headache and tears welled up in his eyes. He ran upstairs and slammed the door. He held his pillow over his face and screamed as loud as he could. He refused to let himself cry, it was too big an injury to cry over. His dad had betrayed him, replaced him, abandoned him. The last three years, were they a lie? All of that talk about family and trust—what an idiot he was! He swore at himself as the anger roiled in his head, making his headache worse. Then he had an idea. A crystal clear idea.

He flipped open his laptop and clicked on the email from Miles. It had several attached PDFs for the application to the Overseas Student program and a link to the school. Everything he needed was there. All he had to do was get three letters of recommendation from his teachers, a transcript of his marks, a cover letter explaining why he wanted to attend and why he should be chosen, and then the inevitable parental permission. That one may have to be faked; Jacky wasn't telling his dad about this application, not until after he was approved.

"I'm so out of here," he said out loud. His head and his heart agreed.

He heard them coming in from outside. He heard their voices downstairs as Kerry said goodbye. He heard the door close and his dad's footsteps on the stairs. He tapped on the door and opened it.

"Hi ,Jacky, I didn't hear you come in," his dad said.

Jacky switched his screen to Facebook before the door opened. He didn't look up from the screen. "Yeah, well, I saw you had company so I just came upstairs."

"Sure," his dad said. "How was practice?"

Well, other than the fact we are flying to BC to play for the Royal Family, he didn't say. "It was . . . um, same as usual," he said.

"Okay, good night," his dad said, closing the door.

There was no sleep for Jacky, not that night. He stared at the wall, the darkness of the ceiling playing memories in his mind. All the joy of the last three years, all the love and respect that they supposedly shared, all a lie. It was hard to comprehend. How could his dad be so deceitful, so full of it? Why would he do that to his only son? They were a unit, a partnership, he and his dad. At least that's what he had thought, up until that night, until he heard the conversation he wasn't supposed to hear.

But maybe his dad hadn't lied to him. Maybe he just said that because he was infatuated, convinced he was in love with Kerry. Who the hell was she anyway, coming into their lives and pushing the memory of his mother out of his dad's head? Everything would be normal if it wasn't for Kerry, the new bitch from hell who was sinking her claws into his father, he seethed.

I'm tired of being alone. His dad was never alone, unless he wanted to be. He was ignoring the fact that Jacky was always around. If he wanted to be with Kerry so much, then the best thing would be for Jacky to disappear. Well, he now he could take care of that.

27

Crazy Town

The sound shocked Jacky out of his sleep. It was dark and he was struggling to wake up. He could hear people's excited questions and a loud banging coming from somewhere. In the time it took to untangle himself from his makeshift bed, pull on his coat and run outside he imagined an endless stream of possibilities for the disturbance. Ranging from helicopters to gunshots to an avalanche, nothing made sense. When he emerged from the plane's door, the image he saw still didn't make sense.

It was Rick, the big drummer, wearing the band's bass drum strapped to his chest. He was standing in the middle of the open area beside the plane and hammering the drum with his muscular arms and yelling at the top of his lungs.

Boom boom—"C'mon down. Bring it on. Come get me, let's go"—boom boom.

The sound was deafening; Jacky could feel it thumping through his body and echoing off the mountains all around them, which was obviously the point. He was trying to cause an avalanche. Rick was officially out of his mind.

The adults ran at Rick and tackled him, while yelling at everyone else to get back inside the plane. The last ones in were the men still struggling with Rick. They had taken the drum off and left it outside in the snow when they pulled the door shut. That wasn't good for the drum, Jacky thought, but no one said anything. Silence fell over the group as everyone waited for Armageddon to fall. Minutes ticked by.

Nothing, no avalanche, no rumbling, not a trickle of snow, only silence as the last of the drum sounds echoed away into the distant mountains. After what felt like an hour, but could have been a few minutes, Rick began laughing like a crazy man. His face was bright red, and he looked high on something.

"Nothing," he bellowed, "I told you, nothing happened." He looked at Jacky with a face that was wild, eyes wide, a demonic smile and sweat pouring off him. He pointed, his face intense, "Ha ha! You see! Jacky was right. Now we can do what he planned. We're going to make some noise and get out of here."

Rick kept laughing, shaking off the adults who were holding him, and pushed the door open. He ran to the middle of the field, jumping in the snow and dancing around the drum. He could be heard through the open door screaming and laughing like a drunk. Everyone else followed him, looking up at the snow and at each other. Then they looked at Jacky who was looking at the co-pilot, who looked like he had eaten a porcupine. Everyone else seemed to follow Jacky's stare and soon everyone was looking at the co-pilot expectantly, waiting for some kind of answer. He scanned the faces staring at him and exhaled loudly, throwing his hands in the air.

"Do what you want," he said and stormed into the plane. They heard the cabin door slam.

Mr. Stewart looked at the group and smiled happily, "Well, then, with Mr. Connelly's permission, we'll haul out the pipes tomorrow. Everyone go back inside and get some sleep. Tomorrow's going to be a long day." Everyone cheered.

No one had any idea what time it was but it was night. The group started moving back into the plane, although no one was going back to sleep any time soon. Mr. Stewart watched as Rick hauled the bass drum back into the cargo hold and secured the door. Jacky stayed outside, staring up at the night sky. The stars filled the sky with a fantastic light show and the cold bit at his skin, helped by the slight breeze that moved the trees. He had to go in. He was cold, but this moment was one that he wanted to keep, to burn into his memory. He was sure they were finally going home.

"Inside, Jacky, let's go," Mr. Stewart called him out of his thoughts. As Jacky walked past him through the door, Mr. Stewart put a hand on his shoulder and spoke quietly, "Thank you." Jacky nodded and walked past.

"Wasn't me, thank Rick," he said.

Crazy Rick just saved their lives.

28

The Piper on the Mountain

They started preparing early the next morning. The mood was upbeat; everyone was as excited as if they were about to play a concert. This was their last and best shot at saving themselves, even though there was as much chance of the experiment failing as succeeding. The rest of the food was handed out, and the remaining water was rationed for each player to give them enough strength to play and stay hydrated. Even though it was going to be cold, the act of playing would keep their core body temperature up. They planned to play in shifts to avoid anyone being out too long. Their faces and fingers would still be exposed and their feet would be cold standing in the snow.

Mr. Stewart brought everyone together outside the plane; he was back in his normal role as band leader. They did their pre-performance warm-up and breathing exercises and reviewed the order of songs they would start with. It seemed a bit weird to have a playlist when they were basically making noise to be heard, but Jacky knew Mr. Stewart wanted to keep everyone's spirits up by maintaining discipline.

"All right, now we've played in the cold before but this is a lot colder than normal. You have to be aware of your hands and feet; don't stay out so long that you get frostbite. Also, everyone must keep moving so you don't freeze on the spot. Drink water regularly but sparingly; this is all we have. Also, pipers, protect your reeds. They will play fine once you start, as will your drones and chanters. You need to come in after your shift and thoroughly dry them out and keep them warm under your coats. If you freeze your reeds, they will get damaged so dry them thoroughly before playing again."

"As a bonus," he continued with a big smile, "we've been able to set up a fire pit using some parts from the plane. We're lighting it up now. Go ahead Rick."

Rick and Terry were piling branches on a piece of metal several feet away from the plane. On Mr. Stewart's signal, they lit some paper and the fire began to burn. Everyone cheered when the flames started to catch the wood.

Mr. Stewart continued, "I've checked with Mr. Connelly and the fuel for the plane has thickened enough that there is no chance of an explosion, which was the concern up to now." He paused and looked serious, "I don't have to tell you how important this is, and how proud we are of you for stepping up like this. The plan should work, and we have every confidence that it will; now it's up to you. This has been an adventure but we would all like it to end, today, right?"

Everyone cheered and ran into the plane to retrieve their instruments.

The bagpipes were stored in their cases in the overhead bins so they hadn't been exposed to the extreme weather outside. They were cold but kept dry, so they would play. The drums had been stored in the luggage compartment, which was colder than the inside of the plane, so they were brought in to warm up enough that the metal sides wouldn't give the players frostbite. The bagpipes were brought out of their cases and wrapped up in each player's coat to warm them up.

Jacky pulled down his case from the bin and opened it. The gloss finish of his new pipes filled him with mixed emotions. They were a gift from his dad, after Mr. Stewart advised Jacky that he had already outgrown the old pipes that Sergeant MacGregor had given him. They went to several stores that sold pipes and eventually ordered this set from the factory. The first day Jacky held them and the first time he played them were his happiest moments. They sounded loud and proud and played so well that they made him feel like he was a better player. Now he was counting on them to help save his life. Jacky assembled the instrument and bundled it into his coat, next to his shirt. They were so cold he gasped, but he held them close. He laid out the cloths he used to dry the inside of the pipes, along with a backup set of reeds so he could swap them out during shift breaks. Then he headed outside.

As he exited the plane, he almost walked into Nadine. She was clearly waiting for him to come out. Jacky walked quickly past her and stood away from the group by the tail section of the plane. The morning sun was bright but still lacked the warmth he was hoping for. The pipes were still cold next to his skin, but he held them close, pacing in the snow and humming to himself like a mother rocking a child. Nadine followed him.

"See, if you have faith then things work out." Nadine stood beside him, also holding her pipes under her coat. This was what he was trying to avoid. Nadine's lectures about religion and faith and how everything happens for a reason.

"Not now, Nadine. I don't want to talk about it," he said in a forced calm voice. She stood her ground, stepping closer.

"I believed that God would help us and He has, through you. You didn't die because I rescued you and now this. That's what I believe, whether you want to hear it or not."

That was the push too far. He felt his temper start to rise as he turned and faced her. "First of all, it was my idea; no one else gave it to me. Second, we don't know if it's going to work so hold off on sing-ing "Amazing Grace." And if you're so quick to credit God for all the stuff that happens then why don't you blame Him for causing us to be stuck up here in the first place?"

Nadine's face dropped. Her confident grin changed to an angry grimace. She didn't back away but stepped even closer, and her eyes narrowed, "People make mistakes, Jacky, people cause accidents. God put us here because we could have crashed and died otherwise." Jacky shuddered, he knew that was true but he chose to think of it as luck, or the pilot's quick thinking.

"What you call acts of God, I call fate," he said.

"Call it what you want," she said, "His hand is working through you, even if you don't believe it." She was pointing her finger at his face for emphasis, making her point literally. Others were looking at them, and Jacky was silent. He didn't want anyone overhearing the discussion. Seeming satisfied, Nadine backed off.

"I don't understand you," Jacky was still simmering. Nadine leaned back against the plane and clutched her pipes closer. She didn't speak as she looked up at the sky. Then she took a deep breath and started to talk softly.

"A few years ago, I was about nine, I think, we were at home watching TV when a man broke in the patio door. He was on drugs or something but he had this wild rage in his eyes. He was yelling something incomprehensible; we couldn't understand but he was raging like an animal. We all ran to the kitchen, and my mom called the police while my dad stood up to him. I was so scared. My dad was trying to talk to him, but this guy kept coming toward him screaming. My sister was crying, and my mother was yelling on the phone while my dad and this guy started fighting. My dad pushed him away from us, and the guy started swinging and throwing things. I was afraid he would kill my dad but he got a good swing at the guy's face. The man fell backwards on the floor, hard. We stood there watching him, waiting for him to get up but he didn't move. My dad went to check on him." She looked at Jacky, her eyes were wide and she was shaking. "He was dead. My father didn't kill him; he had a heart attack or something. At that moment, I knew that God had saved us and I have been grateful every day of my life since then."

Jacky had to swallow hard; letting that story set in to his mind. He had newfound respect for Nadine; having survived a situation like that would change anyone. But still . . .

"He was probably a drug addict, Nadine, he could just as easily have walked in front of a bus. That's not proof . . ."

Nadine turned on him with wild eyes and yelled as loud as she was able, "God saved us, Jacky. Don't tell me what to believe." She stormed away from him with everyone staring. Heat rose up through his body. He pulled the pipes from under his coat. "These are warm enough now, are we going to play or not?" he demanded, walking toward the group.

They lined up in a semicircle with the pipers facing away from the plane, spreading out so the sound would carry in all directions.

The drummers were behind them, also spread out. They were dressed warmly, but it was going to be a long day. Everyone was ready, waiting to start. Larry Walford took his place at the front and tapped his bag, bringing his drones to life. Everyone else followed suit, and the mountains around them filled with the sound of bagpipes as they started to play "Scotland the Brave." The drums kept the tempo as the band played for the trees, for the snow, for the animals and the wind and the spirit of the pilot who lay in his snow-covered grave. They played and the sound echoed from the mountains to the forest to the sky. The world was full of the sound of music.

After two, half-hour shifts, they were cold and tired. Everyone including the co-pilot was watching the sky hopefully. Mr. Stewart stepped in and told everyone to take a break. The band members went inside the plane to put down the instruments, and the pipers set to drying the various parts of the bagpipes. The adults managed to warm some water over the fire enough to make tea. This was the first warm thing they had to drink since the salty soup they had after they landed, and it was welcome. Jacky held on to his cup with his bare hands, the feeling in his fingers gradually returning. He hid his disappointment; he had hoped for results by now.

"As wonderful as it is to hear you playing again, there is no way we can keep this pace up." Mr. Stewart was taking advantage of the fact that the group was standing by the fire warming up with tea. Someone found a supply of sugar in the plane and had added it to the tea to help keep their energy up. Even though they had been playing steadily for an hour with no real results, everyone seemed to have forgotten that they were playing for their lives with no guarantee that anyone else was out there to hear. It felt more like a regular concert, albeit a very long one. Even though the band members were tired, they were still anxious to get out and play again.

They rotated like that for the rest of the morning, taking shifts, warming up and going out again. The sun had traversed from the east and was hanging over the mountains in the western sky. In a few hours, the players ran out of songs after playing through their regular set several times. They were getting overtired and goofy, running on warm, sugared water after they finished eating the rest of the food. Pretty soon they were just playing random songs from the radio and getting into squealing competitions with each other. Any semblance of order was completely lost as the pipers were all playing their own melodies and the drummers were hammering away like machine guns. The noise was beyond unbearable, especially the drums. The hammering bounced off the mountains and hit Jacky's ears almost to the point of being painful. Except, he realized, most of them had stopped playing and were looking skyward.

Those weren't the hammering of drums, they were helicopters.

Two yellow helicopters passed overhead, their huge rotors thumping the air and echoing off the distant mountains. They hovered, appearing to be checking out the group, and then moved away. The group started cheering and jumping in unison, except Jacky, who was still standing in his position, staring in disbelief. It worked; they were saved. It was over.

Nadine ran to him, squeezed him in a painful bear hug, kissed him on the cheek, and ran back into the plane. The mix of noise from the crowd and the helicopters that were still hovering nearby was clamorous. Jacky saw the co-pilot emerge through the plane door, look up at the sky and then back at Jacky. He nodded and gave Jacky a thumbs-up. Jacky still hadn't moved.

He had one more thing he needed to do at that moment and with the group being distracted and ignoring him, this was the best opportunity he was ever going to have. He put the blow pipe between his lips and filled the bag. His face was numb from playing excessively, but he was determined. He tapped the bag, and the drones sang again. He began playing the first song he had ever learned, "Highland Cathedral," the song he had to master to play for his dad at the Police Games. The bagpipes had saved him, more than just this once, and he wanted to make amends after thinking he wanted to stop playing them. He played because he loved this song and he loved the sound of the bagpipes. Gradually, some of the other band members joined him in the song until most of the band were playing, and it seemed like the trees and mountains played along. The rescue crew started lowering themselves from the hovering aircraft with first aid supplies and stretchers. They wouldn't have known what to expect when they arrived, but it was definitely not a musical performance by the pipes and drums of the New Caledonians. The rescuers stood and watched as the band finished playing. Some of them recorded the performance on their cell phones. It was an unusual sight.

When the band finished playing, the rescue team cheered. Then they started gathering everyone up to prepare to leave. In a few minutes, they started hoisting people up to the helicopters with their instruments. The nightmare was finally over for the band members, but not for Mr. Connelly, the co-pilot. They knocked down the snow cairn and put the pilot's frozen and wrapped body into a black, zippered bag as he stood next to it. Jacky kept his distance but watched as the bag was hoisted up with the co-pilot.

They cleared the site with incredible efficiency. They had to leave anything large, including Rick's bass drum, behind. There were protests from some of the members who were told to leave suitcases and anything they couldn't carry, besides their instruments, at the site. After an exciting lift in a basket dangling from a cable, Jacky was sitting in the cramped helicopter, wrapped in a warm blanket and squeezed between bodies. They rose into the sky quickly, and he watched as the wreckage of the plane and their home for the last few days disappeared from view. Soon the site vanished behind the snow-covered peaks of the surrounding mountains.

29

Airbourne

The search and rescue team flew the castaways to Prince George to be checked out at the University Hospital. There were several cases of mild frostbite and dehydration on top of the bruises and cuts they got from the initial crash, but no one in the band was seriously injured. The flight attendant had to have surgery on her arm as it had multiple fractures. The greatest needs for most of them were food, bathrooms, and electrical outlets. Band members were scrambling to plug their phone chargers into any available outlets. Then came the phone calls, and the inevitable crying and high-pitched, excited talking of people connecting to their families after being cut off from the world for a week. The hospital was as accommodating as they could be, but the rush of people overwhelmed the already full emergency room. Mr. Stewart and Mrs. Walford were running around, shushing people who got too loud and comforting those who were overwhelmed. Some of them needed to lie down and rest. Rick had used up his medication and flying in a cramped helicopter took all of his strength to keep from climbing out the window. After the group members were checked out and had called home, Mr. Stewart brought everyone together to meet in a room the hospital provided for them.

"Okay everybody, quiet, please," Mr. Stewart began. "Thankfully we're all okay. I've conveyed our sympathies and our thanks to Mr. Connelly and Mrs. Fournier, our flight attendant. Once they're finished operating on her arm, they're flying home." He paused, "We've been through a lot together over the last few days, and I know we all want to get home right away. We're arranging a flight back to Vancou-ver where most of your parents will be waiting to take you home." There was a loud cheer. Mr. Stewart raised his hand for quiet. "But first, we have to eat." Much bigger cheer. "A very nice restaurant in town has offered to feed us all, and there's a bus waiting out front to take us there. So come along everyone."

There was another loud cheer and a rush to pick up bags and cases as the group surged out the main doors. Jacky wondered if there was enough food in this city to feed this mob of starving teenagers.

The restaurant was set up buffet style with endless amounts of food and drinks and desserts. The chef standing at the end of the meat run with his large carving knife cutting roast beef had to replace the roast so many times, he eventually ran out and they had to settle for ham. Mrs. Walford was reminding everyone not to overdo it as they hadn't eaten properly for a few days and they could get sick. The advice wasn't going very far as the food vanished quickly. Jacky ate two full helpings of roast beef, vegetables, potatoes, soup, and dessert. He was so full it hurt to breathe and he went outside to walk it down.

The air in Prince George was full of smells and sounds that Jacky knew were among the everyday, regular things he lost track of while they were up on the mountain. He was used to the subtle sounds of the wind blowing through the tree branches and snow crystals hitting the side of the plane, the perfect silence of the mountains. He remem-bered seeing thousands more stars and the sky itself being darker at night, a brighter blue in the daytime. And the freshness of the air. There was such an absence of odours up there he remembered smell-ing the pine trees and the subtle odours of the snow as it melted in the sun. Here there was a hum underlying everything. The sound of traffic and trains and machinery was constant, and the heavy smells overwhelmed his senses. He liked the normalcy of it, but the differ-ence was stark now that he had returned to civilization.

He heard the rest of the band members climbing back onto the bus, laughing and belching. Jacky joined them, sitting next to Nadine at the front of the bus. The doors closed, and they drove away. The group quieted as they started moving. The lights of the city slipped past as they watched, taking in the activity of people doing normal things. It was amazing how fascinating it was to see regular people living their lives with no idea how it felt to be without the things they took for granted every day, like electricity and freedom of movement, and warmth. Jacky felt the satisfaction of being on solid ground. He was relieved everyone in the band was alive and, other than a few days of their lives and a bass drum, they hadn't lost anything. Except for the pilot. There was a tragedy, but he died a hero. So that was something.

He was sitting next to Nadine, but they hadn't spoken during the ride. He wondered if she was still mad at him, expecting an apology for what he said. He remembered that argument and how it ended but he also remembered how she had kissed him when the helicopters arrived. Now she wasn't talking, she just stared out the window. He didn't know what to do, talk to her, apologize, or say nothing and let things be. It was a tough choice.

That was the biggest change to happen over the course of this whole experience; Jacky's relationship with Nadine. Before they flew off on this excursion, Jacky hadn't said more than a few words to Nadine and hadn't thought of her, even in passing. She was just one of the band members. Then she saved his life; that changed things. He responded by yelling at her about religion and then she kissed him. It was all very confusing. He was pretty sure they were friends now but he didn't really know how she felt about it. Maybe she expected him to say something or maybe he was just imagining things and she didn't care one way or the other. It would be nice to have some kind of sign.

"Did you have enough to eat back there?" he asked.

"Why because I'm so fat?" she said staring out the window.

Jacky sat up and looked at her, "No, I didn't say—" She slapped him on the chest, grinning at him.

"Oh, learn to take a joke once in a while. I love food and I ate like a starved bear. It was so good I couldn't help myself."

Jacky laughed and sat back. "I didn't even taste it, I was so hungry. I'm probably going to explode and you'll find food all over the place and no sign of me."

"Gross," Nadine said as she looked out the window.

"I think I'd like to go back there sometime," she said quietly, as if to herself.

Jacky leaned in, "Sorry, what? Back there, to the mountain? Hmm, I wonder if you can."

"You can do whatever you want as long as you set your mind to it," she said.

Jacky sighed and closed his eyes. He answered his own question. She wasn't mad at him; he had nothing else to add.

Nadine poked him in the ribs, waking him as the bus pulled up at the airport.

"Time to go home," she said as she stood up, nudging him out of the seat.

They collected in a group by the main doors with their luggage and instruments. Airport security and the airline people met them there and checked their names on a list, took their baggage, and directed them to follow a guard who led them to another bus waiting outside the building. They were going directly onto the plane rather than the usual route through airport security. Jacky regretted not using the washroom before they got on the bus. Once everyone was loaded on, they drove out toward the plane. It was a jet, thankfully, and the band members ran up the stairs in a mad rush to grab the best seats.

While they were in the terminal Jacky saw a few people with cameras watching them and taking pictures. Did the media hear about them and were they going to be in Vancouver waiting to ask them questions? That could be awkward.

The bags were loaded, and the jet was rolling down the runway and into the air in little time. Everyone was plugged in and playing games, listening to music, or watching movies before the wheels lifted off the ground.

Vancouver spread out underneath them like a carpet of lights, made brighter by the night sky. When the pilot announced they were preparing to land and they should put on their seat belts, every window had a face glued to it staring out at the city. Traffic moved around rapidly, buildings climbed into the sky, ships sat out in the harbour. When the wheels thumped on the ground and the reverse thrusters roared, the band burst into applause and cheering. The flight attendants looked both amused and puzzled as they prepared to disembark. The plane rolled for several minutes around the building looking for a gate. When it finally came to a stop, the seat belts snapped off and everyone was standing, anxious to leave well before they were supposed to. They had to wait for several long minutes before someone finally opened the door and they poured out into the building.

Vancouver International Airport was an interminably long building filled with a maze of hallways, stairs, and more hallways with signs promising an eventual escape down the way. Jacky fumed at the endless corridors, desperate to get out. He was tired of sitting, tired of being in transit, and he longed to see his dad. He could only keep moving with one foot in front of the other following the directions of the signs. He rounded one last corner and walked through the sliding double doors that emptied into the waiting area. They were greeted with an explosion of sound and a wall of people rushing toward them. So many people were calling, it overloaded Jacky's senses, distorting the sound and images to blurs and noise. He turned slowly to look at the faces, looking, searching. A second later he was wrapped up and squeezed in his dad's arms. Jacky recognized his scent, his feel. He could hear his dad's voice, muffled through his coat. He wrapped his arms around his father and held on for life. The uncertainty, fear, anger, all the emotions he was feeling and all the internal struggle to find words evaporated. He was with his dad again; everything was right.

"Thank God you're all right," his dad whispered. Jacky felt his father's sobs through his coat. They held each other for a long moment, and then his dad stepped back and looked at him. "I think you've grown."

"Dad, it's only been a few days," Jacky grinned. He hoped it was true.

"A few days too long," said his dad, sniffing as he wiped his eyes.

Mr. Stewart approached them. Jacky's dad greeted him and they hugged, patting each other on the back. In the bright lights of the airport, Jacky could see the worry and stress of the last days still showing on Mr. Stewart's face.

"Welcome back, Vince," his dad said. "Hell of a trip."

Mr. Stewart sighed, "Yes, and not one I care to have again. But we came out of it okay, didn't we, Jacky?" He patted Jacky on the back and smiled. "Your boy showed some real leadership out there, Murray. He'll have to tell you about it, but I want to thank you, Jacky. And you know why." He tapped Jacky on the shoulder and walked away to speak with the other parents.

Jacky's dad raised his eyebrows. "Sounds like you had an adventure."

"Yeah, Dad, but I'm really tired. Can we go now? Where are we going, anyway?"

"We're staying at the Sheraton by the airport over there. We'll fly home tomorrow morning. You definitely want to have a shower when you get there. Hoo," he waved his hand at Jacky and winced.

"Thanks Dad."

They retrieved his backpack and case and walked out the front door to the waiting shuttle buses.

Their hotel room was huge, with two queen-sized beds, a large-screen TV, and, best of all, a massive bathtub. Jacky filled it, opting for a long soak rather than a quick shower. Lying submerged in the water, he could feel his muscles slowly relaxing. He scrubbed the dirt from his face and feet, his legs were sore as was his back from sitting in various aircraft all day. He was sure there was still some ice deep inside that had yet to thaw. When he climbed out, his skin was pink but the water was black. He rubbed himself dry, dried his hair, and brushed his teeth. That was the best feeling of all. After almost a week, he could finally feel normal again. When he walked out of the bathroom, his dad was lying in bed watching TV. Jacky climbed into the large, comfortable bed for the first time since he left home. It was warm, inviting, and he wasn't sleeping in his clothes for once, or curled up like a dog on a seat squeezed between an armrest and the wall. He looked at the TV screen and saw video of the band members walking into the airport and the crowd of parents greeting them. He didn't see much of it; he was asleep before he knew it.

He woke slowly, like coming out of hibernation. He took stock of where he was and reassured himself he wasn't on the mountain. He had moved around in his sleep so much the pillows were on the floor and the blankets were wrapped around his legs. His dad was already showered and getting dressed when Jacky lifted his head and tried to speak. What came out was a dry squawk.

"Yeah, good morning," his dad answered, pulling on his socks. "You better get a move on. We have a long flight ahead of us, and I'm sure you want breakfast." Jacky started to untangle himself from the bedsheets. His pyjamas were soaked with sweat, and he needed to use the bathroom.

"I brought you some clean clothes. Don't take too long in there, we have to go," his dad called through the door.

"Could we please have your attention for this short safety demonstration," the smooth voice over the video playing on the seat monitor in front of him switched to French. Jacky ignored it and checked on his phone to see if the last of the pictures he took had uploaded to Instagram. The airport wifi was slow, and it took a long time for the files to upload. They were almost done, about 85 per cent; Jacky figured they would probably finish before he had to turn it off, but there were enough of them up for his friends to get an idea how things were up there. The texts, messages, and emails were starting to come in. Jacky didn't bother reading them; they would all be the same questions anyway. He'd take care of things when he got home.

His dad had been reading news reports on his phone all morning, looking for any mention of the rescue. There had been a few of them, some pictures as well but he was still looking. Finally the doors were closed and the plane began to move so they turned their phones off and waited to take off. The chatter on the PA systems and this video playing on the screen made it impossible to talk so they waited. Once they were in the air and the announcements for the refreshments were made, it was quiet enough that they could hear each other.

"Why don't you start from the beginning?" his dad said, with a broad hint of his anticipation.

Jacky pondered, putting things in order, "Okay, we landed in Vancouver and got on another, smaller plane. It was loud and cramped, but I thought we would only be in it for a couple of hours."

His dad nodded, listening intently. Jacky ran through the chain of events, all of them, including falling off the mountain and being rescued by Nadine. The challenges of keeping busy, the rationing of water and food. He showed his dad the pictures on his phone of the site and the mountains. His dad didn't say anything except for the occasional "uh huh." When Jacky got to the part about playing the bagpipes, he downplayed his part of it. He focused instead on Rick's tirade with the drum as the point of action. He wasn't looking for praise.

"So that's how they found you?" his dad asked.

"Yeah, the sound of bagpipes can carry for miles," Jacky said. "It was all we had left to try; there was no other option. We were getting pretty scared up there. There was no more food, and the plane was half buried in the snow. It was—" he choked on the word. His dad's face was white. He might not have realized how dire things were up on the mountain.

Neither spoke until the flight attendant appeared beside them. "What would you like for lunch?" she asked.

After their sandwich trays and drinks were cleared away, Jacky tried to change the subject.

"What's been happening with you?"

"I've been a nervous wreck, sitting on the phone and the computer looking for information on where you were," his dad said, reaching into his carry-on bag on the floor and pulling out his iPad. "I've been saving every news story and report I could find. Have a look at this." He opened a page for the newspaper story that the plane had been reported missing and they started searching. There were several more, similar stories in other papers and websites, and on some foreign news sites like the BBC, which had a story that the Prince of Wales was deeply concerned about the missing plane and the safety of the people on board. Other reports showed the weather in the area and how they had to cancel the search due to dangerous conditions in the area.

"They said a cold front moved in unexpectedly to the area you were flying in. They thought it would travel farther north, but it ducked down and settled in over the mountains. The island you were flying to was fogged in and freezing cold. After two days, they started speculating that the plane may have crashed into the ocean and started looking there." His dad's voice caught, and Jacky knew he thought they were dead. He flipped though more pages. "This one came online last night." He turned it to show Jacky: "Sounds of Bagpipes and Drums Summon Rescue from Mountain."

"When they called to tell me they found the plane and everyone was safe I grabbed some clothes and ran to the airport to get here," his dad said, happier. "I don't even know if I locked the door. We might have an empty house when we get back," he grinned.

"It won't matter, as long as the house is still there," Jacky said. Everything was okay, nothing was changed. He looked out the window and waited to get home.

Back Home

The doors opened to the luggage claim area with the usual sound of people greeting each other. Jacky avoided the groups gathering and headed for the luggage carrousel. When they retrieved their bags and started for the door, Jacky saw Kerry watching for them, waiting by the car in the pickup zone. His heart fell. He had managed to put her completely out of his mind, hoping she wasn't going to be around. He stopped and looked back at his dad, who was a few steps behind.

"Why is she here?" he said, not masking his displeasure.

His dad did a double take, stopped, and stared at him. "Excuse me?"

"Why does she have to be here now?" Jacky whined. "We just got home. I thought we could be by ourselves for a while."

His dad paused for a moment, frowning and said, "She's our ride, and she lives with us now." He stormed out the door.

"She what?" Jacky stared in disbelief. Then he followed his dad out the door. He put his bags in the trunk while his dad and Kerry hugged and talked. Jacky climbed in the back and closed the door, breathing hard. After a moment, Kerry got in the passenger side. His dad put his bags in the trunk and slammed the lid. Then he sat down and slammed the car door, making his feelings known. Jacky felt exactly like he did before he left, which meant it was Kerry's fault. His dad started the car and drove, not looking back or speaking. Kerry turned around and gave Jacky a smile.

"It's good to see you back safely, Jacky," she said, obviously trying to start a conversation. "We were worried about you."

"Hi," he replied. "Thanks." He stared out the window. Kerry looked at his dad and shrugged. They spoke in short bits of conversation, but it was clear his dad didn't want to talk either. Kerry gave up and looked out the window.

The drive seemed to take forever. Jacky had been looking forward to getting back home but he wasn't anymore, not now. They pulled up to the house, and Jacky went immediately upstairs. He had nothing to do but unpack, put his clothes in the laundry, and catch up on the local gossip. He had already been looking at Twitter, Instagram, and Facebook between flights, but there wasn't a lot happening except people were asking about the accident. He didn't feel like talking about that yet. What was worse, he realized, was his only real friend was probably going to school in the UK without him. Thinking about that and missing the deadline for the application made his heart sink. It really did feel like the world was out to ruin his life, and coming back home to find Kerry living there and his dad fawning over her was enough to make Jacky want to vomit. He was an outsider in his own home, and his own school. The only place he wasn't unwanted, ironically, had been on top of a mountain. Well, that's over with, he thought, better get used to being alone.

He heard arguing downstairs, Kerry's raised voice and his dad's lower-pitched voice in response. He didn't know what they were saying but he knew what they were arguing about. Then the front door slammed and a moment later Kerry's car drove away. He knew what was coming next.

"Jacky," his dad's angry voice carried through his door. "Get down here."

Jacky closed his laptop and shuffled down the stairs. His dad was in the living room standing by the window staring out. Jacky sat on the sofa and waited. His dad paced in front of the window a few times then turned to Jacky.

"Explain to me, please, why you're being such a complete ass about Kerry. Why are you so against me having a relationship?" he demanded.

Jacky looked back at him coldly. So this was the way they were going to do it? He was the victim, here; it was his dad who had the explaining to do. Those thoughts broiled in his mind while he sat lock-jawed on the couch. His dad was still waiting with the identical expression on his face.

"I don't know, Dad. I was thinking maybe—you know—because this is our house, that we might talk about it before she moved in. I thought I had some say in what happened around here."

His dad walked to the dining room, carried one of the chairs over, and sat facing him. The tension between them had not been this high since his mother died, back when things weren't going well in their relationship. That situation had escalated to his dad going to hospital with a heart condition. Jacky never stopped feeling guilty about that. This was different. Jacky was in the right this time.

"Whether you approve or not, Jacky," his dad started, "Kerry and I are very much in love. We're planning to get married."

Jacky waved his arm in the air. "Well, that's just great. It's all decided, then. Perfect." Jacky's stomach hurt. The heavy sarcasm in his voice did nothing to hide his pain. That was it, then? Everything was completely disintegrating, and he no longer belonged in his own family, his own home? A sickening, sinking feeling filled his chest, and he lost control of his emotions. Tears rolled down his nose and his face burned.

"Why does that upset you, Jacky? I don't understand." His dad's tone changed. He looked lost. Jacky quickly wiped his face with his sleeve and sniffed.

"After Mom died, I was sure you didn't want me around; you seemed mad at me all the time. And then we started talking and understanding each other. We've been so happy since then, Dad. We did stuff together, we talked, and we went places. We—we're a team, and I thought it would be like that forever. We were like a real family." He dropped his face, red and soaked with tears, in his hands while his body jerked with silent sobs. His dad brought Jacky a box of tissues from the kitchen, then he sat looking at Jacky, waiting for him to calm.

"Why would you think that I love you any less because Kerry is around?" he asked after a moment. "She doesn't replace you or your mom in my life; no one can."

Jacky leaned forward, unable to hide his anxiety. "But she does, Dad. Since she came here we don't do things like we used to. We can't even sit and watch a movie or go out without her coming along or you having to check with her first. You spend all of your time with her and now I'm just a third person around here." He blew his nose and wiped his eyes, trying to regain some composure.

His dad sat quietly, thinking, while Jacky was sniffling. The silence was getting loud. Jacky wished he could go to his room. This was a pointless conversation, and he wanted it to end. His dad sat back and cleared his throat.

"Jacky, I've apologized more times than I can count for the way things were after your mom died. I told you how worried I was about doing the wrong thing that I ended up making mistakes. I'm only as good a father as I can be, Jacky. I am a product of my own upbringing and I tried very hard not to be the man my father was. You understand that, don't you?"

Jacky nodded, still wiping his runny nose. His dad rubbed his hands together, a habit he had when he was stressed. "After your mother died, we promised there would be no secrets between us. You remember that?"

Jacky agreed and sniffed. His dad continued.

"You're growing up, Jacky. You won't need me to guide you and protect you for long. You'll be going to university in a couple of years. Who knows where you're going to end up. But you're the one who'll be leaving, Jacky. I'm dug in here; this is where I'm staying." He seemed to be waiting for a response. Jacky said nothing. His dad got up and paced.

"While you were gone, your friend Miles called here. He just heard about the plane crash so he was pretty worried about you. I told him you were fine and on your way back home. He asked me to tell you to give him a call. When I asked him what he was calling about he told me all about the private school you were applying to. So now maybe you can tell me about this secret plan of yours."

He was looking right into Jacky's eyes. He didn't seem angry but he wasn't happy either. Jacky knew what he was thinking. Not telling was as bad as lying, that's what his dad said before. It was after the concert at the Police Games and after his dad heard the whole story about Jacky's bagpipe lessons and all of his plans to play a solo for him. His dad said he was both impressed and disappointed. He loved the surprise but he missed out on the preparations and the months-long process of Jacky learning to play the pipes. He said he would have enjoyed the concert as much even if he knew it was coming. But the end was the same; they found new strength in their relationship and a new openness in their communication.

"I believe that you can do whatever you set your mind to, Jacky," he had said back then. They were having dinner at their favourite restaurant. "Let's neither of us make that mistake again," his dad had proposed. "We have to be open and honest with each other and then no problems will come between us." They agreed on that and, for the next three years, that arrangement worked well. Problems were dealt with and no one lost their temper. But then Kerry came along, and she was a problem that was growing between them. But his plans to covertly apply to go to a foreign school, to be accepted and then tell his father about it, that was a betrayal.

Jacky excused himself and went up to his room. He opened his backpack and dug out the brochure for the Academy in the United Kingdom and took it down to his dad, who read it and put the papers on the table.

"I thought you hated the idea of boarding school," he said.

"I did, but that was before I knew what it was like. Besides, it specializes in science. That's what I want to do, honest to God." Jacky was earnest.

His dad nodded. "Really? Okay, I get it. But why didn't you tell me about this before? And why pick a school so far away?"

Jacky thought about his answer. He could say that it was the best school for science, which it was. He could say he didn't want to tell him anything unless he knew for sure, but that would be all lies. He made a promise, no more lying.

"I was angry about Kerry and I wanted to get away from here." It didn't feel any better to say it, especially when he saw his father's reaction. His face dropped and he swallowed hard. Jacky did the same, and then he tried to take it back. "That was how I felt before. I don't care about that now."

His dad didn't move or change his expression. He spoke with no emotion. "Why?"

Jacky sighed and fell back into the cushions. "Because it doesn't matter anymore. I missed the deadline for the application while I was stuck on that mountain. I can't go anyway. There's no point even talking about it. It's a special program to qualify for advanced placement in university. I'll just have to stay here and finish high school, and do it the normal way." That was it; the whole plan had failed. The dream was over, and Jacky was probably going to end up at a lousy university while his dad was happily married to Kerry. It was punishment, he was sure of it. Fate had a way of getting even with him. Or maybe Nadine was right; God was punishing him for being selfish.

Kerry walked in the front door and froze, her hand still on the doorknob. "Sorry, I thought you'd be finished. Do you want me to go?"

Jacky's dad was still looking at Jacky, and then he rose from his chair. He moved to the table and pulled another chair over.

"No, Kerry, come here and join us. This involves you, too," he said, pointing to the chair. Kerry closed the door and walked over, eying Jacky cautiously.

"Okay, I'm not sure what I'm supposed to do," she said as she sat, pulling off her coat.

"You don't have to do anything." Jacky's dad sat and waved to him, "Jacky, tell Kerry what you told me."

That startled Jacky, his face suddenly hot. What was he doing? Jacky's nerves were humming like guy wires in the wind. His dad must want Jacky and Kerry to duke it out right here. Kerry looked— confused? Nervous? Was she worried about him? That was weird. He was ready to take his anger out on her but he couldn't, that would be wrong. He decided to talk and let her react as she would.

"I—uh—I told my dad that I feel like you've come between us. We had a really great relationship, but now all he cares about is you. It's like I don't matter anymore."

Kerry raised her eyebrows and looked at Jacky's father, then back at Jacky.

"Interesting," she said, turning her head and staring at her hands. This wasn't anything like Jacky expected. The room was very quiet for a long time. Kerry pulled off her coat and faced Jacky again.

"What you just said was almost exactly what I said to your dad when I walked out the door a half hour ago. I think that may be the point he is trying to make. You and I have been forced together in this—relationship, and we're all of a sudden supposed to get along." She shot Jacky's dad a quick look, and then continued.

"I'm not your mother, Jacky. I can't replace her and I'm not even going to try. I won't be your stepmother either. I would just like to be—how about friends? I think we have a lot in common, and not just your dad, although we both love him. I hope you and I can find a way to make things work between us."

A lot in common? Make things work? What was she talking about? Was she blaming him for interfering in their relationship? That was crazy. Why was he even having this conversation? He already knew his opinion didn't matter anymore, why did he have to get along with her as well? That was never going to happen. Jacky said nothing.

His dad spoke up. "Jacky, you know about my father and you know from experience I'm not the best person to talk about feelings or emotions, but I do love you. I am the luckiest father in the world because you're my son. I also miss your mother, believe me I miss her all the time, but she never expected you or me to be unhappy, or lonely. I still have feelings. I want to be in a loving relationship again, and Kerry and I really love each other. I know your mother would understand. I'd appreciate if you would try to understand as well."

That was the kind of conversation that made Jacky want to leave the room. He wasn't comfortable with having this kind of open-secrets, family discussion in front of Kerry but he also knew, like it or not, she was going to be staying. He sighed, lifting his hands in an exaggerated shrug.

"Who cares what I think, Dad? Nothing's going to change. You're going to get married and I'm not going anywhere. It doesn't matter how I feel about it."

I should have just stayed on the mountain, he thought.

"Yes, it does," Kerry interjected sharply. She looked angry. "If you think I'm going to live somewhere where I'm not wanted, with someone who hates me, you're both wrong."

Both Jacky and his dad looked startled. His dad started to say, "Kerry, he doesn't—" but she stopped him.

"No, I've had to put up with difficult relationships before and I'm not going through it again." She looked at Jacky. "Jacky, I love your father and I want to be with him, and I want to be part of your life, too, if you will let me. But I'm not going to force myself on you or the relationship you have with your father. I don't want that any more than you do."

There was an awkward moment where no one spoke. Kerry started to rise. "I think I'm going to go. You two should talk this over and decide what's going on."

Jacky's stomach squeezed itself into a fist. Suddenly everything was on him, just like on the mountain. He hated himself for having this conversation. He could have just shut up and played along. He was right about what he said earlier. None of it mattered because his father was in love with Kerry. Even though he wasn't going to go to the Academy, Jacky was still going to a university and he was still going to major in science. All of this arguing was a complete waste of time, and he was wasting it. He stood up.

"No, I'm the one who's being an asshole. Yes, I want you to stay and be with my dad. I promise not to—not to be miserable about it. I just had a really major disappointment and I'm bitchy. That's all, I'm going upstairs. Good night."

He walked up the stairs expecting his dad to call him back or something but there was nothing. He walked up to his room and closed the door.

31

The Circus Comes to Town

Even though the band members were back home and trying to get on with their lives, the echoes of the accident and the rescue didn't fade away. Some of them had to get counselling to deal with their fears and night terrors. Some of the parents had questions about the charter air company they hired and the maintenance of the plane. Some wanted to sue. Terry quit the band, reluctantly, as it was his parents who pulled him out. He was pretty broken up about it. And then there was the media.

Like a tidal wave that rolls over the helpless inhabitants trying to pick up the pieces after an earthquake hits the shoreline, the media response to the news of the plane crash and the return of the victims was overwhelming. The local TV stations, radio, and newspapers covered the story with pictures and interviews, with Mr. Stewart representing the band. But then the circus arrived. Reporters and camera crews from major networks in almost every country showed up to talk. They wanted longer stories; they wanted inside stories and their own angles. CNN showed an entire recreation of the crash in 3D animation, which was weird because the official report of the accident wouldn't be out for several months. Mr. Stewart was constantly on the phone or in front of cameras talking to the media from the United Kingdom, Australia, Japan, the Netherlands, France, Germany, South Korea, and all over the United States. Freelance reporters were continually hanging around looking for a story and talking to everyone associated with the band. The schools finally had to arrange security to keep them away from the students.

It wasn't just the regular media that were adding to the momentum of the story. Online sites posted articles and pictures of the group without any authorization by the band. One of the rescuers had recorded the band playing on the mountain with their phone and posted it on YouTube. It ran with commercials, so someone was making money on it. The video trended for over a week with over twelve million views and counting. Then came the comical and insulting posts on social media. Parodies of *Lost* and *Gilligan's Island* were everywhere, and there were joke animations of Sasquatch being chased away by bagpipes and another where a jet launched a missile at the pipers and blew everything up. It wasn't funny at all and the idiots and jokesters were ruining the story. Mr. Stewart sent emails to all the band members advising them not to talk to the press and to ignore it all until the "lowlifes on the Internet" lost interest and moved on. He also begged anyone who was having trouble of any kind to get help. He included the names and numbers of recommended counsellors.

But the story of the pipe band marooned on the side of a mountain that was ultimately rescued by playing bagpipes had caught the public's attention. Twitter became abuzz with hashtags like #Ihearbagpipes, #bagpiperescue, #frozenpipes, and #piperonthemountain. Other than the events of the crash and the rescue, people wanted to know about the brave teenagers who survived and ultimately saved themselves. Who were they, how did they feel about their ordeal, what happened up there? Someone from a company in California phoned Mr. Stewart to offer to buy the option to make their story into a movie. It was getting to be too much for Mr. Stewart. He talked to the band parents and said he was getting tired of reporters and of telling the story over and over. He wasn't the only one who was tired of the attention.

Someone told someone in the news that it was Jacky who came up with the idea to use the bagpipes to help with their rescue. Some people started calling him a hero and using his picture from the band's website and his Facebook page for their story. That made Jacky's dad angry as they pulled every image of Jacky that they could off the web as quickly as possible. It was too late as so many of them were out there and photographers were constantly taking shots of him wherever he went. All of the online services Jacky used for keeping in touch were suddenly dangerous. He almost laughed at the irony that after surviving a plane crash in the mountains, his greatest danger was from the media after he was at home. The phone started ringing with reporters looking for an interview with Jacky and asking for pictures from the accident. That was when Kerry stepped in to take control.

"She's worked in news for years and knows how to handle these vultures," his dad said, waving his hand to the stacks of paper messages, emails on the screen, and the flashing voicemail light on the phone.

With Kerry in charge, they organized a few interviews with some recognized news channels and media sites with Jacky and Mr. Stewart. Kerry was standing nearby ready to pounce if any questions were out of line. Jacky was just getting used to Kerry living in his house and now she was his manager. Life was really strange. He did what he was told and stuck to his script for each one. Then he'd go back to school and try to forget it.

Jacky was getting most of the attention and he was surprisingly calm once the questions began. He knew what he had to say and had no problem controlling the conversation once the cameras were on. At first the whole experience was surreal, so many people seeming to be so amazed about something that Jacky knew was very straightforward—they were in an accident. They survived and they were rescued. The reporters asked pretty much the same questions, or variations of them. How did you feel? Were you afraid? How did you know the bagpipes would be heard so far away? If they asked a question he didn't want to answer he would deflect and talk about something else. Most of them seemed to be surprised or impressed that he knew so much about the physics of sound and could explain in such detail. They wouldn't use it, of course, it wasn't interesting. At least his science teacher, Mr. Lee, would be impressed if he saw it.

The real excitement happened when Jacky was invited to appear on *Mandy* in Los Angeles. When the call first came, Jacky's dad wanted

to

refuse them. This was all too much, and Jacky needed to get his own life back.

"Like go to school, band practice, do homework, all the normal things he usually does, when he's not being famous," he said. They were sitting at the table eating dinner when Kerry told them about the call. "Besides, it's an afternoon talk show, isn't it? Not the kind of thing Jacky needs to do."

Kerry laughed, "*Mandy* is an afternoon talk show like Tim Cook is the CEO of an electronic toy company. Believe me, she's big and Jacky really wants to go."

"Why, he's not a performer," his dad continued, refusing to give in.

"Jacky wants to get into a good university; he needs every opportunity he can get to build up his resume. Notoriety is a good thing for him." Kerry turned to Jacky. "Right?"

Jacky hadn't seen a full episode of the *Mandy* show but he'd seen enough clips on YouTube to know how popular she was and how much fun they had on the show. Why wouldn't he want to do that? He nodded, still eating.

His dad sighed and drank some of his wine. "My celebrity son." He shook his head. "You know what they're calling you?"

"Who?" asked Jacky.

"The whole world. You're the Piper on the Mountain. You have your own hashtag and everything. That should be worth money," his dad grinned.

"Don't laugh," said Kerry. "I've already registered the domain and the trademark."

Jacky and his dad stared at her. She shrugged. "Just to make sure someone else doesn't do it first and try to cash in on you," she said. "It would be a shame to see an action figure of Jacky at ToysRUs and not make any money on it."

Jacky laughed. She obviously knew her stuff. He never would have thought of that.

32

Investigations

Jacky repeated, at every opportunity, that it was the pilot who deserved the title of hero. All the media attention was on him, and Jacky didn't like that their story was being rewritten by the news and social media giving him all the credit. Pilots dying to save the lives of their passengers wasn't as interesting as a sixteen-year-old singlehandedly saving everyone on the mountain by playing bagpipes. Stupid as it seemed, that was the way they were selling it.

When Jacky and Kerry arrived home from Los Angeles they agreed, no more interviews. They would refer any more calls back to Mr. Stewart. Fortunately, the interest had worn off and the circus had moved away. Jacky felt better about Kerry. She helped him all through that whole awkward media thing. He would have been eaten alive, for sure. She was okay to live around, too. She wasn't a slob like he and his dad were, but she had some annoying habits.

Jacky was more concerned about getting back to his previous normal life and getting caught up on his school work. He was going to double down on his averages and make sure he would qualify for a scholarship. Without the boost from the Academy, he would have to try harder to get in to a science program at a good university.

Captain Connelly's funeral was held in his home city of Fredericton, New Brunswick. Jacky read about it online and was looking through some of the pictures that were posted. He was disappointed he couldn't be there. The band sent flowers instead. At least they had a piper there for the service. Looking at the pictures of Captain Connelly's family mourning was hard, but he did anyway. It was as close to being there as Jacky was going to get. He pulled out his own pipes and performed a vigil for the pilot in the backyard.

When the government investigation into the plane crash began, everything started to get ugly. The investigators interviewed Mr. Stewart and Mrs. Walford and started talking to every one of the band members. They asked for copies of any pictures or videos that were taken at the site and during the flight.

Jacky had seen pictures of the site online with all kinds of guesswork by reporters and experts on what had happened. His science teacher gave him an explanation of what might have caused the plane's engines to fail and how they were able to land safely without power. Jacky was fascinated. It was all so complex but it made perfect sense. Why didn't the media talk to Mr. Lee?

He didn't like the speculation that implied Captain Connelly may have had health problems or made a bad call flying through the cold weather. Some reports questioned whether the plane was properly maintained. They criticized the search and rescue crews for taking so long to find them and the government for cutting back their budgets so the crews didn't have the resources. Kerry told him these were people with other axes to grind, other agendas who were using this as a way to attack the government. Jacky was infuriated.

Unfortunately for them, the only people he was able to vent at were the accident investigators, who got the full brunt of Jacky's indignation. The lead investigator was a tall, dark-haired lady who spoke with a French accent, so Jacky had trouble understanding everything she said, and her assistant, who was a shorter man who didn't speak much and wrote a lot of notes. Jacky didn't even wait for the questions.

"Why are you being so hard on Captain Connelly?" Jacky demanded right at the start. "He did a great job of landing that plane safely after the engines failed, why are you accusing him of being careless?"

The inspector sat back and held up her hands. "Excuse me? What are you talking about?"

Jacky pulled the pile of newspaper clippings and printouts of web pages from his backpack and put them on the table. "That, that's what I'm talking about."

She picked up the papers and flipped through them. "We are not the ones who are saying these things. This is the media trying to get clicks; they will say anything even though they know nothing. That is the purpose of this investigation, to find out what happened on that flight. Don't read this nonsense."

She dropped the papers in a garbage can and returned to her notes. "Let's start again. How do you know he landed the plane safely? What did you see? Try and remember everything."

Jacky thought back. The plane hit turbulence and they climbed. He heard the engines accelerating and felt the plane rising. They told everyone to put on their seat belts. The plane settled for a while but started jumping violently. Everything flew around, and the flight attendant was hurt. No, she was injured helping someone. The plane was bouncing around very hard. Then the first engine stopped. The pilot came on the PA system and told them they were going to land until the storm passed. They turned; he felt it. The other engine was working harder. Shortly after that, a few minutes maybe, the other engine died, too, and the co-pilot came on the PA—no, he came out and talked to everyone, explaining what was happening, and instructed us on preparing for an emergency landing. Everyone was scared and got very quiet. Without the engines going the only sound was wind and the hydraulics that operated the wing flaps. Jacky could see the ground and the snow and the plane turning left and right while it was gliding down. It felt like they were floating. Jacky remembered looking out the window and seeing the snow lit up by the plane's landing lights. It was strange, to be so calm just before all hell broke loose.

The co-pilot told everyone to brace themselves, put their heads down. Then the plane hit something, and then it landed and bounced. That was when Jacky was hit on the head by something loose that was flying around in the plane. He blacked out for a short time. He woke up after the plane stopped and everyone was panicking in the plane. A split second later an avalanche hit and the inside of the plane went dark.

He explained all of this to the investigators who were writing furiously even though they had a digital recorder taking down everything he said. The investigator finished writing notes and pulled out a diagram of the plane, pushing it in front of Jacky.

"Please mark where on the plane you were sitting." He put an X on his seat on the picture and pushed it back. She looked at it, put it away, and turned off the recorder. Jacky assumed the interview was over. He decided to say what he was thinking.

"I have a theory on what happened," he said. The woman stopped and looked at him, blinked twice, and sat down.

"Oh, you do. You're aware that an investigation like this can take a long time and we won't speculate on the results until it's completed. But you already know what happened? Why do you think that?"

Jacky shrugged, "No, I said I have a theory. I researched it as a science project. I plan to study physics at university so I figured, why not give it a try."

She crossed her arms. "A school project, indeed. Okay, give me your hypothesis." She shook her head at the man next to her who was waving the pen over his notebook, unsure whether to write it down.

Jacky pulled out his notebook and handed it to her. He explained, pointing to the diagrams as he did, "That design of airplane allows it to handle wind and snow so that wasn't the problem. The shaking was caused by ice forming on the wings, which the pilot controlled using wing de-icers that are designed to inflate and break off the ice, but it kept icing again faster than he could remove it. Captain Connelly said he was going to fly above the storm, but it started shaking worse as we climbed. Instead of avoiding the cold front, I think he flew through a pocket of super-cooled water, which is colder than freezing and needs a place to attach itself to become ice. When the plane flew through the moisture, it entered the engine's air intake and clogged it with ice. The engine was already cold because of the storm so there was no way that heat from the engine could melt the ice."

The investigator shrugged. "Impressive. You've spent some time on this, I see. Well, it's too soon in the investigation to say if you're right, but it sounds like a very plausible scenario. It would certainly explain a lot." She started to rise and stopped, "I understand it was your idea to use bagpipes to attract the search and rescue teams." That was obviously off the record, too; Jacky was relieved.

Jacky shrugged. "Yes, I know it was dangerous but—"

She looked confused. "Why was it dangerous?"

"Well, we might have shaken up the snow overhead and buried everyone," he said. "That was why we didn't do it earlier."

The investigator considered that and then shrugged. "I suppose that was a possibility, but the noise of the helicopters would have done that as well and they didn't. So, it probably wasn't a real threat. We know the rescue crews couldn't find you. They flew by that area several times and couldn't make visual contact. They came after they heard you play. So I think you made the right decision."

"You mean we could have come home sooner?" Jacky was startled.

She shook her head. "There's no guarantee of that. The mountain range is very large; they were there at the right time. You can't think in terms of maybe or might have. Things turned out well this time, except for Captain Connelly. Be happy about that. And keep working on your science; you are very good." She smiled and Jacky left the room.

As he walked back, he realized that reliving the experience had reignited the emotions he felt up on the mountain—the confusion of the crash-landing, the frustration of being stuck up there, the euphoria of seeing the helicopters. Even though it was over and he was safely on solid ground, Jacky was surprised that he could remember those feelings so clearly. It was like a video on his hard drive that he could watch and relive anytime he wanted. Ironically, he never thought he would want to but the experience was less frightening in his memory. He could never forget it but he wasn't afraid to remember it.

Normal Life, Interrupted

The interest in the story was finally dying out and life was returning to normal for Jacky, as much as was possible with a new person in the house. When he saw Miles at school, Jacky asked him if he was able to get accepted to the Academy. Miles grinned.

"Yeah, I filled out the application form and threatened my dad I was going to work for his company if I didn't get in. It's amazing how fast he gave me his credit card." He smiled at Jacky and then his face dropped. He looked down at his feet again and changed the topic. "Um, I saw the new Avengers movie, did you see it yet?"

Jacky shook his head and kept walking. "No, I want to make sure there's no plane crashes in it first. There aren't any planes crashing, are there?"

Miles laughed. "Everything crashes. And explodes. And yet somehow they all come through alive and win." He paused again. Miles seemed to be so worried about what he was saying he couldn't finish a thought.

Jacky laughed. "Yeah, well, I have a lot of catching up to do. I probably don't have time to see movies anyway. I'm glad you got in the Academy. At least one of us did."

Miles grunted a vague agreement. They walked the rest of the way in silence. They were both dealing with disappointment; Jacky wouldn't be going to the United Kingdom and Miles would be going there alone.

Band practice started up again a few weeks after they got back. Although several of the members had been getting therapy to deal with the trauma of the whole thing, they all came back except for Terry, who tried unsuccessfully to get his parents to change their minds. The band office had received calls from other players wanting to join as well as stacks of letters and emails of congratulations and support from other bands around the world. Mr. Stewart and his wife had posted most of them on the board and on the walls coming in from the doors; there were so many. It was nice to see all the support from other pipers. The players didn't say much coming in; most of them seemed to want to get back to normal and try to put the whole experience behind them. Some of them looked sideways at Jacky. He could tell they didn't like that he was getting all the attention after the rescue. He knew how they felt; he didn't like it either, but he said nothing. The only exceptions were Rick who grinned at him when he arrived and Nadine who asked about his trip to Los Angeles. She was a huge *Mandy* fan.

They gathered in a circle and started with their breathing exercises first, then Mr. Stewart stood in front to address the group.

"Hello, everyone, welcome back," he started. Everyone grunted in response.

"How come you shaved your beard?" asked Rick. Several others laughed, and Mr. Stewart rubbed his cleanly shaven face.

"You can blame Mrs. Stewart for that. She said either I shaved or I can go back and sleep outside, seeing how I was starting to look like a mountain man."

There was more laughter; it felt good to relax and laugh. Everyone knew what was coming next; no one wanted to talk about the crash again.

"All right," Mr. Stewart said, waiting for silence. "There are some things we need to discuss, but only briefly. I want to get back to playing as much as you do. First of all, I am very sorry for what happened. I know it was an accident and no one, including two professional pilots, could foresee what happened, but I am still responsible for your safety. The other thing I want to say is thank you. Thanks for keeping it together while we were stuck up there, even though I know it was very hard on all of you. But also thank you for being brave, standing out there and playing the pipes and drums like the world champions you are. You may have saved us. We can't be sure and it's not important, but you did it and here we are."

He took a breath and pointed to Jacky, "I also want to thank Jacky and his stepmom-to-be, I guess?" He looked at Jacky for verification, but he just shrugged. Kerry's exact role in his family was still to be determined. Mr. Stewart laughed. "I was absolutely buried in phone calls and emails from the media all around the world. I don't know how to deal with them and I couldn't keep up. Fortunately Jacky's future stepmom is a professional in that business and she stepped in and rescued me. I know that some of you think Jacky was getting an unfair amount of attention from this. I want you to know that the only reason that happened was someone told them that he was the one who came up with the plan to use bagpipes to summon the rescuers. That was the hook they needed and they went after him. I saw how much he had to put up with and I'm grateful he took the bullet for us." He looked at Jacky and frowned. "Although, even you have to admit going to California and being on TV was over the top, Jacky." That broke the mood and everyone laughed.

"All I know," Mr. Stewart finished, "is that I never want to see another TV camera or reporter again in my life. Now, let's play."

From that point, it was just like any weekly practice. Like the event never happened. When they were finished, as they were putting their instruments away, Mr. Stewart called them together for one more thing. He handed envelopes to each of the players with a big smile on his face. He looked like he was holding the world's greatest secret. He pulled a piece of paper out of his pocket and smiled.

"There was one more letter we received recently that I need to share with you, and with it, some news. Please take these envelopes to your parents. It's good news, trust me." He opened his letter and read:

We are deeply sorry to have missed the New Caledonians at the festival in British Columbia and were terribly concerned when we learned of your accident on the way there. We followed news of the search closely and we were increasingly concerned that they were unable to locate the accident site. Our prayers and hopes were with you during that ordeal and also with the search and rescue teams who were rigorously looking for you.

We were greatly relieved to hear of your rescue, as, no doubt, were the thousands of people in Canada and elsewhere who were anxiously awaiting any word on your condition. We were very saddened to hear of the passing of Captain Connelly, a decorated veteran of Canada's armed forces and whose actions contributed to your safe return.

We thank God and good fortune that you were rescued safely and are back, safely in your homes.

Deepest regards.

Mr. Stewart looked up at the group and read the name: "His Royal Highness, the Prince of Wales."

Mr. Stewart paused for a moment and put the letter in his pocket. "There's another part of this letter that goes on to say that we have been invited, as the prince's guests, to attend the Edinburgh Tattoo in August. We're going to Edinburgh." He raised the letter over his head and cheered along with the band members.

The Edinburgh Tattoo is one of the greatest showcases of Scottish music anywhere in the world. It features one of the largest collections of bagpipes and drums assembled in one place, with a spectacular fireworks show afterwards. The band members were jumping and hugging each other. Jacky stood in the middle of the celebrations, his head reeling. Edinburgh, guests of the prince? The band members were talking over each other and sharing high fives when he was suddenly tackled by Nadine, who hugged him tight with her substantial strength. He had the air squeezed out of him and was having trouble breathing. He hugged her back, thumping her on the back as a signal to loosen her grip. She did and he sucked in air. Nadine looked up at him, her face broken in a wide smile and bright red with excitement.

"Don't you dare," he said, pointing at her. "I had nothing to do with this."

She laughed and ran to hug someone else.

Jacky ran home to tell his dad and Kerry about the trip. He rushed in the door, breathing hard and red faced and saw his dad and Kerry talking in the living room. They looked up at him as he dashed in, holding his case and the envelope. They were smiling happily. They must have already heard the news. How the heck did they do that? Unless it was something else. He paused for a moment and swallowed, trying to decide what to say.

"Hey, Jacky," his dad said, still grinning. "How was practice?"

"It was great. So you've heard, then?" Jacky asked, unsure. His dad's face looked puzzled as he cocked his head.

"Heard? About what?" *That answers the first question*, Jacky thought.

"Never mind," he said. "What's going on with you guys? You look excited about something."

His dad glanced at Kerry and squeezed her hand. "Well, we got some good news that sort of involves you, too," he grinned. "You're going to have a new brother or sister. Kerry is pregnant." They looked like they had won the lottery.

He dropped the case and the letter.

What?

Jacky decided that it was a good thing. He could see they were happy about it, and they were still waiting for a reaction. He had some good news to share, too. He crossed his arms and frowned.

"Aren't you supposed to wait until after the wedding?" He shook his head. "You do know that I took sex ed. I know how it happens." His dad laughed and Kerry turned red. She didn't look comfortable talking about it, obviously, but his dad was too happy to notice.

"You're absolutely right, Reverend, that's why we've moved up the wedding to this summer. That way no one will know," he whispered.

"Only those who don't know how to count," Jacky said. "Congratulations, I'm happy for you, really. I have some news as well." The laughter stopped as they paid attention. Jacky handed the envelope to his dad.

"The band has been invited to play at the Edinburgh Tattoo in August. By the Prince of Wales."

His dad's face lit up again. "Edinburgh? That's fantas— Wait, this August?" Jacky nodded. "Do you know when?" His dad opened the envelope and pulled out the letter. They read the letter together and disappointment was clearly written on Kerry's face.

Jacky noticed. "You don't have to change your plans because of me. I don't have to go."

His dad put down the letter, got up and hugged Jacky. "Of course, you're going. That's so great, Jacky. I'm proud of you. We'll work things out, don't worry."

"Thanks." Jacky glanced at Kerry but she was still looking away. He figured she was mad or upset so he picked up his case and started for the stairs.

"I have an idea," Kerry spoke up. Jacky stopped and turned. She didn't look upset, she was just thinking. "Why don't we all go to Scotland together? That way we can watch you perform and then have the wedding there."

"Are you sure?" Jacky's dad asked, still standing. "None of the guests will be able to make travel plans at such short notice."

"I don't care about guests," she said. "We didn't have that many to invite anyway. I'd sooner just be with my new family. Besides, I do have some family over there. My cousin works for the Canadian consulate in Edinburgh. She's been trying to get me to come over for ages. Maybe she'll agree to be my maid of honour."

"Jacky, is that okay with you?" his dad was asking him, as if Jacky was the one making the decisions.

"Yes." *Of course*, he thought. Why not? This was great. "You guys haven't been to Scotland. I could show you around. Or have you?" He looked at Kerry. She shook her head.

"Nope. I've been to London lots of times when I was a reporter. I actually met the Prince of Wales there once. I would love to see Scotland. Now, if you will excuse me, I'm tired. Good night."

"'Night," said Jacky as he picked up his case to follow her upstairs.

"Hold on a second, Jacky," his dad said. "Sit down, I have to ask you something."

Jacky sat. *What now*, he thought.

His dad sat next to him after grabbing a beer from the fridge. He offered Jacky a Dr. Pepper, which he took.

"That's a lot to take in, all of a sudden, isn't it?"

"Yeah," Jacky said. "It is, but at least it's good news."

"Um hum, it is. I want to ask, are you still planning on quitting the band?" His dad looked at him seriously.

The last time Jacky talked about that was on the mountain. Then the craziness that happened and the change at home overshadowed it. He hadn't thought about it but he hadn't changed his mind.

"Yes, I think so. I still have to focus on my courses to qualify for a scholarship," he said.

His dad nodded and took a drink. "You remember what I told you about my father and his obsession with work. I know some of that rubbed off on me; I find myself getting single-minded about a job and the cost of everything else. I know I did that a lot when you were young. I hoped you weren't going to pick up that habit, but maybe it's in our DNA."

He turned and faced Jacky. "It's not necessary to give up something you like for something else you think is more important. You have the ability and the time to do more than one thing. Actually they say the more you do the better your brain is at taking in new knowledge. Look, I know you were disappointed that you didn't get into the school in the United Kingdom. We all have disappointments in our lives, things that hurt when we lose them. The biggest one for me was losing your mother. But there were others. I've never told you this but we never wanted you to be an only child, like I was. I wanted you to have brothers and sisters, but every time we tried it failed. Your poor mom was so upset because she lost three children by miscarrying. Every time a baby died inside her a little of her died, too. Then you came along and you thrived. She took that as a sign and stopped trying for any more. I felt bad about it but I understood how she felt. So now, my getting married, having this baby and spending these next few years with you, before you become an adult and go off on your own, this is me trying to carry on with my family, my new family. You remember what Angus said, family is the most important part of your life."

Jacky was watching his dad. After all their years and all of the talks they had since his mother died, Jacky was still finding out stuff about him.

"You want me to stay with the band?" he asked.

"All I'm asking is that you think about it. Make an informed decision and don't assume that wanting to go to a good university and be a good scientist means you have to give up everything else. You don't give yourself enough credit, Jacky. You play the bagpipes, you play the guitar, and you used logic and physics to save everyone up on that mountain."

Jacky groaned.

His dad laughed. "I know you're tired of hearing about it, but you did, it's a fact. That shows how you think. A brain like that needs many, many things to work on to stay vibrant." His dad stopped and held up his hands. "I'm done, that's all I want to say. Just promise me you'll have a long think before you pull the plug."

"Okay," Jacky said. He took his can of pop, grabbed his case, and climbed upstairs. His mind was spinning and he still had homework to do.

34

Edinburgh

More than anywhere else in the world, Jacky loved Scotland. Of all the places he had seen while travelling with the band or with his dad, this country was magical. Every historic legend he'd read about, every medieval role-playing game he'd played involved battling the invading hordes and ancient magic that reminded him of that place. It was all there—the castles, the legends, the prehistoric standing stones, the dates that were carved into the walls of the buildings, and the stories told on plaques mounted on the walkways.

Talk about epic battles. The history of Scotland was written by them. Jacky read up on the history of the Fraser clan; they had immigrated to Scotland from France and fought in the early battles against the English kings with William Wallace and Robert the Bruce. The whole history of Scotland was about defending itself against invaders and overlords, with the last big battle being fought in Culloden in 1746. That ended Scotland's fight for independence and ultimately led to Jacky being born in Canada. But Scottish spirit never dies.

Jacky had been to Glasgow a few times and travelled around the west coast islands with the New Caledonians but he had never been to Edinburgh. That city was divided into two areas, Old Town, which looked exactly as its name implied—ancient looking buildings and cobblestone streets perched on the hill above the newer part of the city. Even New Town looked old, except it had sleek-looking trams travelling up the main road. Everything in Edinburgh was heavy, gothic, and historic, but it wasn't dull. Every year in August, the city became a circus as the streets filled up with tourists and performers of every kind. The ancient Edinburgh Castle, perched on top of the Royal Mile, was festooned with lights and a massive stage for its annual Edinburgh Military Tattoo, which filled the night sky with music, lights, and a blazing fireworks show.

Jacky arrived in Edinburgh with the band after flying through Toronto and Amsterdam, catching a bus to Waverley Station, which stood between the old and new towns. They walked to the hotel two blocks away in New Town. By the time they tossed their luggage and instruments in their rooms, the band members were wired having been awake for more than a day. Mr. Stewart suggested they may want to rest first, have a nap before heading out into the city, but that wasn't going to happen. He made sure that they all had his phone number programmed in their phones and had maps of Old Town and the route to their hotel handed out before they left.

"Watch for traffic coming from the right," he called out to them as the band members poured out of the hotel, heading for the Waverley Bridge. The old section of the city was perched on the hill above them with buildings seeming to grow up from the rocks. The walls were stone with gothic designs everywhere and blackened with time and smoke. The bridge outside the station that stretched over a long, green park was a mass of tourists, double-decker buses, and taxis. Everywhere were the sounds of the city. A mix of traffic, trains, voices, and music that seemed to come from every direction. Jacky could imagine horses trotting up the streets or pulling carriages. The place just looked untouched by the passing of time.

People were streaming up and down the Royal Mile with the occasional taxi or delivery truck crawling through the horde of pedestrians. Jacky looked both ways, trying to decide which way to go first. There was a lot to choose from. On the top of the hill was the castle. The view down the hill looked like something out of Harry Potter with its old buildings made of stone, Scottish flags flying everywhere, and hundreds of colourful gift shops. A small crowd was gathered around a man dressed as Braveheart, with a sword and his face half painted in blue. Further up were Merlin and some druids in long, brown robes with hoods standing next to a Stormtrooper wearing a kilt. There were solo pipers playing at different spots up the sidewalk to the castle.

He passed Nadine coming down the hill, carrying large bags filled with souvenirs, and wearing a Scotland T-shirt. She was beaming, taking pictures of everything she passed.

"Look," she said, reaching into her bag, "I got a knit scarf, a wool sweater, and some Scottish toffee. They have haggis-flavoured chips, too. I'm off to find the Elephant House Restaurant; it's not too far from here."

"What's that?" Jacky asked.

"It's the restaurant where J. K. Rowling wrote *Harry Potter*," she said. Jacky looked doubtful. "Just the first one."

"Oh, okay. I was going to say that would be an awful lot of coffee," Jacky said.

"Ha, ha, funny. It's just down this way. Do you want to come with me?"

He was going to refuse, beg off and let her go, but he was hungry and eating street vendor food wasn't appealing to him. They wandered down the street and found the restaurant, just a short distance from the main road. Sure enough, it said "home of Harry Potter" by the window. Inside was swarming with people but they had lots of tables and counters to eat at. Jacky saw newspaper clippings and pictures of J. K. Rowling all over the restaurant. He ordered a sandwich and ginger beer and sat with Nadine at a small table. She was still giddy with excitement. She stacked her bags under the table, pushing Jacky's legs sideways. He looked down at the colourful heap of paraphernalia.

"Why are you buying so much stuff?"

"I'm doing my Christmas shopping while I'm here. You can't get any of this at home."

"Smart," Jacky said. The food was good. He could have probably eaten two sandwiches. He took a drink of ginger beer.

"Are you still going to quit the band?" Nadine ambushed him with no warning. He almost spit up his drink.

"Nadine, don't jump me like that." He wiped his face.

"Are you?" She wasn't letting go.

"I don't know. A lot has happened since the accident." He stopped. His normal reaction would have been to avoid the subject, but he didn't want to. He may have been tired but he knew, after everything they had been through, he could trust Nadine. "I was trying to get into an overseas high school when we had the accident. I lost my chance to apply because we were stuck up there. I haven't decided what I want to do yet. Literally everything has changed since the accident."

"For the better, I hope," she said.

"I don't know," he said, shrugging. "I mean it, it's been nuts since we got back, and I haven't figured out how I feel."

"Hmm," Nadine grunted. "I hope you change your mind. Sometimes if you have a choice to make it's easier to say you're too busy than to face it. You're here; you're having a good time. You play really well and you're smart enough to go to a foreign school. Seems to me a guy like you wouldn't have to choose between doing something he wants and something he enjoys."

He had no answer to that. She was dangerously close to repeating what his dad had said to him, but coming from Nadine, it made sense. Why did he want to quit? He wasn't sure anymore.

"Okay, I'm going to go up to the castle and look around. Good luck shopping. See you later," he said. She was eating an apple pie. She smiled with her cheeks full and waved.

He walked to the Royal Mile and up the hill toward the stone gate that led to the Edinburgh Castle. This was the only castle he'd seen in real life, and he wasn't going to miss his chance to look around. The building was a military fortress. Its displays showed the uniforms and guns they used over the centuries. They had the largest cannon ever made that could flatten any ship attacking in the harbour. They also had a jail and the torture chamber on display. He stepped outside in the open courtyard and saw the immense lighting and seating area for the show.

As he walked back down the hill, he felt his lack of sleep catching up with him. He was overtired and needed to get some rest before they had dinner. His dad and Kerry were meeting him at the hotel when they got in the next day. For now he was sharing a room with one of the other guys in the band. He headed back to the hotel, wishing they had picked one closer to the castle. It was a long walk down the hill to the bridge and on to the hotel.

At dinnertime, everyone piled into a bus and drove through the city, past the newer old buildings to a restaurant that was large enough to facilitate all of them, with food that was closer to what they were used to: burgers, fish and chips, and chicken. Most of the band had managed to get some rest but a few of them had stayed up exploring. They were the ones falling into their food.

Mr. Stewart stood up and demanded everyone's attention. "All right, band members, finish eating and we'll get back to the hotel. I want everyone to go straight to bed and sleep, no Netflixing or Facebooking. Sleep. I want every one of you up and ready to go at eight o'clock tomorrow morning with your instruments. Don't bring your uniforms in the morning; we'll be back later to change before you play. They're going to feed us breakfast at the site, and we're going to use the time to practice so we can get familiar with the field." He paused as the chatter was getting louder; he waited for silence. "Remember, we're here as guests of the Royal Family and of this city. We'll be performing in front of a lot of people who don't know us but have heard how great this band is, so their expectations are going to be very high. There's no excuse for being tired and not performing at your best. It's going to be a very long day tomorrow; get a good sleep tonight and make everybody back home proud. All right?"

A big cheer from the band members filled the room, and everyone returned to their food and chatter. Some of the members ran back to the dessert tray to scoop one more helping of cake and pie before they had to leave. Jacky was still fighting to keep his eyes open. The bus returned everyone to the hotel, and Mr. Stewart stood guard by the door to make sure all the band members went up to their rooms and didn't wander off with the crowds on the street. This city obviously didn't sleep at night, especially when it was so warm and lively. Jacky closed the window to keep out the noise of the partiers and the traffic and was asleep before Randy, his roommate, was out of the bathroom.

"Jacky, Jacky. Wake up." Randy was nudging him. Jacky struggled to wake.

"What?" His voice sounded thick as an old smoker.

"Get up, it's time to go. It's almost eight o'clock."

"Oh, crap." Jacky rubbed his eyes and climbed off the bed. "I need a shower." He stumbled into the bathroom and into the narrow stall. He stood under the shower and hit the button to turn it on. The shower used an electric pump that heated the water on demand, which meant the first bit of spray was cold enough to numb his chest. Jacky gasped as the freezing water hit his skin. It took a minute to warm up, but he only had a little time to clean up and get dressed.

"You better hurry up, man," Randy yelled into the room. "Mr. Stewart said not to be late."

Jacky was scrubbing his hair as fast as possible. The water was just getting warm. He was dried, dressed, and downstairs waiting for the bus with everyone else in fifteen minutes. Not bad when his body was still hours behind in another time zone. The cool morning air helped his brain to clear. He was so worried he'd sleep in and was going to miss things until he got downstairs and saw how tired everyone else looked. At least he wasn't any worse off.

The bus carried them to the gates of the castle. As the band members were led through the entrance, everyone was craning their necks to take in as much of the old structure as possible as they passed. They walked by the spectators seating to the staging area, a vast courtyard surrounded by high stone walls. They carried on to another room inside the castle where the smell of food welcomed them. They gathered by the door as a woman holding a binder and her assistant, a man wearing a kilt, approached. She spoke to Mr. Stewart then addressed the band members.

"*Fáilte*, welcome," the lady said. "We are so happy you were able to join us here at the festival. And we're excited to welcome you all here in Edinburgh. I know you've been to Glasgow but I think you'll agree that this city is a little different than what you've seen before."

Most of the band members nodded and grunted in agreement. The lady continued: "The annual Edinburgh Military Tattoo has featured the top pipe bands from around the world, but this is the first time we've featured a band invited by the Royal Family, which makes us doubly proud to have you here. So again, welcome."

The man stepped in. "Now we've put on a fine Scottish breakfast for you, including haggis for those of you who are a bit adventurous. Then we invite you to a complimentary tour of the castle, so you can see all of the wonderful displays of Scotland's past military history."

The band members cheered. Jacky smacked his forehead, realizing he could have seen more of the city instead of touring the castle yesterday. He sighed; didn't matter, he could stand to see the castle again.

They filed into the dining room and feasted on breakfast, everything from granola and fruit to sausage, eggs, haggis, and blood sausage, with stacks of dry toast and small jams. Jacky was hungry enough to try some of everything. He liked the haggis; it had a nice spiciness to it that made him forget he was eating a sheep's organs. The blood sausage was dry and bitter. The eggs were good as was the toast, no matter how cold it was.

They were assembling the instruments and getting ready to practise when the lady with the binder reappeared. "If I could please have your attention for a moment. We have a special surprise for you. You're about to have a visit with His Royal Highness, the Prince of Wales. There are a few things I need to explain to you first so you understand the proper etiquette for meeting the Prince."

She explained the details of what they were supposed to do and not do when greeting and speaking with the Prince. The instructions just made Jacky, and most of the others, nervous. They just stood at attention and waited. The lady left the room and came back a few seconds later and spoke with some formality in her voice.

"His Royal Highness, the Prince of Wales."

The prince entered the room followed by a small group of assistants and security people. Other than being mobbed by Nadine for a selfie, Jacky couldn't think of any threats to the Prince in that group. He spoke with Mr. Stewart first, then they started meeting the individual band members with Mr. Stewart following closely reciting each of their names to the Prince.

Nadine was so excited she was vibrating. Jacky was surprised to find the Prince looked and sounded like a regular person, a well-dressed and well-spoken regular person. He didn't know what he was expecting. He stood and waited until Mr. Stewart introduced him to the Prince, who shook his hand warmly.

"Oh, so you're Jacky Fraser? The infamous Piper on the Mountain I've heard so much about?" The Prince grinned as if sharing a joke. Jacky smiled back, restraining a grimace.

"Yes, sir, that's me."

"Well, I'm very pleased to meet you. I'm pulling your leg, of course, but I understand you played an important role in saving your bandmates. Your parents must be very proud of you."

"Yes sir, they—" He paused, almost correcting himself, but he didn't. "They are. I knew that bagpipes would be heard from a long distance. It was our only option," Jacky said. The Prince smiled, seeming impressed.

"I do love the sound of the pipes," said the Prince. "I wonder what that must have sounded like, playing in the high mountains like that. Simply marvellous, I imagine."

The memory came to Jacky's mind in an instant—the sound of the bagpipes playing into the cold, clear air echoing back from the distant mountains, as if answering in their own voices.

"Yes, it was, sir—um, Your Highness," he fumbled. The Prince nodded and smiled, moving on to shake Larry Walford's hand. Jacky exhaled; he was so nervous that he was going to blow it but a little stumble wasn't the end of the world. He remembered that moment on the mountain again. He wished he could have recorded it, to catch the sound of music bouncing from the mountains around them, echoing back at different points depending how far off they were. He knew the physics, he knew how sound worked, but it seemed like there were three times as many pipers playing up there. It felt, for the moment, like they weren't alone.

Playing at the Edinburgh Castle was an eerie mix of old and new. Technicians were still working around them as they stood in the centre of the field practising their performance. There were many rows of seats for the event around the courtyard of the castle with large-screen monitors and lights everywhere. With the seats empty in the daylight, the staging area looked like an empty football stadium with enormous stone walls behind it. The sound of the pipes echoed nicely off the walls and made the band sound larger than it was. They ran through the set twice and rehearsed the marching without playing until they were comfortable with the space.

After an hour, they were as ready as they were going to be, and other bands wanted the space. They were scheduled to play early in the evening so they had a few hours to kill. Mr. Stewart warned them not to wander off around the city but to take it easy and be well rested for their performance that night.

As they were packing their instruments and preparing to return to the hotel, Mr. Stewart tapped Jacky on the shoulder and pointed to the door. "Jacky, your parents are here."

He waved and they joined him.

"How's it going?" his dad asked.

"Great," said Jacky. "I got to meet the Prince. He listens to the news, apparently." He finished packing his pipes and picked up his case. "I have to go back to the hotel now. Where are you guys staying?"

"Not far from here," his dad said. "Before you go, there's someone we want you to meet." He pointed to the door and started walking. Jacky fell in behind them, past Rick who stared at him curiously. Jacky held his arms akimbo, to say *I have no idea.*

The lady with the binder led them to an office and closed the door after them. A man was standing by the window. He was another well-dressed, older man with white hair. Jacky was about to ask what was going on when the man turned and greeted him.

"Ah, Mr. Fraser, do come in." Jacky assumed he was talking to his dad, but, as he looked, his dad and Kerry had hung back by the door. Jacky walked in, and the man approached, holding out his hand. They shook.

"You are John Fraser, are you not?" the man asked.

"Yes, um, Jacky, actually. Call me Jacky," he said, uncertain about what was happening.

"Pleased to meet you, Jacky. My name is Dr. Wellesley, and I'm the chancellor at the BIAS, the British International Academy of Science. I understand you've heard of us?"

What? Jacky looked back at his dad who winked and smiled. How was this possible? That was the director of the school he wanted to apply to.

"Y—yes, sir, I've heard of it. I tried—I mean I was going to apply there."

"Yes, I understand that," the chancellor said. He pointed to two chairs, and they sat, facing each other.

"You have an interest in science, do you?" the chancellor asked.

Jacky nodded, holding his excitement in. "Yes, it's my favourite subject. I've been doing extra work in physics to try to get a scholarship."

"That's very good," said Dr. Wellesley. "From what I hear you are quite good at applied physics as well."

Jacky sighed. He was talking about the bagpipes on the mountain. Jacky couldn't get away from the hero label but he wasn't going to argue with the head of the school he wanted to go to. "Yes, sir. That's true."

"Could you explain that to me? I only know what I heard on the news," said Dr. Wellesley.

Jacky gave him a short version of the accident and playing on the mountain to attract the rescue.

The chancellor raised his eyebrows and cocked his head. "So you used physics of the bagpipes to alert the search and rescue because the electronic forms of signalling had failed."

Jacky nodded. "It also helped improve everyone's morale. We were getting depressed just waiting."

Dr. Wellesley chuckled. "So you're a scientist *and* a natural leader. You impress me, Jacky."

Jacky's face flushed, and the chancellor continued, "You may have guessed that we've heard about you from a number of sources. I had my assistants check with your teacher, Mr. Lee, and he recommended you very highly."

Jacky was listening, and his stomach clenched; he knew what was coming, he hoped.

Dr. Wellesley continued, "We also spoke with your Science Outreach instructor to get a second recommendation for your application and we are happy to offer you a scholarship to attend the Academy of Science."

"Bu—but I missed the deadline, I wasn't able to—" Jacky stuttered.

The chancellor interrupted, "I would consider being in a plane crash and stuck on a mountain to be extenuating circumstances. Had you been able to submit the application as you intended, I'm certain you would have received serious consideration. As I say, we've seen your marks, you do qualify. This isn't an exception to those rules, Jacky, only that you were unable to submit it on time. The only question is, will you take us up on our offer?"

So that was it? He got his wish? Jacky was about to say yes, to put everything back as it was before. Then he stopped. A weight landed on his chest so suddenly, he almost gasped. Things weren't as they were before; everything had changed. Before, he was angry. He wanted to be away from home, from his dad, from the disappointments in his life. Now, that was changed and he wanted something else.

Everyone was waiting. The chancellor cocked his head.

Jacky cleared his throat and spoke slowly, "I do want to, yes sir, but—" He paused again.

The chancellor said, "But?"

Jacky looked back at his dad and Kerry who were watching him, waiting. "I can't believe I'm saying this," he said, turning back to the chancellor and shaking his head. "I wanted to come to the Academy because I didn't like things the way they were. But a lot has changed since then. I'm going to have a new brother or sister, and tomorrow I'll have a new stepmom. I'm applying for a scholarship at Waterloo University in Canada. Mr. Lee thinks I have a good shot at it." He shrugged, "And then there's the band. I can't really abandon them."

Dr. Wellesley pointed to Jacky's dad, "Would it change your mind if I told you it was your father who wrote to us and explained the situation, and told us how much you wanted to attend the Academy?"

Jacky laughed, and shook his head. "No, but I think he just wants my room for their new baby."

Dr. Wellesley laughed, getting up. "Fair enough, you've made your decision, then."

His dad walked over to Jacky and squeezed his shoulder. "Jacky are you sure, it's okay, you know, we support whatever you decide to do."

Jacky nodded. "Yes, I'm sure. I'm sorry, Dr. Wellesley. You came all this way for nothing."

"That's not a problem at all," Dr. Wellesley said. "I wanted to meet you, after hearing so much about your adventures on the mountain. I wish you the very best of luck, Jacky Fraser. I hope to hear wonderful things about you in the future."

"Thank you," Jacky said, shaking the chancellor's hand. His heart was a battlefield of emotions. His dad and Kerry hugged him as the chancellor left them alone.

"You never stop surprising me, Jacky," his dad said.

They took Jacky for lunch at a restaurant just down the hill from the castle, then they dropped him back at his hotel. He intended to sleep but he gave up on that and went for a walk instead. The Princes Street Gardens stretched along the valley between Old Town and the rest of the downtown. The calm of the park being situated between the busy downtown area and the constant noise rolling down the hill from Old Town was the perfect analogy of his life at that moment. Everything was busy; everything was new and old. Part of him was unhappy with his choice to give up the scholarship to the Academy, yet another part was happy that things were going to stay as they were. He would be moving on in a year anyway; he hadn't changed his plans, just his feelings. He hated Kerry and her intrusion into the life he and his dad shared. Now he liked her, appreciated her anyway, for everything she had done for his dad, and for him. He knew she had something to do with contacting the chancellor and she helped him through that media nonsense after the accident. He was wrong about her.

Things were still changing; he was going to have a sibling. Sharing the house with another kid may be a pain but everyone he knew had brothers and sisters and they seemed to like it. He still remembered what it felt like to meet so many relatives in Inverness.

He stopped to look at the ominous monument built for Sir Walter Scott. It was heavy and dark but only because of the effects of time. Up close it was really quite beautiful, with a statue of Scott himself writing and contemplating with his dog sitting beside him under the high, cathedral-shaped monument. It was an interesting contradiction. Here was a man who wrote words on paper, a simple act of thought transposed into print, working in what he believed to be quiet contemplation. But his words carried so much weight and appeal to so many people—these people—that they built a huge masterpiece of architecture of him to honour and revere his memory.

"It is what it is, right, Sir Walter Scott? You do what you can do and people will remember you as they choose."

It was time to go back and get ready.

Blow Down the Castle

The Edinburgh Military Tattoo was a huge production that had been presented every year since the 1950s. By then the event was the largest in the world with over 200,000 people attending the performances in Edinburgh and millions more in over thirty countries watching on video. The members of the New Caledonians stood in stunned silence when they saw the venue lit up and full of people. The castle itself was the backdrop for the performers, and the walls of the ancient building were lit up with such an array of colours that it seemed to be as alive and full of energy as the thousands of people packed in the seats. The stands for the spectators formed a large horseshoe in the main court-yard of the castle grounds, and there were no empty seats to be seen.

As it was opening day, the show began a little later and ran well into the night with a fireworks display that promised to be legendary. The sun was beginning to set, and the sky was just light enough to see the clouds. The members of the band had been fed and run back to their hotel to change and get ready. They knew once they walked into the castle grounds they were about to play their largest show. The New Caledonians were scheduled early in the evening and each of them, including the normally overconfident drummers, were awed by the size of the crowds and the sheer number of pipers, musicians, and performers. There were drummers, dancers, and performers of almost every type of music from around the world.

The knowledge that the Prince of Wales and other members of the Royal Family were there was foremost in Jacky's mind. He was more nervous about making a good impression with them than the thousands of audience members. Jacky looked at the other band members to see how they were doing. Most were like him, breathing slowly, staying calm and focusing on the music they had to play. They were guests at the Tattoo, not scheduled performers, so they did not take part in the massive collection of pipe bands that opened or closed the show. The opening act was a light show and parade of hundreds of pipers and drummers marching through the grand entrance of the castle to the grounds. The music seemed to shake the city, and the roar of the crowd lifted the sound level to beyond maximum of Jacky's hearing. He held on and let the sound wash over them.

There was a signal and the band members started getting into formation. Jacky took his spot and looked around quickly to make sure everyone was there. He saw Mr. Stewart talking with a man wearing large headphones and holding a clipboard. It was time, and Jacky felt that familiar icy cold thrill through his stomach that happened just before they performed. He first felt that when he stepped out to play his solo. It scared him then, but now he welcomed the feeling like an old friend. He knew they would play well and their performance was world class, that's why they were there in Edinburgh. That and the other part about the plane crash. Whatever, the past was the past, and here and now was spectacular.

They got their signal and the pipers tapped their bags. The collective drones of the pipes hummed, and the drums struck the first beat. The New Caledonians marched out on the field playing "The Highland Wedding," a quick-paced song that started their set. They performed their well-practised moves while transitioning seamlessly from one song to the next. As the last song ended, the crowd cheered with the sound echoing from the walls of the castle and the distant buildings in the city. The band stood in position as the announcer told the crowd their story. Jacky couldn't hear the words but he could guess. International award–winning Canadian youth band, plane accident, survival in the snow and cold, and the inevitable piper on the mountain. The crowd stood on their feet and cheered noisily

Then the band played the piece they had added to their show after the accident. The pipers fanned out in a large semicircular shape with the drummers forming the base, exactly as they had done on the mountain. This time, Larry started solo, playing "Going Home," a sad, moving song to honour Captain Connelly. They arranged this with the organizers of the festival. After a verse, the rest of the band joined in and the people running the fireworks set off a special display of six white rockets that shot across the sky with a single one shooting straight up in the air, a traditional send-off for a fallen pilot. The crowd cheered and stood as the drummers hammered out a quick beat and the pipers began playing "High Road to Gairloch." They marched off the grounds, while the audience continued to clap along.

Once they packed their instruments, the New Caledonians ran up the stairs to their reserved seats in the stands. They were high enough to see the whole field and hear everything as the sound boomed off the walls. The night was a feast for their eyes and ears. Colours played over the castle walls while the performing area filled with military bands from countries around the world doing synchronized drum-ming, complicated marching formations, and dangerous but fascinating acrobatics with guns and bayonets. Irish and Scottish dancers created a moving pattern of colours with their bright costumes and high-energy dancing, barely touching the ground as they kicked and spun. There were African troops in browns and greens; Middle Eastern groups in long, white costumes and exotic instruments; Jamaicans with steel drums; brass bands from the United States; Celtic music with rock bands; Chinese dragon dancers in neon pink and blue; and stunt performers on motorcycles jumping over each other. The sound and movement just kept coming as Jacky tried to take it all in. Finally, the amassed pipe bands from around the world, in every imaginable colour of tartan, grouped together to play the grand finale and a march off the field to a light show of fireworks that lit the sky and booming echoes that bounced off every building and hill around the city.

When it was over and the last of the echoes of the fireworks rolled into the distance, the band members wandered down the Royal Mile with the rest of the crowd. The pubs were full, and the sound of music and people talking poured out the doors. Street performers and musicians were spread out down the hill with clumps of people standing around and dropping coins in their boxes. The persistent thump of bass from the clubs couldn't compare to the beating Jacky's ears had taken at the castle. His eardrums rang from the noise. He couldn't believe they played on that field as part of that incredible show. His body was vibrating from the excitement and the vast amount of sugar he'd consumed. He was exhausted and sore from standing and his throat was raw from screaming in the stands, but he didn't want to go to bed yet. Sleep was going to come quickly so he resisted as long as he could. He didn't want this night to end.

Role Reversals

The plans were made for the wedding to happen two days after Jacky's concert at the castle. Kerry's cousin had arranged things at Dundas Castle, a former aristocratic home outside of Edinburgh. Jacky would fly home the next day while his new parents drove north on their honeymoon to Eilean Donan Castle and a tour of the highlands. The day after the concert was still busy. Jacky had to move into the hotel with his dad and go to the wedding rehearsal in the afternoon.

That morning, the band was checking out of the hotel and loading on to the bus to the airport. Jacky was standing at the doorway waiting for his dad to pick him up when Rick stepped outside with his backpack and spotted him.

"Hey, aren't you coming to the airport with us?" Rick asked.

"No, I'm sticking around a couple of days with my parents," Jacky said, still not used to saying *parents*. "They're getting married tomorrow. I'll come back after that. Are you ready for the long flight home?"

"You mean am I going to go crazy and tear the door off the plane, yeah, I'm ready," Rick said, smirking.

Jacky sighed, "I'm sorry I called you crazy. I didn't mean it."

"Yeah, you did, but that's okay," Rick said. "Everybody got crazy up there, even you."

"Yeah but, you know if you hadn't actually gone nuts with the drum we never would've got out of there," Jacky added. "You're the real hero, Rick. Which makes me wonder why you told the reporters that I was the guy who came up with the idea."

Rick laughed. "Well, you handled it better than I could. I was getting sick of people asking me about it. I don't need the attention. Hey, are you staying with the band next year? I heard a rumour you were quitting."

Jacky grinned. "Yeah, I'm staying. See you back home." He waved as his dad pulled up in a rented VW.

"Hey," said his dad as Jacky got in and closed the door.

"Hey," said Jacky. "So what are we doing?"

His dad pulled out of the lot and drove down the main street. "The rehearsal is at one. You and I have to pick up our suits and head out to Dundas Castle. We have a little time to kill before then, so I figured we could see some sights while Kerry and her cousin get ready. I really don't want to be hanging around waiting."

Jacky laughed. His dad was actually nervous. "What are you so worried about? It's not like she's going to say no."

His dad rubbed his chin. "I don't know, Jacky. It's not the wedding itself, it's the rest it that follows. I'm going to be a new dad again, just when I'm starting to get the hang of living with a teenager."

Jacky shook his head. "I don't think you have anything to worry about."

They drove to the hotel and dropped Jacky's bags. They were free to explore. They drove through Old Town, crossed into New Town and down to the harbour. They passed the ship *Britannia*, then followed the shoreline to a village called South Queensferry and parked. There was a dock with tour boats tied up loading tourists for a cruise.

"You want to take a ride?" his dad asked. "This will be your only chance to go on the water for a while."

Jacky agreed and they climbed onboard with a load of tourists; Germans, French, and Dutch, and maybe some Americans. The boat cast off, and the tour guide started talking to them, pointing to different sites around them including the three bridges they were passing.

The massive Forth Bridge, its bright red steel structure forming three large lens shapes, resembled an oversized DNA model more than a railroad bridge. Next to that was the normal looking Forth

Traffic Bridge and the Queensferry Bridge, the newest one.

"Pretty amazing, isn't it?" said Jacky's dad, staring up at the beehive of traffic above them. They were at the front of the boat, stand-ing in the wind while the other tourists stayed at the back of the deck.

"Sure," said Jacky. "They love their bridges. Three of them, wow."

"Okay," his dad said, turning his face into the breeze and the light spray from the water. "I know it's not the most exciting thing you've seen, but I love being on the water. I find it very relaxing. Probably the fisherman in me."

"I think so," said Jacky. "I like it, too. It's different."

"Yeah." His dad faced him, leaning on the rail. "By the way, we want to give you something, sort of a wedding gift for the best man." He held an envelope out for Jacky.

"Oh, yeah?" Jacky said. "What's that?" He turned away from the wind and opened it, pulling out two tickets.

The Red Hot Chilli Pipers, tonight, in Edinburgh.

Jacky stared at the tickets in disbelief and then hugged his dad. He lifted his arms and howled into the wind. His dad grinned at the other tourists as they laughed.

41

Ending at the Start

After the wedding rehearsal was complete, they drove back to their hotel to change. The wedding would happen the next day then Jacky would board a plane for home while his new family ran off on their honeymoon. He was looking forward to having the rest of the week on his own before life started into its new routine, whatever that was going to be. After changing, they walked together up the Royal Mile to Deacon Brodie's Tavern for dinner. It was surreal to be acting so normal when everything was about to be so different. It was easy to see how much in love his father and Kerry were. Jacky was just happy to have his own room at the hotel.

After dinner, Jacky and his dad stepped out of the hotel in jeans and T-shirts and caught a taxi. The music hall wasn't too far away but nighttime came pretty quick and they didn't want to get lost on Edinburgh's labyrinth of roads. It turned out that it was easy to find, with the lineup outside the hall that snaked around the block. Fortunately, they had advanced tickets and walked in past the lineup.

Regardless of how many people were outside, the room was already packed with a flurry of activity, people wandering around, finding seats or goofing around, technicians setting up cables and mics, the big screens flashing the Red Hot Chilli Pipers graphics and recorded music filling the air. It was already loud enough to have to yell to be heard. They had seats close to the stage. Jacky figured that must have cost a bundle but he wasn't going to say anything. This concert was going to be worth every dime. His dad was looking around at the room. Jacky guessed he probably hadn't been to a rock concert in a while.

The place was thick with anticipation. As far as Jacky could see, the Red Hot Chilli Pipers fans covered the gamut from old rockers his dad's age to ones younger than him. Clearly Bagrock was a lot more popular in the United Kingdom than it was back home, but it was catching on. The Chilli Pipers were just back from a tour in the United States. It was strange that people thought Jacky playing bag-pipes in a rock band was a novelty back home; they didn't have a clue. Still, Jacky was amazed by the sheer numbers of fans packing this hall to see the Chilli Pipers. He knew his dad didn't know what to expect, and it was exciting to anticipate his reaction. Jacky watched hours of concert footage by the band on YouTube and knew most of their songs by heart. This was going to be a great night.

Both Jacky and his dad bought T-shirts at the souvenir stand. His dad pulled his over his own shirt while Jacky did a quick shirt switch, one of the advantages of being male in a crowded concert hall. He almost wore his kilt, but he changed his mind at the last minute. It turned out he would have been in the majority, half the guys he saw were in kilts.

"Aren't you going to be hot?" Jacky asked his dad, who was already starting to sweat.

"Probably but I've got lots of water. Don't worry about me," hi dad said, raising his voice over the recorded music. "This is pretty amazing. I had no idea these guys were so popular."

The crowd was warming up to the music, and Jacky was stomping his feet in time. It quickly built in volume until the band appeared on stage in an explosion of sound and light.

The crowd were instantly on their feet, jumping and cheering at the first beat. The band played straight through an exhaustive list of songs before they let everyone catch their breath. Jacky was standing with the rest of them, cheering and waving. He snatched a glance toward his dad who was having just as much fun, cheering and swaying with the crowd. He was getting red faced and sweaty. Jacky thought he had to keep an eye on him, mindful of his heart condition. As if he heard

Jacky's thoughts, his dad pulled off the T-shirt, took a long drink of water, and grinned at Jacky.

He hadn't noticed the band had stopped playing and the leader was talking. Jacky wasn't listening; he was looking at his dad. He was suddenly aware that the room was silent and everyone was looking at him. He looked up at the stage where the piper with the microphone was pointing at him.

"Come on, laddie, you're holding up the show." He was waving Jacky on stage. Jacky looked at his dad and the crowd, who had started slow clapping. His dad gave him a push.

"Go on, Jacky. They're waiting for you."

Jacky started walking hesitantly toward the stage. It didn't make sense but he walked on, climbing the stairs up the side. A stagehand helped him up and put a wireless microphone in his hand, pointing him to the front and gave him a push.

"Come on up, Jacky, we're not going to bite," the piper said, drawing laughs from the crowd. Jacky knew the place was full but, from the stage, the sea of faces was staggering, and they were all looking at him. The piper held out his hand.

"Hey, Jacky," they fist bumped. "I'm Kevin, and this, ladies and gentlemen," turning to the crowd, raising Jacky's arm like a boxer, "this is the Piper on the Mountain."

The roar of the crowd filled the room and his ears. Jacky felt the heat rising in his face. He understood what was going on. His dad and Kerry managed to pull this whole thing together under his nose. He realized everyone was waiting for him to say something. He lifted the microphone to his mouth.

"Oh, you heard about that, did you?" It was an honest question, but the laughter from the crowd and the smile on Kevin's face showed they thought he was being ironic. He grinned back, his embarrassment disguised as modesty.

Kevin took over. "Well, unless you've been living under a rock, you probably know who Jacky is. If not, then Google it. Suffice it to say Jacky here saved the members of his band from an icy death—with bagpipes!" Another roar from the crowd. Kevin turned to face him. "So Jacky, we'd like to make you an honorary member of the band for tonight. We know you don't have your pipes with you but we thought these might do in a pinch." He handed Jacky a new set of bagpipes. They were glassy black with shining silver ferrules and the band's trademark red tartan. Jacky held them in awe, unable to say a word.

"Would you like to play something with us," Kevin asked, and Jacky froze. This wasn't happening; he was not going to play bagpipes with the Chilli Pipers.

Oh, yes, he was. His head was spinning, as he brought the microphone to his mouth and said the only thing he could think of.

"Oh, yeah." He raised the pipes over his head facing the crowd, who cheered their approval.

Kevin said, "What do you know?"

Once before, three years ago, when he was about to step out to play in front of a large crowd of people and his father, Jacky almost quit because he feared failure. This time, in the same situation, he had no such fear. He was ready to rock.

"How about 'Thunderstruck'?"

Kevin laughed. "Of course. Take it away, Jacky."

Jacky handed the microphone back to the stagehand, then fixed himself with his new pipes. He blew, he closed his eyes, tapped the bag, and started playing. He knew the song by heart. The first part was a quick pattern, usually played on the guitar, but Jacky mastered it easily. The guitarist joined him, matching him note for note. The crowd clapped a quick double beat with the drums and then the rest of the band joined in with a punch. The guitar growled, the drums pounded, and the pipes wailed while the crowd howled. They were standing and clapping over their heads as the lights waved back and forth over the room. The sound was so loud Jacky couldn't hear himself playing but it no longer mattered, his hands knew what to do.

He thought he wanted to quit this? That was crazy.

He was right where he belonged.

Acknowledgements

It is very hard for me not to fill a book's worth of pages listing everyone who has helped me in the long process of writing this book. It very nearly died in process several times as I struggled to bring this story out to the world through various publishing challenges. What you have read in this book is the net result of many supportive and encouraging conversations I have had with authors who have a great deal more experience and knowledge than me, but who still took the time to share helpful information on writing and story with this struggling newcomer. I promise to buy and read all of your books.

This book exists thanks to the work of industry professionals. Thanks to Morgen Bailey (morgenbailey.com) for editing and story consultation, Magdalene Carson (newleafpublicationdesign.ca) for the cover and book design, Nancy Syrett for line editing and formatting.

Thank you to Laurel Deedrick-Mayne (www.awakeforthedreamland.com) for her time and suggestions. Thanks also to Val and David Heide, my trusted beta-readers.

One does not write about crashing an airplane in the mountains without finding out how it happens. I was able to fly, freeze up and crash land an airplane in the Canadian Rockies with technical input and consultation from Jon Lee, who is an expert in aircraft crash investigations.

Information on handling bagpipes in the cold was provided by John Walsh, bagpipe maker in Antigonish, Nova Scotia (www.johnwalshbagpipes.com).

To Michael Korb, (www.highlandcathedral.de), co-composer of my favourite bagpipe song, *Highland Cathedral,* danke schön for letting me include your prized work in my story.

Thanks to the Edmonton Youth Pipe Band (EYPB.ca) and the Red Hot Chilli Pipers (www.rhcp.scot), the greatest bagrock band in the world.

Finally, thanks to my supportive and encouraging children, Christine and Stephen, and my understanding, generous and loving wife, Zoë, who is the reason I've managed to accomplish anything.

About the Author

JIM SELLERS is a freelance writer of fiction, non-fiction and commercial work living in Edmonton, Alberta, Canada. He worked in television for 25 years, writing series, commercials and documentary scripts before writing fiction. *Jacky the Brave* (2013) was his first published novel.

Jim lives with his wife Zoë.

info@jimsellerswriter.com
www.jimsellerswriter.com

www.ingramcontent.com/pod-product-compliance
Lightning Source LLC
Chambersburg PA
CBHW032013050726
47590CB00006B/2151